John N.

Richard Totino

When I lived in Saratoga Springs, New York, I had the honor of belonging to a group of selfless and dedicated people who gave of themselves to assist others. This group was and still is known as LASAR, or Lower Adirondack Search and Rescue. This group is a self-trained assembly of people primarily form Saratoga and Warren counties in the Lake George region of New York who assist the New York Forest Rangers in the search and rescue and too often recovery, of people who get lost or go missing in but not restricted to, the Adirondack Mountain region of the state.

Defined as "ground pounders" this group responds to the needs of the Rangers when trained and certified manpower is needed. In addition, they have trained and certified K-9 teams that augment their human team efforts.

The individuals in this group will go to the extreme with their efforts to find a missing person and are equipped for searches in all terrain and weather conditions. It is what I learned from being a member of this group that I drew upon for much of this story and it is to this group of "friends" that I dedicate this book.

Contents

Chapter 1

"What the hell is that?"

"What?"

"That, dumb ass!

The two local men continued to walk out onto the ice-bound surface of Lake George, nestled in the Adirondack Mountains of Upstate New York. It was ice fishing season, and they had all the equipment they needed to spend an enjoyable day on the ice, even though the air temperature was hovering just slightly below zero degrees and the wind was a brisk fifteen miles an hour. To them, just another winter day to enjoy the great outdoors.

They were launching their day's activity from the public beach area on the southernmost point of the lake, located within the Village of Lake George, destined to see far more than normal activity in the weeks ahead. At this time of year, early in January, instead of white sand, the entire beach area was buried with well over a foot of snow. It is not unusual for this time of year in this part of the country. If there was anything certain you could bet on in this part of New York state at this time of year, it was the cold. Bone rattling cold, knee-knocking, butt puckering, nose snot freezing cold!

The two men, still dealing with the lingering effects of the party they attended the night before, turned toward the dark, round object perched on the ice about a hundred yards offshore. Against the sparkling white lake surface glistening in the early morning sunshine, the object, whatever it was, stood out clearly enough to be seen and draw their attention.

The ice covering the lake moaned and groaned, moved by the wind as they approached the dark lump to check it out. They were curious to find out what the object was before boring their first hole in the more than two-foot-thick ice. Their pace cautiously slowed with every step they took closer to the object, increasing their befuddlement.

As they got closer, they were drawn in by a mysterious magnetic force compelling them to determine what the out-of-place object was. Their brains already knew what it was, but wouldn't yet accept it. What the hell was it, and why was it out here on the ice? When they were about ten yards from the object, their brains finally clicked in and admitted what their eyes were telling them. It became crystal clear what it was fouling the pristine surface of the lake.

"Oh, my God!" the man closest said.

"What the fuck!?" the second man uttered, stunned by what was in front of him.

With one more step, the first man turned and puked up the remains of the beer, pigs-in-a-blanket, hot Buffalo wings and pizza from last night's party, along with what little of the scrambled egg and greasy bacon breakfast he had eaten before approaching the ice.

"It's a man's head!"

"Oh, my God, man. It's… it's a fucking head! It's a human head."

Anchored in place by the sight lying out before them, they couldn't move. Their gaze froze on the head of a human man positioned upright on the ice, surrounded by a pink circle of blood. The eyes were open and staring back at them as if awaiting their arrival to have a conversation. They quickly turned back toward the shoreline, dropped the tow ropes attached to their equipment sleds and ran like hell, screaming like two little girls.

Fifteen minutes later, the south end of the lake was lit up by flashing red, blue and white lights mounted atop every type of law enforcement and emergency response vehicle imaginable. Local police, county sheriff, state police, as well as officers from the State's DEC, Department of Environmental Conservation, because the lake was a part of the vast Adirondack State Park. Fire trucks and ambulances added to the mix, completing the total chaos. Every volunteer first responder with a light mounted on top of a pick-up truck within twenty miles was there to add to the show.

The snowy mist of frozen crystals traveling across the lake in the frigid wind bounced the flashes of the spinning lights, creating a disco appearance hanging over the village. It was like Saturday night at the Legion Hall.

The various government agencies present would spend hours fighting over who would control the unfolding events. The Village police took the position that the obvious crime took place within their jurisdiction. The county sheriff said no that the village stopped at the water line, and the lake was within the county. Therefore, it was their territory. The state police took pretty much the same stance against the sheriff's department. Finally, it was the DEC officers who claimed jurisdiction since the lake was a part of the state park.

The head didn't care! It was just as dead. It sat there, taking in everything going on around it, appearing as if the body that once attached was standing beneath the icy surface with only its head sticking up through a hole in the ice.

The debate continued. In the end, it was the state police who prevailed. The agency's Superintendent was, however, smart enough to form an alliance by appointing a committee made up of all the other forces in attendance to assist in the effort. This preserved the all-important political appearance each member was so desperately concerned with. This was going to be a news-maker, and everybody wanted in.

Luckily, the village was almost totally void of any of the tourist population that it survived during the summer months. Most of the people who gathered to see just what the hell was going on were locals. However, it was still very early in the morning, and the village was very close to I-87, the major north-south interstate route between the state capital of Albany and the Canadian city of

Montreal. It wouldn't take much time once the word got out that the flood of gawkers would soon descend upon the well-known vacation village.

There were four big questions being bantered about by all the law enforcement personnel. First, to whom did the head once belong? Second, how did it get out on the ice without anyone reporting it? Third, who took the head from the body it was once attached to? And last, where was the body that the head was so brutally detached from?

The first to be questioned were the two men who discovered the head. They were currently being held in the village visitor's center, a short walk from the scene. It was obvious to the detectives from the state police department that both men were shaken by find. Both had a hard time harnessing the nervous energy that took control of their bodies and speech. They jabbered on, nervously twisting back and forth in the chairs they were forced to occupy. Nothing of any useful importance would be learned from either of these two men.

Those on the ice trying to determine the facts could find nothing of use there, either. There were no identifiable tracks leading to or away from the head that were of any use to them. During the winter sports season, the lake experienced heavy foot traffic from those wanting to walk onto the lake to ice fish. In addition, the beach area was a popular site to park trucks and trailers hauling snowmobiles. The snow on the lake was totally messed up from these machines racing across the surface. And lastly, the north wind that constantly blew, drifting snow erased history every few minutes. The combination dashed all hopes of finding a usable shoe or boot tread pattern left by the culprits.

So, the immediate concentration focused on question number one. Who was the original owner of the head? To find the answer to this most important question, the head had to be moved off the ice to a crime lab. The headquarters for the New York State Police and the location of their facilities were in Albany, about an hour's drive to the south. Much less if you happened to have flashing lights and very loud sirens on your vehicle.

Two medical lab technicians approached the head carrying what looked to be a shoe box. They bent over and attempted to lift the head and place it into the box. However, they found that the head was frozen to the icy surface. Surprise! Surprise! It was currently zero degrees, with the wind blowing about ten to fifteen miles per hour. Things tended to freeze at this unGodly temperature.

After a couple of unsuccessful attempts to dislodge the head by lifting it by hand, a helping soul approached the pair with what looked to be an old-fashioned flat and wide coal shovel used years ago to stoke the furnaces inside of the homes bordering the lakefront. Flat, wide and deep, this style of the shovel was now most often used to remove snow from driveways and front porches. Human heads from frozen lakes were a bonus feature.

One of the techs took the shovel and attempted to scoop up the head. His first stroke failed, as did his second. The third dislodged the head and sent it bobbing across the ice, bouncing to a stop up against one of the ice fishing sleds left by the two local fishermen. The two unsuccessful attempts by the techs to dislodge the head were immediately followed by the up-chucking of numerous folks watching the gruesome show of high-tech medical work from the shoreline. The moans and groans of those losing their breakfast were reminded me of something similar to a Charlie Chaplin comedy routine on the ice.

A bloody human head bouncing across a frozen lake is enough to flip a few stomachs this early in the morning. Greasy eggs along with a couple of equally greasy strips of bacon, then add in a little oatmeal with bananas topping it off, and most people didn't stand a chance to hold anything down.

Very near the lake's beach area, there are boat docking facilities. The lake tour and dinner cruise boats used these facilities when operating during heavy tourist summer months. Right now, the docks were empty, abandoned to the winter ice that would crush the boats if left in the lake during the cold months. The boats were stored somewhere safe and dry. Their absence left a wide area of unobstructed lakefront, great for those interested in watching the goings on out on the ice.

Unnoticed, standing amid the docks, stood a group of four men intently watching all the activity near the beach. The way they were standing, almost with arms touching one another, they were all dressed exactly alike. It was clear to anyone interested that they were together. They weren't talking, just looking…. Observing with great interest the proceedings taking place on the ice just a short walk away.

They were all identically dressed. They were all wearing black. From head to toe, black. But, black clothing in sub-zero weather, was not entirely uncommon and drew no immediate attention from the other locals crowding the area to see what was going on near the beach. What was odd was that it wasn't just one man dressed in black. It was four standing side by side as if dressed in some sort of uniform.

As if on cue, the small group of men turned and walked away. They walked west toward Route 9, the main street running through the village of Lake George. They then turned north, walking toward a small park located near the middle of town. When they reached the park, they got into a plain, unmarked, dark white Ford Econoline van. The van pulled away from the sidewalk and headed north, disappearing as it drove beyond the village.

They would be back!

Chapter 2

Approximately six or seven miles north of the village, there was a secluded compound where a number of very private, very expensive homes were tucked in along the eastern side of the lake. It was less than a half-hour ride by boat to reach the settlement. However, because of the twisting, winding mountain roads, it took nearly an hour to reach the same destination by way of the most direct and only partially paved road route.

Originally built by an early 1900s business tycoon, the settlement was now the location for about a dozen high-priced summer getaway homes. All but two were owned by some rich downstate big business executive types whose attitude was that they would honor the little people in the community with their presence every now and again. Some of the homes were used annually, and others hadn't seen their owners for several years.

The owners of these homes were smart enough to know that, stuck up here in the remote mountains, their investments required protection from the local yahoos out looking for a Saturday night run of fun. They also knew that their homes needed to be maintained on a regular basis. The cold winter and hot, humid summer conditions on the shore of the lake took a toll on any and all types of dwellings. Expensive, highly taxed retreat homes included. Even if the 'King' was not in residence, the castle still needed attention.

It helped that they were all wealthy and smart enough to afford a full-time caretaker who both guarded the area and performed regular maintenance. As a part of his compensation, he was provided with one of the two "other" homes on the property. Until fairly recently, he and his wife were the only full-time residents of the compound.

The compound is accessible by watercraft or by way of a very long, narrow and winding one-lane, heavily monitored dirt road. Or, for the highly motivated, by a cross-country hike through, over and around some very rugged mountains. The limited access made the complex reasonably secure from outsiders. Many locals weren't even aware that it existed.

At the road entrance to the property, there was a six-inch heavy-gauge steel pipe filled with cement that was anchored to steel-reinforced posts at either end, buried more than ten feet into the ground. The pipe acted as a barrier that could be lifted out of the way to allow vehicles to enter the property. There was a counterbalance on one end to aid in the lifting. The entire barrier was painted bright yellow for visibility as well as to appear as if it were a forest service structure to add emphasis to its function. It clearly announced a warning of "DO NOT ENTER."

In addition to the barrier, there were other types of electronic monitoring systems strategically spaced along the dirt road's fifteen-mile length to provide an early alert to any uninvited vehicle approaching unannounced or unwanted. Just inside the pipe barrier, hidden only a couple of inches below the surface of the road, was a remotely controlled spike strip. If it were triggered, it would spring to the surface and puncture the tires of any approaching vehicle passing over it.

The pipe barrier itself looked exactly like those installed by the state's forest service, limiting access to protected lands. Many people who approached the barrier believed this to be the case with this bright yellow painted pipe, and it was enough to turn them around for fear of messing with the state government and not just a local resident's private property.

Mother Nature also aided in the protection of the settlement. The road leading to the estate from the nearest paved highway was narrow and difficult to drive and over fifteen miles long. Any speed over twenty-five miles an hour was risky. Even for those who knew the road with all the twists and turns along its entire length, it presented quite a challenge. Thus, the hour-long travel time from the village of Lake George.

In the winter, the road was very often covered with snow ass hole deep to a long-legged giraffe. Although maintained by the county, because of its remoteness and limited population, it was at the bottom of the priority list for snow removal. With no children in residence and, therefore, no school buses traveling its length, the road was often the last in the county to be plowed. Sometimes, it could be impassable for days following a storm, limiting winter travel to snowmobiles until cleared and ATVs during those months with no snow.

In the spring and fall, the rains made for very slick driving atop the slick mud created from the clay-filled mountain soil. The locals would describe it as 'slicker-than-snot.' And, during the hot summer months when it was dry, the dust clouds kicked up by any passing vehicle would blind the driver, causing many a wreck along the way. The ravines along both sides of the road were littered with vehicles that plunged over the edge, driven by those too stupid or too arrogant to slow down.

Lake George's waters contain ice on average for one-third of the year. The months there was no ice, the best, safest and fastest way into the compound was by a boat launched either from the village or from directly across the lake in the town of Bolton Landing, home of the century-old posh Sagamore Hotel, once the vacation destination for the "rich and famous."

The purpose of dealing with all of this inconvenience was simple…. Seclusion and privacy. Those who owned property within the estate possessed the money or, fame or, worldly status or self-inflated egos that pressed them to seek seclusion. They did not wish to be pestered by the 'little people.' And they had the money to pay for the luxury. After all, they were legends in their own minds.

But, all the privacy measures in place were not intended for the property owners only. Officially, there were only two people who lived within the complex on a full-time basis. They were Bob and Sally Herman. Bob was the caretaker/guard of the estate. His wife, Sally, often assisted him and provided some housekeeping services for the homeowners or an occasional guest or family member of an owner who might pop in for a weekend visit.

The Hermans had been in residence for almost fifteen years, living in the house provided for them as a part of their compensation package. They were also provided with a very necessary four-wheel drive vehicle, a small boat, a snowmobile and a four-wheel drive ATV. All were necessary for getting around in this remote environment as well as to fulfill their duties and responsibilities. Their income was substantially enhanced by the only other permanent resident of the compound.

In addition to those having large investments to protect within the complex, the location and conditions made it a very attractive place for another unofficial full-time resident. A former government assassin who owned the second of the "other" homes within the compound.

Lucas Martin! Known to the few who knew of his existence as John N. Anderson, also unofficially resided here. He inherited a very comfortable medium-sized log home on the property. He was the adopted son of a very wealthy family who took him in purely to satisfy their need for social justice. When his adoptive parents died, he inherited a small fortune along with the cabin. His fortune grew substantially as the result of smart investments and also from the fees he collected as one of the deadliest men in the employment of the U.S. government.

He was recruited into government service while in college to become an unspecified "government agent." During his service, he had two sources of income. One source was via his sales commissions for roaming the world as a high-profile industrial chemical salesman. This was the 'cover' for his real job. He was also paid exorbitant fees as an assassin. Paid by the government to 'eliminate' the problem of people around the world. A little over a year ago, he was assigned the mission of killing the Canadian Prime Minister.

It didn't happen. Lucas Martin, aka John N. Anderson, detected and brought down a totally illegal plot drummed up in the mind of the then President of the United States. The president's plot also included the elimination of both John and his control agent, Kristin Blake. The President had ordered their death as part of the plan to conceal who was behind the plot to assassinate the Canadian head of state.

In John's mind, this was a fatal mistake on the part of the president. Killing the Canadian Prime Minister was an illegal mistake. Targeting him .….was a fatal one.

The solution was in John's control. Threatening him had a price. A very steep price. The president and his top aide who ordered the political hit were no longer active citizens of the United States of America. Their sole function was now to fertilize flowers growing in the national cemetery from six feet beneath the surface.

The irony of the plot was that John had hoodwinked a fee of over fifty million dollars on the pretext of completing the president's original illegal mission. Adding this fee to his already substantial bank account, John found himself to be an extraordinarily wealthy man. And, for the very first time in his life, he was in love. Deeply, madly, head over heels in love. The recipient of his attention being his former control officer, one Ms. Kristin Blake.

After manipulating the destruction and elimination of both of their employment personnel file with the help of yet another government insider, he and Kristin withdrew from the world of government service and intrigue by taking up residence within the secluded estate on the eastern shore of Lake George, New York.

With their personnel file deleted from all government records, they no longer existed. Simply evaporated. He particularly was a distant memory in the minds of the very few who ever even knew there was a John N. Anderson. He was, as he liked best to be, a ghost. A puff of smoke in the breeze. He was alone. Lived and survived alone. Traveled the world and lived his double life…..alone.

Over a year had slipped by since the beginning of his new life status. During that time, life had settled into a level of normalcy that he had never known before. As such, everything was new to him. In his previous existence, normal was abnormal. He was soaking up every day, every hour, every moment of his new life. More and more each passing day, he found peace in a world where he had once found nothing but death, violence, and chaos.

Each day was a new adventure enhanced by the presence of Kristin Blake. He sensed within himself the love for her that expanded every morning when he looked upon her face resting on the pillow next to him. Now, as his wife, she not only brought love into his life, she brought peace and purpose.

Kristin, too, had lived a hollow life. The only child of a single mother, she had little to do with her father. He was a drunk who had abused her mother repeatedly before being sentenced to prison for manslaughter. He got into a fistfight in a bar and ended up killing a man by hitting him in the head with an empty beer bottle. She hadn't seen him since his sentencing to prison.

She grew up fast. By the age of eighteen, she was on her own, making a living by waiting on tables in a local dive. She worked her way through an online college until she was awarded a B.S. degree in criminology. She made an application to an unnamed federal agency and was eventually hired into an entry-level position. The agency sponsored her in a continued education program, and she completed a master's degree from VCU in Richmond, Virginia.

After completing the process of obtaining a security clearance, she rose quickly through the ranks, bypassing many of her contemporaries because of her intellect and performance. She was smart, good-looking and driven with a 'take no prisoners' approach to her job.

Her childhood and adolescent years made her a prime candidate for recruitment by one of the shadow agencies that preferred to hire people with little if any, personal life. She fit the bill perfectly and quickly rose up to be promoted to the very sensitive position of a control officer. She was the desk-ridden counterpart to an unacknowledged, non-existent, unofficial government assassin. In her case, a man known as John N. Anderson. A complete enigma to the entire world… except her.

This morning, John N. Anderson had left her bed early and was outside of their cabin loading his arms up with firewood when he heard a vehicle approaching. He looked up to see Bob Herman driving into the compound in his four-wheel drive GMC Sierra pick-up truck. The two men had a very long, very intertwined relationship dating back to the time they served together in the U.S. Army.

After exiting his vehicle, Bob approached John. "Morning John".

"Morning Bob. Where have you been?"

"Had to run into town to pick up a couple of things at the hardware store. Got delayed by all the police activity."

"What police activity?" John asked, his alert system immediately kicking into gear.

"Seems like a couple of hungover local yahoos going ice fishing found a head on the ice."

"Head? You mean like a human head?"

"Yeah, about a hundred yards off the town beach. They spotted it as soon as they got on the ice. Noticed it right away because it was so dark against the snow on top of the ice."

"Who is… or should I say, who was it?" John asked.

"I don't think they know yet. Seems like every cop within fifty miles has gotten involved and there's a fight over whose jurisdiction the situation would fall into. When I left, my head was still on the ice. I could just make it out from where I was."

"What about the body?" John asked.

"Don't have a clue. I got out of town as quickly as I could. Downtown was filling up with police vehicles and rubberneckers, and all I wanted to do was get the hell out of there."

"Did you hear if there were any leads as to who put it there?"

"Didn't hear. As I said, I just wanted to get out of the village as soon as I could. It was crazy with both law enforcement and gawkers trying to sneak a peek."

"Stay clear of that mess, Bob. We don't need to be involved with anything like that. I don't want to have people snooping and crawling around here because of this."

"Don't worry. I don't have any interest in that kind of crap."

With that said, each man turned and went about the task they were doing before Bob's arrival. Bob headed for his work shed with a sack from the local hardware store while John hoisted a bundle of firewood and headed toward his front porch.

Waiting inside, Kristin had seen the two men conversing while she sipped a cup of hot chocolate. Once John entered and placed the wood in the wood box next to their stove, she asked him what was up with Bob.

"He was telling me that there's a lot of commotion in the village. A couple of hungover local guys found a human head on the ice. Cops everywhere scrambling to figure things out."

"John!" she reacted with alarm.

"No! Don't worry. This has nothing to do with us", he said, taking her in his arms to belay her concerns. "We're fine here. It has been over a year, and our world has been very quiet. There's no reason to think this is connected to us in any way. Just relax."

"You're sure? Or are you just saying that to make me feel good?"

"I'm sure," he said with as much conviction as he could muster. He believed what he was telling her. But, in the deepest part of his brain, there was a flake of doubt. His past was not one easily left behind.

Chapter 3

All was quiet for the next few days. On the fourth day following the discovery of the head, Gretchen Black, an important long-time friend-confidante-mother-like figure in John's life, drove into the compound. Besides Bob and John, she was the only other person in the world who had direct access to the compound. 'Gretch,' as John called her, worked for him as a housekeeper, cook, nurse and most anything else that he needed in his life to survive, including doing most of the grocery shopping for the entire compound.

Deep down, she knew what Lucas did for a living and why the rest of the world knew him by another name. She knew but would never admit that she did. But she didn't want to know the details of his life or his activities. All she cared about was that he returned. More than once, he managed to return broken and in need of being nursed back to health. She was the for him and administered to his every need without asking any questions or wanting any answers.

She acted as another set of eyes and ears that John depended upon to keep informed as to what was taking place in the local area. She owned a small restaurant not far from where the dirt road leading to the compound met the state highway. Serving only breakfast left her lots of hours in her day to do other things. In addition, she worked as a part-time employee for the village police department. Her 'insider' position provided her with access to all the local information of potential importance to John.

Lastly, she was the person John trusted most in the world, even more than his trusted friend Bob, maybe even more than his new wife. Gretchen helped raise him. She was his adoptive mother's housemaid and replaced his parents after they died. She became a replacement mother and, with the approval of the local court, ran John's inheritance until he came of age. She never had children of her own. John, or Lucas as she knew him, was the closest thing she had to a son.

Today's visit was to deliver a weeks-worth of groceries to both Bob and John. Bob's wife Sally was very capable of doing her own shopping, but if she dared attempt to do so, she would risk Gretchen's wrath. After all, Gretchen had been a main character in John's life and the running of this compound for over thirty years and wasn't about to be replaced by any 'Johnny-come-lately, or, in this case, a Sally-come-lately. If you hadn't been here since John was a little boy, you were considered an intruder.

So too, Kristin was totally capable of doing the shopping for her and John. But, once again, John's life was sacred territory to Gretchen. She justified continuing to do "her job" by insisting that Kristin didn't know her way around the area yet and didn't want her to get lost up here in the expansive north country. In her mind, it would take Kristin forty or fifty years to learn her way to and from the closest grocery store. After all, it did require two turns along the way. Her role worked for all three of the women! A classic case of "If it ain't broke, don't fix it."

The three women got along wonderfully… so long as they followed Gretchen's structure and didn't try to upset her role in the life of the compound or that of Lucas Martin, aka John Anderson. She was the queen of the compound and they were the ladies in waiting.

She knocked once on the door to John's cabin before kicking it open with her heavy boot. It didn't matter to her if John and Kristin were running around naked or not. Her arms were loaded with bags of groceries, and she was on a mission. That's all that mattered. Kristin jumped up to assist, and John came from the rear of the cabin to pitch in.

"Hi beautiful," he greeted her with a smile, kiss on the cheek and exchanged a big hug once her arms were free of grocery bags.

"Don't beautiful me, young man. You have a real beauty in your life now. You don't need to be kissing up to me anymore. I'm an ugly old hag now."

"Come on, Gretchen," Kristin jumped in. "You know no one can replace you in his life. Not even me."

"Yeah! Yeah!" she replied joyfully. To Gretchen, these were her kids. She wholeheartedly welcomed Kristin into her life and, more importantly, into John's. She hated thinking of calling him John. To her, he was still the little boy she knew as Lucas, and he always would be. She had to fight her initial impulse to call him Lucas so as not to upset his second life.

"What's new in town?" John asked her.

"Well, the police have finally identified the head those two yahoos found on the ice last week."

"Really? Who was it?"

"He was a priest."

That got John and Kristin's attention.

"A priest!?" John reacted.

"Yep. A retired priest from Saratoga Springs. Lived in the St. Clements retirement home next to the church on Lake Avenue. Old guy in his mid-eighties. Been retired for many years. Originally came from somewhere down in Ulster County. Near Kingston."

"What about his body? Any luck finding it?"

"Nope. Rangers got the L.A.S.A.R. team out. But no luck so far."

"What's L.A.S.A.R.?" Kristin asked.

"Lower Adirondack Search and Rescue. Best search and rescue team in the whole damn state," Gretchen answered. "They're thinking the body was dumped somewhere in the woods. Only after this much time, they're thinking that the coyotes and bears have finished it off. Not much hope of finding a whole lot if the critters got to him. But, you know that L.A.S.A.R. bunch, John. They'll keep looking until Rangers tell them to stop. It's just what they do. Greatest, most dedicated, the best-trained bunch of ground pounders ever put together."

"How's Larry?" John asked as the two women busied themselves, putting groceries away. Larry Norton was the former President and Captain of the L.A.S.A.R. team.

"Not too good. Getting old like the rest of us."

"Is he still active with the team?"

"No, his wife kind of put a halt to that. The middle of the night calls from the Rangers, along with his general health and age, have all taken their toll on him. He still attends our monthly meetings and he still supports the Rangers when they need his radio equipment. And he still runs his mouth with all his stories. But that's about it."

"Too bad. He's a good man."

"One of the best," Gretchen added, choking up slightly over the thought of her old friend. "Known him a lot of years. Never be another like him."

"Stay for dinner. I'll whip up something special just for you," John said to her.

"Can't. Got too many things to do. Got to get Bob's groceries to him and Sally. Then I've got to get back to my place. Don't want to be out here after dark. Roads freeze up and get slicker than owl crap this time of year. Once the sun goes down and the cold moves in, driving gets more like ice skating. Kristin, you might want to take a look at some of the specials I picked up this week. Price Chopper had some nice items on sale this week in the frozen and produce areas of the store."

"Keep me posted on what's going on in town with all this turmoil, Gretchen. I need to know if it gets close to us in any way," John instructed her.

"You bet. See you guys in a few days. Oh, Kristin, there's something special in that small brown bag. One of your husband's favorites," and with that, she was gone, leaving John and Kristin alone again.

"Are you worried about what's going on in town?" Kristin asked him.

"No. Just needs to be cautious and stay informed," he answered. "Let's see what's in the little bag."

Kristin opened it to find two chocolate-covered custard-filled eclairs.

"I love that woman," John proclaimed, staring at tomorrow morning's breakfast.

The following morning provided more bad news. Just as John and Kristin were about to leave their cabin for an adventurous day of snowmobile riding on the lake, John's phone rang. Gretchen's number appeared on the screen.

"Good morning, Gretch. Oh! and thanks for the eclairs. They were great!"

"You're welcome, but I've got some bad news, John," she began curtly. "There's been another incident in town. They found another head on the ice. A couple of kids having a snowball fight saw it and started throwing snowballs at it until they got close enough to see what it was. Then they ran home, and their parents called the cops."

"Where was it this time?"

"That's another thing. It was found in almost the exact same spot as the first one."

"And I assume no one saw anything."

"Right. Not a soul. Apparently, it was placed there during the night just like the first one."

"Has it been I.D.'d yet?"

"Not yet. Local cops have secured the area and are waiting for the state guys to show up and take over."

"Damn!" John exclaimed. "How did you find out about it?"

"Friend of mine on the local PD gave me a call. I asked her to keep me in the loop."

"Stay clear of this, Gretchen. Don't get any closer than talking to your contact. Otherwise, keep away."

"Don't intend to get any closer. Got too much to do taking care of you… and your beautiful woman. In case you haven't noticed, I think the world of her."

"Thanks, Gretch. I know you do, and that means a lot to me. I'll see you soon."

He turned to find Kristin standing nearby, listening to his end of the telephone conversation.

"Is everything okay?" she asked him.

He filled her in on the details Gretchen had given him on the telephone. He could see the concern painted on his wife's face. One thing both of them hated and was feeling that they were in the dark, not having all the information available concerning events in their lives. It made them feel very exposed and vulnerable.

"I think our snowmobile ride will include a visit to the village. We'll stay way back out of the way, but I'd like to get a little closer look and a sense of what's going on."

"Isn't that a little risky, John?"

"Shouldn't be. I have been totally inactive and out of sight for almost a year and a half now. No reason to think anyone even knows who we are or where we came from. You know how things work in D.C. We're old news. Our fifteen minutes of fame is long over, thank God. The administration changed and along with it, most of the agency bigwigs. They've moved on, and we have to do the same.

"And besides, we'll have our helmets on, so our faces will be totally covered. We'll be just another couple of onlookers gawking at the activity. We'll be fine. I might even take you to one of my favorite pizza joints in town for lunch."

They left the cabin and walked down to the shoreline where Bob had parked his big snow machine. John asked if he could use it for a few hours. He pressed the electric start button and straddled the seat motioning Kristin to do the same. Soon, they were flying down the lake at over sixty-five miles per hour atop the flat snow-covered ice.

Kristin silently marveled at the scenery surrounding her. She felt as if they were inside of a crystal snow globe. The cold air biting at her skin wherever it could sneak through any opening in her protective face mask and helmet made her tingle and feel alive. Life in the North Country could to hard. But it was beautiful all the same. The ice, the snow, the cold, the surrounding mountains, the fjord scenery surrounding her new world, all the pieces fit together. Each is a part of the other. Like a new fashion outfit, she would wear to the winter ball. The dress, the shoes, the purse, and the jewelry were all necessary and not complete without the other.

What a wonderful winter wonderland this area is, she thought to herself. How wonderful it was to be here with the man she loved and how lucky she was to have found him and her new home. She hoped he would come to understand how much she loved him and loved living here with him. How excited she was about their new life.

Within a few minutes, they were closing in on the south end of the lake. They could see the various police and emergency vehicles that had been driven out on the ice to surround the scene. As in most cases, the response to an event, any event like this, was overdone. Where maybe three or four official vehicles would represent the necessary response, there were always four or five times that number present. Typical government response. Overkill for a killing.

No different at this incident. They could count nearly twenty sets of flashing lights. Police cars, ambulances, and fire trucks. John wondered why multiple ambulances were necessary to deal with a single human head already detached from a body no longer in need of medical attention. How many band-aids and medics did it take to fix a severed head? Were any of the EMTs going to screw the head back on and say, "Okay, all better, you can go home now!".

And why were fire trucks necessary when there was no fire, and the incident took place on a lake filled with water and covered with ice and snow? Guess it had to do with the 'boys and their toys' syndrome.

As they approached the south end of the lake, police directed them toward the western edge of the shoreline, away from the cordoned-off area. John stopped as he neared the boardwalk leading to one of the local restaurants. Every inch of the sidewalk and the street was jammed with dozens and dozens of people trying to catch a glimpse of what was going on. The crowd buzzed with all kinds of speculation as to the who, what, when, where and why this was happening. *This was Lake George! A quiet little mountain resort town in Upstate New York! This wasn't the big city where there were criminals. This was Lake George. These things didn't happen here!*

After parking his snow machine on the ice near the shoreline, John led Kristin on a meandering walk among the crowd. He wanted to pick up as much information as he could from the crowd's buzz. He led her toward the area where the police and medical personnel were concentrated to see if he could hear anything of importance. He heard nothing.

He then led Kristin toward the center of town. There were far fewer vehicles on the main road and almost no pedestrians. Everyone was trying to cram into the limited space closer to the morbid scene on the ice. Every possible vantage point was crammed with an onlooker.

Across the main street near the center of the village, he took her into an Italian pizza restaurant where they could order pizza with a variety of toppings by the slice. Once inside, they each took off their helmets for the first time.

They each ordered two slices of pizza. John ordered a Stewart's Crème soda to drink, and Kristin ordered a Diet Root Beer. While waiting for their order, Kristin decided that it was a good time to ask John a question that had been on her mind for some time.

"John, what's the 'N' for?"

"The 'N'?"

"Yeah, the 'N' in your name. You know, John N. Anderson."

"You really want to get into that now?"

"Yeah! Why not?"

"Nothing!"

"What do you mean?"

"Nothing," he repeated.

"Well, if you don't want to tell me, just say so," she responded with a minor attitude.

"It stands for nothing," he repeated.

"It's got to stand for something!"

"I mean nothing."

"Yeah, okay, I get it! You know, I am your wife now. You don't have to cop an attitude with me over this. Don't you think it's okay if you share it with me?"

"It's nothing!" he repeated.

"Okay, I said I get it. Just drop the subject."

"Kristin, it stands for nothing. N-O-T-H-I-N-G, nothing." He leaned toward her so no one within earshot would hear him. "When I took my operational name, I was told that I needed to have a middle initial to put on my fake I.D. I couldn't think of anything, so I put an 'N' for nothing. So, the 'N' is for Nothing. My entire operational name became John Nothing Anderson."

"You've got to be kidding me!"

"Nope!

"You are kidding me, right!"

"I'm serious, I became John N. Anderson. Given what I did, don't you think it's an appropriate name? I spent most of my life trying to be unseen, to blend into a crowd, to be …... nothing. So, there you go. Yours truly, John N., for nothing, Anderson. Simple! Like I've been telling you for months, I'm a simple man."

She looked at him in wonderment. "You are anything but simple, Mister Nothing. You are the most complex and complicated human being I've ever known, and that's why I love you so damn much. Now, let's get out of here. Take me back to the cabin. I'm in the mood to screw your brains out this afternoon."

After wolfing down their pizza, the check was paid, and they were speeding across the ice again within minutes with a new sense of urgency.

Chapter 4

Two days later, John received another call from Gretchen.

"Hi, pretty lady," he answered.

"Hey, John. Got some news for you."

"Okay, go ahead."

"Got a call from my police friend concerning the second head."

"Yeah?"

"Well, it wasn't another Catholic priest."

"That's good news, I guess," he replied.

"Well, yes and no. This one was a Lutheran priest."

"Whoa! That's a bit too coincidental."

"I'd say. He was from a church up north near Plattsburg. Been missing for a couple of days. A much younger man, only in his late forties."

"What about a body?"

"Nothing. Rangers and police are looking everywhere, up north near Plattsburg as well as in the area surrounding our village. They're spread a little thin. They're also searching the lake. So far, they've come up with nothing."

"The lake? All thirty-plus miles of it?"

"Yeah," she answered. "They are out there with a four-wheeler, snow machines and on foot. They've pulled in every Forest Ranger in the Northern Tier of the state, as far away as Buffalo. It's a cold, tough job. They're going to be at it for quite some time. I'm sure they will be buzzing by your place sometime or other. Might want to keep an eye out for them."

"Okay, keep me posted if you hear anything new," as he said goodbye.

He turned to Kristin and filled her in on the news.

"What are you thinking?" she asked him.

"Two things. Two clergymen, that is no coincidence, and I think there will be more. Someone is sending a message."

"To you?" she asked.

"No, I don't think so. I can't imagine any message to me that would involve clergymen. I think this has nothing remotely to do with me. The location is probably a pure coincidence. I think this is some crazed nut or group of nuts making some sort of a statement. We need to be informed so that it doesn't sneak up on us while we're staying as clear of the whole damn thing as we possibly can."

"I agree," she replied.

But it wouldn't be that easy. Exactly one week later, John's telephone alerted him for the third time.

"What's up, Gretch?"

"They're coming your way!"

"Who?"

"The police. A whole shit load of them. There's been another killing…… another head has been found."

"Where?"

"Same place. This time it was a woman."

Just as she spoke, John could hear a loud commotion coming from the direction of the lakefront. He looked through his front window to see half a dozen snowmobiles rapidly approaching the compounds from the ice.

"Got to go, Gretch. They're here."

Kristin came running to join him at the window. "What's going on?"

"Gretchen just called. There's been another killing. A woman's head was found this time."

"But who are these people, and why are they here?"

"Police, but I don't know why."

As they stood watching from within their cabin, they saw Bob exit his house and calmly walk toward the edge of the lake, where the shoreline buried itself beneath the ice. John watched as the snowmobiles came to a stop, practically surrounding Bob. There were two men on each machine, one civilian and one uniformed law enforcement personnel. John could distinguish at least three different uniforms: state, sheriff and Forest Ranger.

One of the state officers removed his helmet and began talking to Bob. John would stay back away from direct contact with the police until and unless it was absolutely necessary. Bob was the known face of the compound in the community and John would leave the discussions up to his trusted friend.

The conversation went on for almost fifteen minutes. The officer, who was clearly in command, pointed toward the lake several times as well as toward the compound area, including John's cabin.

Finally, after shaking hands with Bob, all the men re-mounted their snow machines and headed back out across the ice. Bob remained standing where the conversation took place until all the machines were well out on the ice and away from the compound. He then turned and headed toward John's cabin.

John opened the door before Bob got within fifty yards of his front porch. He stepped outside to hear what Bob had to report.

"What's up?" he asked his long-time friend.

"Another head was found early this morning."

"Yeah, I know. Gretchen called to warn me just as the posse came buzzing up the lake."

"Did she tell you it was a woman?"

"Yeah."

"Well, they know who it is this time. One of the state guys knew her. She's an Episcopalian priest from Albany."

"Another priest?"

"Yeah. There's a real pattern developing here," Bob said.

"WOW!" John exclaimed. "I presume they haven't found a body yet."

"Correct."

"Okay, so why did they come flying up here as if their butts were on fire?" John asked.

"Well, seems that this time, there was a trail. The state police helicopter picked up a fresh snowmobile track in the snow covering the ice. It led in this general direction. Their checking every possible place it might have pulled on or off the ice. Ours is one of the few places along the east shoreline where someone can access the lake. They're headed over to Bolton Landing right now to question people over that way. Wanted to know if we had seen or heard anything during the night."

"Did you?"

"No. Sally and I finished off a bottle of wine with dinner last night and hit the sack pretty early. I slept like a log until this morning. I don't think I would have heard anything unless it drove through our bedroom."

"I saw you pointing up this way."

"Yeah, they wanted to know who else was in residence in the compound."

"What did you tell them?"

"The truth. That one of the owners and his new wife were here, but that you didn't have a snowmobile and that mine was locked up all night. Told them that I had the keys to the house where no one could get them without me knowing it."

"Did they buy it?"

"Sure, they did. I'm the good guy around here. Besides, one of the rangers that were with that group spoke up and told the state guy that he knew me really well."

"Where were they headed next?" John asked.

"Like I said, across the lake toward Bolton Landing. They're going to question the guests at the Sagamore to see if anybody there saw or heard anything. Don't think they'll be back this way."

"We'll see!" John said as he turned to walk back to his cabin.

When he entered the warm environment, Kristin was waiting.

"What was all that about?"

"Take a guess."

"Another head."

"You got it."

"Why did the police come here?"

John explained what Bob had relayed to him concerning the conversation with the police. She could tell by the expression on his face that John was more concerned than he was willing to share with her.

"John, you're worried about this, aren't you?"

"A little. Like I told you, I don't think this has anything to do with me or with us. But, when it starts getting close to us, I begin to worry. I'm very uneasy about visits from the police, and if they wanted to search the compound... well, I'd have a problem with that. There are things I have stashed here that I wouldn't want them to find. Besides, I get a bit nervous knowing that there's a serial killer or killers operating in my neighborhood. I'm primarily concerned about your safety".

"I understand," she replied. "But, we're just two people living their lives in our beautiful home. Can't you get rid of the things you don't want them to find?"

"Yeah, I could."

"But…?"

"But I won't."

"Why not?"

"Some things are not replaceable and others….I just won't."

"I think I understand," she added. "So let's just leave it at that and make damn sure no one can find anything you don't want found."

"Sounds good, Kristin. But cops are never that easy to please. If they start sticking their noses into our presence here, we'd have to come up with a lot of explanations like who's John N. Anderson when the title to this cabin and our marriage license is in another name? When did we come here? How long are we planning on staying? And each question would lead to another. That is what makes me nervous.

"This is very difficult for me. Being here, being with people, having you in my life. It's all so strange for me. I've spent most of my adult life alone and isolated. My first reaction to anyone in uniform was to run and hide. If anyone tried to get close to me in any way, all my alarms went off, and my training kicked in, telling me to kill. Kill before I get killed.

"Suddenly, everything is different. You, living here in one place, being around people, not running and hiding. It's different for me, Kristin, and it's very difficult. I have to fight to control my initial reactions and not lash out. Not suspect everything and everyone as a threat. And not to meet that threat as I was trained to do.

"This whole thing in the village is getting a bit too close to us for my comfort level. My usual relationship with the authorities is to keep them miles and miles away from me. So, I might have to get out and try to find out what's going on before it comes down on our heads. I don't like surprises. I don't want to be blindsided."

"Do you think we should start by using your real name? Should we start calling you Lucas? Should we tell Bob and Sally and leave 'John' in the dust?"

"Might not be a bad idea. Would take some getting used to".

"John!" she reached out and took his hands in hers. "Maybe we should load up the motorhome and take a trip somewhere. That way, you wouldn't have to do anything."

"Don't worry, little lady. I'm not going to do anything stupid. I just think it might be time for us to establish ourselves as a part of the community. There's no reason for me, or us, to be on the radar of the local or state cops. We've done nothing to draw their attention. And, if what our friend Bruce back in D.C. has been telling me is to be believed, neither of us exists any longer. Our past lives don't exist in the federal records. We're smoke to the rest of the world.

"I think it's time we are born again, so to speak. I like your idea of Lucas Martin being reborn. I think I should get Bob and Sally and call Gretchen in as well and have a conversation about that in a day or two."

Chapter 5

Kristin sat on the couch, brooding for the rest of the afternoon. She was clearly unhappy, uncertain and nervous about what John was struggling with. John knew he had to settle her nerves. He didn't want her to sulk. He would need her help to carry out his plan to assimilate them into the community. He knew they could not exist for the rest of their lives, restricted to the compound using false names. And he knew he could not and didn't want to do it alone.

Sooner or later, they would have to stretch their newfound freedom to include the world beyond the cement-filled barrier pipe guarding their roadway and all the other security in place along the frozen lake shoreline. The two of them, as husband and wife, needed to assimilate back into the local population. They had to become members of the community and take part in local events. They had to become social and rejoin the human race.

He approached from behind her, reaching over the back of the couch to gather her in his arms.

"When was the last time I told you that I loved you?" he asked.

"About a month and a half ago or maybe two," she replied, pouting.

"Oh, it was not. It was more like an hour or two ago," he said, leaning over to nibble on her ear.

"That will get you nowhere," she said.

"Want to bet?" he answered sarcastically. "Always has so far."

"Stop!" she commanded mockingly.

He slid over the back of the couch, landing in her lap, pulling her down to him and kissing her warmly.

"I love you," he said.

"I know you do. And I love you."

"Okay, then, there are two things I want you to remember. First, I would never do anything that would put you in danger. But, neither will I allow anyone to get near enough to you to harm you.

"Second, you have got to remember that I've been living like this for a lot of years. I know all the warning signs. I look for them all day, every day. And I don't see any. So, let's learn to live a little. We've got millions of dollars sitting around in bank accounts all over the world doing nothing. We've got a box full of cash under our bed that's enough for most families to live on for years, and it's doing nothing. And, neither are we. We need to get out and start living. We need to laugh and have some fun."

She hesitated for a moment before leaning down to kiss him again.

"Okay. Then, I'm going to give you a list of the things you have promised me."

"I thought that's what you might have been thinking about all afternoon."

"No. I was thinking about you."

"Me? What have you been thinking about me?"

"John," she began somberly. "I know only what I know about you. But I don't know you. I mean, I know you as a man and now as a husband. I know you have a loving side with very deep emotions. And I know everything that's in your file. I know you as a government agent and everything in your file. I know every assignment you have ever been on. I know what you did for a living, and I know you on a day-to-day level over the past year and a half. And I have fallen totally in love with you and want to be with you forever."

"But?"

"But, I also know there is much more. The part that I don't know is what made you who you are. Not what you are… or I should say, what you were. Or even what you did. Not the government trained and paid assassin I worked with. Not the government agent who traveled the world protecting his country. That's the John Anderson on paper. That's the John N. Anderson that was created. I need to know what made the man I lay next to every night. I need to know Lucas Martin."

He looked up at her beautiful face. Her sparkling eyes melted his defenses. His immediate reaction to her questions was to run. To get up and run. To put up a wall to protect himself. Or to lash out at her. To protect himself by distancing himself from her. He had a conditioned mistrust of anyone asking questions about his history. He wanted to run and hide or turn and kill.

But he couldn't. Not from her. For years, he trusted her as his handler…… his control. Now, he had grown to trust her in totally new ways. He trusted her as much as he loved her, and he couldn't run away and leave this new-found trust and love behind.

He had come to know that she and his feelings for her were what was missing in his life for all the years without her. He took a deep breath and sat up straight on the couch, fortifying himself. Reaching deep within himself for a strength he needed to use for the first time.

"Wow!" he said. "I knew deep down that one day you would ask me that question. I guess I just never wanted to think about dealing with it."

"But, you knew that sooner or later, I needed to know," she stated.

"Yeah, I knew. And you have every right to know. I've taken you into my life and completely changed yours. You have a right to know everything."

"It doesn't have to be right now, John. Not if you're not ready."

"Kristin, I'll never be ready. You don't know how hard it is for me to do this. So, now is as good a time as any."

He stood and walked to the window facing the lake. It was just turning dark outside. He gazed out across the lake for a couple of minutes collecting himself before sitting in a plush armchair facing his new wife. His new life.

"I can't sit next to you for this. If I'm touching you, I'll never get it out. Okay?"

"Okay."

He sat quietly, looking down at the floor. She waited patiently, giving him time to sort his thoughts and emotions.

"I've spent my entire life avoiding anyone knowing anything about me," he began. "The only people who know about my life are Bob and Gretchen. No one else alive knows what you want me to tell you."

"I understand. If you'd rather not…"

He held up his hand to stop her from talking.

"No. I think I should. I think I owe it to you. Maybe even to myself."

Once again, he sat silently, looking down on the floor and gathering himself.

"You already know a lot of my early years thanks to your conversations with Gretchen. She was the formative figure in my early years. She was my anchor, and I learned a lot from her.

"What I became as a man came from those years. However, it was only after I left home and went to college that I began to become the man you have come to know. I had to leave the sheltered life of an adolescent to begin to find myself, to grow into an adult.

"I believe that once a person becomes an adult, he or she should form their own opinions, their own personalities, make their own decisions and take their own direction in life and not blame everything on someone else. It's too easy to use others as a crutch, as an excuse. To do so, to me, is a cop-out. It's a sign of weakness. To blame what I am, what I have become, or what I have done on my parents is a cop-out.

"Sooner or later, we all need to put a hand in the rear of our pants, grab a handful of ass and pull up. There comes a time when we must stop blaming others for everything. Stop using their shortcomings as an excuse for our own. I have no tolerance for people who say, 'I'm a rotten person because of the way my father or mother treated me.' That's weakness, and I have no tolerance for weakness. It makes you weak."

He paused for a moment to calm himself and search for a new beginning. He knew he was rambling and letting his emotions take over. He paused and took a deep breath. He began again.

"The most prevalent thing I remember as a kid is being alone. I was constantly alone. I sought out others, but I never felt like I fit in. I felt uncomfortable, different somehow inferior. Like I had a big neon sign hanging across my chest warning people away.

"I felt as if those I sought out never accepted me because of what I projected to them. My friends described me as a loner. I don't know if others didn't accept me… or if I didn't allow them to accept me. I remember what my high school counselor once told me. He said, 'You need to learn how to let people be your friends.' I don't know if I ever did.

"I did things alone. When I was really young, I would ride my bike for miles along the back roads of the farm country where I was raised. Then, as a teenager, I got into hiking and hunting. The woods became my sanctuary. I would spend all day hiking to nowhere or sitting in a tree stand with a good book, letting the hours drift by, pretending to be waiting for a deer to come within range.

"After my parents were killed, I felt guilty that I didn't really miss them. They were gone, but they had never really been there anyway. It was like wearing shoes without socks. Shoes fit just as well and functioned the same. So, my life without socks really didn't change all that much. I just slipped on my shoes, left my socks on the floor and kept on walking.

"The only person… the one and the only person who ever held me and made me feel loved and safe is Gretchen. To this day, she is special. She saved me from the world and from myself.

"In school, I was the runt of the class until the summer before my senior year in high school. That summer, when nobody was around to see it happen, I suddenly shot up in height and weight. That was the first time anyone took notice of me. However, by that time, I didn't need them. I didn't need to be noticed or accepted. I was fine with who I was. Then I went off to college. Except there, it was me who rejected everyone else. I didn't need them, and I really didn't know how to accept them into my life.

"My time in the Army was probably the best time of my life. In the military, everyone's the same. Everybody starts off the same. Everybody is equal. Everyone is a piece of crap. Doesn't matter how big or tall or fast or good-looking you might be, everybody's the same piece of crap. Everybody starts with a blank slate. It gave me the opportunity to remake myself.

"Sure, as time passes, as you move up in the ranks, things change. But it's a visible change. You know when a guy has stripes on his sleeve, he's different but he came from the same place. He's there, and he has those stripes on his arm because he earned it, not because his daddy was rich, or that he could run fast or dunk a basketball or hit a home run or if you date the prettiest girl.

"It doesn't matter if you're tall or short or black or white; the only thing that matters is if you can be depended on. Can the guy next to you depend on you to shoot the guy who's trying to kill him and you? Could you be depended on to bleed… to die?"

He paused again. Kristin detected that he was switching his internal gears and moving on to another phase of his life.

"When the agency recruited me, it was a natural, almost seamless transition. I may have been a loner as a high school boy, but I perfected it as a college student and soldier.

They put me into a life that required being alone being secretive. That was like falling off a rock for me. The taking of a human life took a bit more of an adjustment. But I had already been in combat. I had already taken lives, albeit from a distance. I had already dealt with the sickness of knowing what I had done, what it was like to kill.

"The first one up close was difficult. It was on one, face-to-face. Up close and personal, as the cliché goes. It's not like on the battlefield shooting at someone who is shooting back at you from a hundred yards away.

"In the military, you are indoctrinated to kill because the other guy is an enemy, That he's trying to kill you and bring harm to your fellow countrymen back home. With the agency… you are indoctrinated to kill because you are made to believe the target is evil and needs to be eliminated. And, after all my years in the field, I truly believe there are evil people in this world. People who need to die. Evil people.

"By the time I could count more than thirty kills, adding one more didn't affect me much. It became just a number. An academic exercise. With each added kill, I became further detached from reality, from the impact of taking a life. I think… from life itself, I became less and less human.

"I withdrew after each assignment. I readied myself for the next one. Planning was everything. If you read popular books about agents like me, their activities are filled with minor miracles. Exotic weapons somehow appear in the most convenient places at the most convenient times. Numerous passports with brand-new identities materialize out of thin air. Money if currencies that just happen to match the country the agent is going to appear in limitless quantities stashed in just the perfect places.

"All of that is crap. It doesn't happen like that. Nothing happens without careful and meticulous planning. Over and over again. Plan and plan and plan some more. And trusted partners don't exist. Fancy wardrobes don't appear in luggage in a bus or airport terminal locker. All preparations are internalized and done alone. One man casts a shadow. Two create a crowd.

"I also became very wealthy in the process. You know the amount of money I was paid. Some assignments would make a Fortune 500 company top executive wonder if he were in the right kind of job. To me, the money meant nothing. I was not able to enjoy myself or the money I was paid. I had no interests, no hobbies and most of all, no one to share it with.

"I had to stay in the shadows. The money just sat somewhere in a bank. It's still there. I didn't spend much of what I was paid. So, the money I earned, along with the sales commissions from my cover job and the inheritance from my parents just built up in the accounts I have spread around the world. I got rich financially… but I was bankrupt as a man. I've learned and come to understand the price of that money.

"I became numb. Financially rich but broke in almost every other way. The only thing that mattered was the successful completion of the mission…. and staying alive. That became the justification for what I did. To serve my country, to eliminate an evil person, and to stay alive. Survive. Vanish until the next assignment. Be alone. Disappear. Stay hidden. Live in the shadows.

"That was how I lived… how I existed until a couple of years ago. You'll remember there was a stretch of about six months when I had no assignments. It was during the change of presidential administrations. The new president hadn't figured out yet who he wanted to have killed. Who were his enemies?

"During that lull, I spent most of my time up here, in the Adirondack Mountains. I hiked and hunted and sat in the woods, freezing my butt off, reading books while sitting in a tree stand or on a cold rock waiting. I'm not sure what I was waiting for, but I knew something had to come along.

"It was during that period that I felt little pieces of me begin to return. What startled me the most was that I didn't even know that those pieces were missing until they began to become apparent to me. I remember playing with a magnet when I was a kid. I remember watching metal shavings move toward the magnet. They kept building and building. That's the way I felt. Like I was attracting all the missing pieces back to me. It was that sense, that feeling of being rebuilt within myself, when I came to realize the reality of what I had been doing for years.

"It was then that I knew that with each life I took, a piece of me died too. It was the return of these pieces, the metal shavings, that made me understand that I had to stop. I had to stop doing what I was doing, or there would be no more me. No more pieces of me, and I would never be able to reclaim those that were already missing.

"It was about that same time I also came to realize that there was someone else in my life that filled a big hole. Someone who presented a piece of me that I didn't even know I had. A vitally important element to me is having a real life.

"When I was in high school, I had such a crush on a new girl who moved into our little town. I fell for her the first day she came to our school. But one of my closest friends began dating her. So, I moved out of the way.

"I had never loved anyone since. It was a piece that I never missed before because, as an agent, I had never been allowed to love. Never allowed to have anyone in my life. Besides, I didn't know about love. I didn't know what love was. I didn't know how to love. You can't miss love if you never had it and you can't love if you don't know how. So, love was not an emotion I didn't understand. I thought of it as more like a duty that one person had to complete for another.

"Until I realized… until I admitted to myself, allowed myself to love you. I didn't realize that you were the biggest missing piece in my life, within me. I knew after the first time I met you that you opened something totally new and frightening inside of me. It scared me. Whenever I thought of you, it scared me. Scared the crap out of me. For the first time in my life, I came to realize that something was missing.

"When the last crazy screwed up mission came along the one involving the president and the prime minister of Canada. It was a God-sent. It brought me in from the field, and all the crazy circumstances that evolved from that mission led me to you. Forced us together. Broke the barrier between us because of our jobs and led me to this couch, to you and to this very moment."

He looked up for the first time. Kristin's gaze was riveted on him. Tears streamed down her cheeks as she absorbed every word he said. Saw the expression painted on his face as he spoke.

They looked into each other eyes for the first time since he began his story. She raced across the room, throwing herself into his arms. They held each other so tight they could hardly breathe. But breathing was not necessary at this moment. Holding onto each other was far more important. It was all that mattered. It was life itself.

Chapter 6

The following morning, he was in his usual place when Kristin went looking for him with a hot mug of coffee in her hand. A light snow was falling, coating everything, including John and the quilt wrapped around him, with a fresh dusting of white powder.

"It's freezing out here!" she said as she leaned over and kissed him lightly on the lips.

"Yeah. It feels great. Gets your blood pumping."

She snuggled in next to him and wrapped herself in the quilt he had taken from their bed. "How about I make you some pancakes for breakfast?"

"Sounds great," he responded scooping her up in his arms and a playful embrace. "Then we're going shopping."

"Okay! That's music to a girl's ears. What are we going shopping for?"

"Well, if we're going to re-join the world as we talked about yesterday, we're going to need a few things that normal people around here own and use. Besides that, we need to have some fun and adventure in our lives."

"Like?"

"You'll see. I'm hungry. How about those pancakes!"

An hour later, with Bob driving them in his truck, they were headed toward Saratoga Springs. The first stop was a Chrysler, Jeep and Ram truck dealership on Maple Avenue, just north of the village, not far from a large school building. Bob dropped them off and headed back home.

John took Kristin into the showroom, and a couple of hours later, they departed the dealership in a brand-new Jeep Grand Cherokee with more bells and whistles than Santa Claus' sled on Christmas Eve. It included more gadgets than either of them would ever learn to use. Paid for with some of the cash that was stashed under their bed.

The next stop was to the south in the town of Halfmoon on Route 9, a little north of the capital city of Albany. The town was named after the ship the Dutch captain Henry Hudson used to explore the river now named after him. It is said that this is about as far north as he could sail before being stopped by the rapids and waterfalls present in the upper reaches of the river.

John pulled into a dealership located on a bluff overlooking the Mohawk River adjacent to the beginning of the historic Erie Canal. The dealership sold both snowmobiles and ATVs. It didn't take long before they were leaving with a flatbed trailer attached to their new Jeep loaded with one each. Two powerful machines, one for ice and one for mud. Once again, both brand-new vehicles were fully paid for in cash and registered to Mr. and Mrs. Lucas Martin of Fort Ann, New York, just as the Jeep was. Welcome back to civilization.

On the way back home, John told Kristin that he wanted to drive into the Village of Lake George to see what was going on. He parked in the parking lot of a motel a couple of blocks away from the waterfront. When they walked down to the area surrounding the beach. There were at least a dozen emergency vehicles with flashing lights blocking the street. John guessed there to be about a hundred people milling around, stretching their necks to get a peek at what was going on.

John took Kristin by the hand and led her toward the terrace of a restaurant that overlooked the south end of the lake. The restaurant was closed for the winter season. No one bothered them as they stood looking over the railing along with a group of locals. They could see police and some sort of medical unit milling around a focal point a couple of hundred feet out on the ice. Additional police units and two ambulances were parked near the beach area.

Everyone in the crowd tilted their heads to whisper into the ear of the person next to them. Each had a tidbit of information exclusive to themselves afraid to be heard by anyone else. Each had a deep, dark secret to tell or the solution to the crime that was too good to share. A town full of junior Dick Tracy all, knowing more than the genius standing next to them and all-knowing a whole lot more than the total contingent of police scurrying about the ice.

John looked out over the crowd, searching for something that might send a signal of some sort. Watching for and finding signs of alarm was a vital part of his past life. It came naturally for him to observe everything that was going on around him. It wasn't always the unusual that stuck out. Sometimes, it was what looked too usual, too ordinary, that gave him concern. Too normal could be abnormal.

For the next thirty minutes, nothing much happened. One police vehicle would leave, and another would arrive. Fingers were pointed in every direction toward unseen points or objects of interest. It became clear to him that the officials working at this crime scene didn't have a clear direction for anything. They were baffled.

There was something that finally caught his eye. Standing not too far from the cruise boat slip, four men stood together. They didn't seem to be talking to each other or sharing anything at all concerning the action on the ice. They simply stood watching. Absorbing everything. Checking not the activities but the people gathered around the lake shore and the surrounding area. He had looked past them a couple of times before he realized their odd behavior. They did nothing that stuck out… which, to him, made them stick out.

All four were dressed from head to toe in black. Not that unusual. But they were all dressed in the exact same black outfits. Same coats. Same hats. They have the same pants and the same gloves. They could pass as a four-man bobsled team, all dressed in uniform. The four moved and swayed as one. A grove of Aspen trees, each separate, but all linked to the other sharing the same root system.

Kristin looked at John, seeing that he was studying the men. "What's wrong, John?" she asked him.

"See those four guys dressed in black down there near the boat dock?"

"Yeah."

"Does anything appear odd to you?"

"No, not really. All wearing the same outfits. Maybe they're brothers or something. Or maybe they're wearing some sort of work uniforms, you know, like from Jiffy Lube or something."

"Yeah. Brothers! Guys are working together. Probably something like that."

Just then, one of the four men, the tallest one, flicked his head to one side. It was a signal of some sort. All four, without a word spoken, like a unit in unison, turned and walked away. John watched as they crossed the street and walked toward a white Ford van parked at the curb a block away. John watched.

They were across the street from the terrace where John and Kristin were standing, but close enough for John to see the definite effort the four made to conceal their faces. Each had a black scarf wrapped around their neck for warmth. Each wore them high enough to cover their faces as if they were riding at high speed on a snowmobile, leaving only their eyes exposed.

They climbed into the white van and pulled away. When the van reached the corner, it turned right, heading north out of town. John lost physical sight of them when the van drove behind the buildings lining the main street. But, he registered the men and the van in his mind for the future.

A few minutes later, he and Kristin returned to their new vehicles and drove home. When they got to their cabin, Bob helped unload the new toys from the trailer.

"Nice equipment!" he said to John.

"Yeah, figured we needed our own. Couldn't keep borrowing your stuff. Now, we can all take off and play together."

"Sally's going to love that. She's been griping to me about getting out with you two and having some fun on the ice and in the woods. She loves snow and winter sports. Crazy woman!"

"Good!" John said. "Let's plan on a day out. How about we take the snow machines and head up north toward Roger's Rock? We can build a fire on the ice and have a cookout."

"Sounds like fun. I'll tell Sally."

The two men went their separate ways for the rest of the day. The only lingering thought either of them had was the haunting image John in John's mind of four men dressed in black with faces covered, climbing into a van and disappearing out of town.

Chapter 7

"Hello," John answered his cell phone.

"We have a problem!" Bob said to him.

"What's the problem?"

"I just got buzzed from the gate. The State Police are here."

"Did they say why?"

"Yeah, they want to talk to you. They asked to see Mr. Lucas Martin."

John's response was delayed by the utter surprise of what Bob was telling him. It took him a few seconds to regain his composure. Why the sudden unannounced visit, and why the reference to Lucas Martin?

"Well, let's not keep them waiting. Let them in, and I'll meet you out front."

It had been almost a week since John and Kristin had been out shopping and viewed the crime scene in the village and their discussion about using his real name. His head was spinning with this surprise visit from the state police. He fought off the 'flight or fight' urge that instantly flashed across his mind and through his body.

"What's up, babe?" Kristin asked as she sensed the tension in his body language.

"State police are here."

"What! Why?"

"Don't know. They want to talk to me. To Lucas Martin."

She sprang to her feet, caught totally off guard by what John had just said.

"Bob went up to open the gate. I'll meet them out front. You stay here. If they see the look you have on your face right now, they might just lock us up forever". He said sarcastically. "Just sit here for a while until I see what's going on."

"Okay," she replied nervously.

"If they come inside, just go with the flow. Got it?""

"Got it!"

John put on his warm jacket and stepped out onto his front porch. A couple of minutes later, Bob pulled up on his ATV, followed closely by an unmarked dark gray sedan with official-looking license plates and emergency lights mounted inside, and four antennae sticking up from the roof and trunk lid.

A man John guessed to be in his early fifties exited the car. He was dressed in a business suit, not in uniform. He was about six-foot-two inches tall and looked as if he just stepped out of the gym. He was very obviously in top-notch physical condition.

John walked down the steps of his porch and approached the two men. Bob spoke first.

"Lucas, let me introduce you to Superintendent Charles Drake. Mr. Drake is the Superintendent of the New York State Police. He's the top cop in the state."

John extended his hand, as did Superintendent Drake. The two exchanged a firm and friendly greeting looking each other directly in the eye with a smile on their face.

"Superintendent, what brings an important man like you out here in this cold weather? How can I help you?" John asked politely.

"Is there anywhere we can talk privately," Drake asked.

"I'll get out of your hair and leave you two to talk," Bob said, excusing himself.

"Thank you," Drake acknowledged. "And thank you for escorting me into the compound."

"My pleasure," Bob replied, looking toward his old friend before he turned and walked away. "Give me a shout if you need me… Lucas."

"How can I help you, Superintendent?" John repeated.

"I need a few minutes of your time, Mr. Martin. Just trying to clear up a couple of things."

"Please, let's go inside. Much warmer than standing out here in the snow," John invited.

When they entered the living area of John's cabin, Kristin came to attention as if barked at by a drill sergeant. Her nervousness radiated across the room. Superintendent Drake couldn't contain his amused reaction to his presence.

"Superintendent Drake, this is my wife, Kristin. Kristin, Superintendent Drake. He is the commanding officer of the New York State Police."

"Superintendent Drake," Kristin said timidly, approaching with her hand extended.

"Charles, please, Mrs. Martin. And please don't be so nervous. I'm a cop, but I didn't come here in an official status. At least, not totally, and I'm not here to arrest anyone," he added with a big grin painted across his face.

"Okay, Charles. And it's Kristin."

"Please have a seat," John said. "Now, what can we do for you… may I call you Charles, or is the first name status reserved only for attractive females?"

"No, Charles is fine with me," he chuckled. "As I said, I'm here in a … mixed capacity at the moment. So, let's keep it informal."

"Good, so what is the purpose of your visit?"

"I would prefer if we talked privately," he answered. "I'm not sure…" he nodded toward Kristin.

"Please be assured, Charles. There is nothing my wife doesn't know about me, so please speak freely."

"You're sure?"

"I'm sure!"

"Very well."

"Oh, one minor thing," John interrupted. "Do you mind showing me your credentials?"

"Not at all," Drake answered reaching in his coat pocket for his identification.

John examined the badge and supporting I.D. documents with a practiced eye. He then passed them to Kristin so she, too, would be satisfied that the man in their home was who he said he was. She then handed them back to Drake.

"You're aware of the situation that has developed in town in the last couple of weeks?" he asked both John and Kristin.

"Yes, we are. Why do you ask?"

"Well, you can imagine that an event, or I should say, events such as these, has everyone on edge. All of the law enforcement agencies are naturally on high alert and sensitive to anything in the area that seems… out of the ordinary."

"We can certainly understand that," John replied.

"When this all began, my department was designated as the agency that would lead the investigation. Therefore, as the head of that agency, everything remotely connected to an event of this magnitude crosses my desk. Particularly, any item that is, as I said, out of the ordinary."

"Understood," John acknowledged.

"Well, because of that high level of sensitivity, there were a couple of incidents in the local area that alerted one of my people involved in the ongoing investigation," Drake explained, clearly measuring his words.

"Excuse me, Charles. It's clear you are walking on eggs with what the real reason is that you're here. Don't! You're too important a person to be here to talk about what's going on in town. Please get to your point."

"Okay," he responded. "About a week ago, you purchased a brand-new Jeep Grand Cherokee in Saratoga. You paid for it in full… in cash. The size of a cash transaction draws attention. Then, on the same day, you purchased an ATV and a snowmobile along with a trailer to haul them on, also paid in full with cash raising a second alarm.

"Together, the transactions totaled nearly seventy-five thousand dollars. Any cash transaction of this size taking place on its own would be cause for concern. Given what's going on with heads being found skillfully detached from their owner's bodies, added to that the proximity of where you live to these murders, I think you can understand the connection and alarm."

John tried to speak, but Drake held up his hand to stop him. He continued.

"When my people started examining these purchases, they found that all three vehicles involved were now registered to a man and woman that no one seems to know. A man who, a little over a year ago, seems to have appeared out of nowhere. So, as good, curious cops, they started looking a little deeper.

"The only documents they could find in the name of Lucas Martin were a newly renewed driver's license, a marriage license, and a deed to this property. However, curiously, that deed dates back over twenty years. By itself, not of much concern. But, when they could find no records of bank accounts, credit cards, doctor or dental records for a guy walking around with over seventy-five thousand dollars in cash in his pocket…. well, you can see why certain questions began to arise."

John tried again to speak and was met once again by Drake's hand held up.

"What also puzzled my guys is that when they began to ask some of the people who live close by if they knew a Mr. and Mrs. Lucas Martin, they all said that they never heard that name. But, when told where this Lucas Martin lived, they all said the same thing, that we must be talking about John…. John Anderson.

"When you add it all up and put it in the midst of a little town in remote Upstate New York where there just happened to be multiple murders in recent weeks, the question becomes who is this guy who's running around popping for seventy-five grand in cash. A guy we can't seem to trace back more than a few months. A guy with no history. Put all that together, and it all lands right on my desk."

John tried to speak for a third time, but again, Drake cut him off the third time.

"Please understand, I've been a cop for a long time. But, before I was elevated to my current position, I spent some time in military intelligence followed by ten years with the National Security Agency. I'm sure you've heard of the NSA. Once a spook, always a spook.

"So, when I looked at everything my people brought to me, my intuitive nature kicked in. I made a couple of calls to several old contacts that I've maintained. After getting the run-around for almost two days, I ended up on the phone with a guy by the name of Bruce LaBue. Do you know Mr. LaBue?"

"Yes, I know Bruce. We both know him," John answered, never losing eye contact with Charles Drake.

Drake continued. "Mr. LaBue was extremely evasive during our initial conversation. When I informed him of the local events, he softened his position somewhat. He didn't or wouldn't tell me anything about you … either of you. What he did say was that if I wanted to know anything, I would do my best coming directly to you and that he believed that you would put my concerns to rest. Then he also added that he believed you might be of assistance to me because of your……previous experience, as he put it.

"The last thing he said to me was that I should be careful looking at your past and that your future was of far more value. Now, you can understand how my NSA spook mentality wrestled with that statement.

"Immediately after talking to Mr. LaBue, I made one last call to an old friend who still works at NSA. I asked her to run your name. She came back to me that the NSA has never heard of you. Had no record of any kind of either a Lucas Martin or a John Anderson. That really got my attention. NSA has something on just about everyone.

"However, when I asked them to run your name," he looked at Kristin. "Well, low and behold, come to find out that you are a former employee of one of the other shadow agencies headquartered in D.C. A certain Ms. Kristin Blake. And your history, what little there is, just happened to show you as a 'control agent.' A very well-trained, highly placed and highly thought of one at that.

"Well, once again, my NSA brain took over. Control agent… controlling who?"

Drake returned his eyes to John.

"I then called Mr. LaBue back and asked him a couple of additional questions warning him by reminding him of my current position. His comments confirmed that you had, at one time or another, worked in some capacity for the U.S. government. Yet, the NSA has no file. That's odd! NSA has a file on every person who ever got close to working for the government. Except you!

"When I heard that, I immediately pulled this entire file from my investigators. I knew there was something concerning you that they didn't need to know about, at least until I personally looked a little deeper. I told them that I would deal with this matter and get back to them if need be. So, here I am…… do you prefer Lucas or John?"

John remained silent. The two men continued to look directly into each other's eyes, measuring each other. Were they enemies… or allies? Kristin was the first to break the tension.

"Superintendent Drake…"

"Charles or Chuck will do fine, Kristin."

"Charles, John can't… won't respond to your questions. I will, to a certain extent. You see, I was…"

"I know who and what you were, Kristin. To my surprise, the NSA did have a file on you. It has clearly been tampered with, and what little remains has been sealed. But, my contact was able to tell me enough of what it contained for me to fill in a lot of blanks."

"Then you know enough to understand why we are here and why we have been living a very quiet life?"

"I think so," Drake replied. The two men continued to study one another. "Let me make it clear to both of you: I'm not here to cause trouble, nor am I here to stir up your life. Most of all, I'm not here to announce to the world who or what you are or were or where you are living. I'm here because, for one thing, I need to know if a man… and a woman… with the sort of background I suspect the two of you have been living in my backyard. Secondly, I need to know that if such an experience is living within my yard, what potential value does it have for me?

"New York State is a big place. I have thousands of people in uniform, as well as additional thousands of civilians, working for me. We deal with every conceivable type of criminal activity you can imagine. Add to that the quagmire of crime and corruption in the metropolis to our south, sometimes referred to as New York City, and you can begin to see why my curiosity brings me to your doorstep.

"There are times in my job when I'm asked by one federal agency or another to look the other way and let them deal with certain issues… like the death of the president last year, just about the time that one Lucas Martin took up residency in said back yard.

"As a cop, I've been puzzled as to why the F.B.I. hasn't torn this country inside out trying to find the person who assassinated the president. I was able to read the file on how rotten a guy he really was and how the Washington insiders have turned on him and, deep down, are really glad that he's gone. But still, assassinating the President of the United States?!

"Kristin, I know from what little there is in your file that you ran a very high-level, deep cover agent. I can only guess who that might have been. And, if I let my imagination run wild, I can only guess what that agent might have done. Since we have just met, and I have a very keen ability to judge people very quickly, I don't want you to tell me about any of your activities and alter my impression of you. However, should either of you wish to confide in a … friend, I can assure you that what you tell me will never leave this room."

This last comment from Drake signaled to both Kristin and John that the man knew far more than he was willing to divulge. It also signaled that he was not here as an enemy. John needed to know exactly what it was that brought him here. He decided to find out. For the first time, he sat back in his seat, hopefully signaling to Superintendent Drake that he understood and did not see him as a threat.

"Okay, Charles," he began. "You have made it clear you know a lot about us. So, what brings you here?"

"John, I need friends, not enemies. I'm not here to threaten you or expose you. If I'm correct, I would believe that I couldn't prove any of what I think even if I wanted to, which I don't. If I'm correct in my assumptions of your past exploits, and I think I am, then you can be a valuable asset to me. I'm here to establish a relationship that we can both live with and use to our advantage. I have a certain… admiration… for men who come from the world, I think you lived in. So, I'm here to make you a deal."

"A deal?" Kristin injected. "What do you consider a deal?"

"A trade. I'd like to trade my confidentiality… as well as gain me as a friend, along with full access to my department, in return for you sharing your experiences with us. Your talents, your insight, and your knowledge of how certain things and certain minds work can be very useful to me.

"I'm a cop. I think like a cop. Cops don't prevent crimes, and we react to them after they have already happened. We are a reactive force. I don't know and, frankly, don't understand the way the criminal mind works. I need your insight.

"Are you calling John a criminal?" Kristin asked.

"No," he answered, looking directly at John. "But his history, his former job, borders on that world far more than mine. It isn't the commitment of a crime that I need to know about, and it's the escape and evasion after the crime has been committed that I need to understand."

He then turned to address Kristin. "In your case, you know the internal workings of the bureaucratic world in Washington, D.C. You know the mentality and the flow of things there. You know where the bottlenecks are and how to get around them."

Addressing John. "In your case, only suspecting what your background included, I believe that your field experience is way beyond the scope of anything we train my people to be involved in. Because of that, you have a far more intimate sense of how some of the people we are dealing with think and act. Their actions and what they will do when pressured.

"I'd like to know that I can call on you, both of you, from time to time for assistance and guidance. In addition, I will offer you a certain degree of official status within the State Police organization. I will swear you both in as special deputy, you will carry a badge and be permitted to carry a weapon and give you access to resources and attend certain meetings.

"As such, you will both report directly and only to me. Your identity will be whatever you want it to be, Lucas… John… Jason Bourne or Double Oh Seven or Howdy Doody, for all I care. I'll leave that up to you.

"Lastly, the file now sitting on the front seat of my car will disappear never to be seen or heard of again."

"Sounds a little like blackmail to me," John said.

"Not intentionally," Drake replied.

John and Kristin looked at each other. Their silent exchange covered a gamut of questions and concerns. Once again it was Kristin who spoke first.

"What about the past?"

"What past?" Drake asked. "There is no past. I just met you. I just bumped into two nice folks who just moved into the area. Our relationship either begins or ends right here, right now. I either pin a badge on the two of you, or I drive out of here and occupy my afternoon by giving some old codger a ticket for doing something stupid while driving around on the back roads of Washington County.

"I don't sit in judgment of either of you. I don't have the right to do that. The past is the past. Our relationship begins right here, right now. If you break the law in my jurisdiction, I'll deal with you as I would with anyone else. But, right now, your life was your life and we begin anew."

"There's something I need to say. Something I need you to be clear on," Kristin injected. "Nothing John ever did was illegal. He never committed a crime. What he did, he was under orders to do by a fully legitimate government agency. He was serving his country under orders of that agency and with their full knowledge and approval."

"Understood," Drake replied. "If I implied otherwise, I apologize."

John silently studied the Superintendent, trying to see beyond the words. Trying to measure his motive. Instinctively, he liked the man. His first impulse, one he had survived on for so many years, was that he liked the person presenting him with this… whatever the hell it was. Offer… deal… new relationship.

Finally, he spoke. "If I were what you suspect, you must know that the methods of such a man are far different from what you are accustomed to. That the results are usually more… final than yours might usually be."

"Understood. That's why you will report directly and only to me. You will take your orders from me and only me," was Drake's answer.

"If we agree, what's next?"

"I like to get to know the people I work most closely with. I would hopefully put you in that category. So, I would suggest that you and your beautiful wife meet me and my equally beautiful wife for dinner. I'm sure she would find you both very interesting and charming. I also trust her instincts. She will give me an insight that I don't seem to have myself. I think she will immediately approve of my newest 'special assistants' and find them very compelling. She's never been wrong."

Kristin read her husband's unspoken reaction. She could sense it in his facial expression as well as his body language. She also knew from living day to day with him that sooner or later, he would go stark-raving mad living within the confines of the compound. He needed to be a part of the events taking place in their lives. He would go bonkers sitting around on the sidelines watching the world go by.

It scared her. To think of her husband exposing himself to the potential dangers that came with any law enforcement job. It scared her far more that he might be discovered. That his past would be revealed. That his past identity and what he did might surface and end up destroying them. But she also knew the man she lived with.

"What time and where would you like to meet for dinner?" she asked Drake.

Chapter 8

Dinner with the Drake's was great! They met and ate at one of the better-known eateries on Broadway in downtown Saratoga Springs. The conversation was easy and pleasant. By the end of the evening, the two women were laughing and carrying on as if they had known each other for years. They swapped girlhood secrets as far back as their first kiss, giggling throughout the entire conversation while John and Charles watched and listened with delight.

For the most part, the men sat by with grins painted across their faces, taking in the interaction of their wives. The give and take between the two men did, however, become easier and more relaxed as the evening progressed and the second bottle of wine emptied. It was clear that the four had a very positive chemistry developing, and all the anticipated tension that could have gotten in the way quickly evaporated. All four seemed to genuinely like one another, and clearly, the basis for a friendly relationship developed before it was time to bid each other good night with promises to repeat the evening soon.

The following morning was a totally different matter. John's telephone rang early. It was shortly after six o'clock when he heard Gretchen's voice burst through his cell phone.

"They found another one. Number four. Same spot on the ice and no sign of who or when. It's a male head again. Cops are already on the scene. You can feel the tension in the air from a mile away. Things are getting really scary in town."

"Who found it?" John asked.

"Not sure. Don't know if it was found late last night or early this morning. Everything is in such an uproar down there that it's hard to get good information. Folks are beginning to panic. Cops are talking about a curfew. They are baffled as to how the heads are repeatedly getting placed on the ice in the exact same spot with no one seeing a thing. I'll let you know more when I hear it."

"Okay, Gretch. Thanks for calling, and please let me know whatever else you find out."

"Will do. Love to Kristin. Bye!"

He disconnected the call and walked into the kitchen to make a pot of coffee. Before he filled the canister with water, his phone buzzed again. He didn't recognize the number, but he had a pretty good idea who it might be.

"Hello."

"Good morning, John." He immediately recognized the voice of Charles Drake. "Looks like we have another head on the ice."

"So, I've heard."

"Really? Your sources are obviously faster than mine."

"They're very limited but good."

"Do you think you could make your way to the scene and start poking around a bit? Hell of a first day on the job, but like the man once said, 'gotta start someplace.'"

"I'll be there as soon as I can," John said.

"Great! I won't be there for a while. The governor wants to talk with me about this case and what's going on. Downstate media is beginning to heat up, and he's feeling a little pressure. He has to pay attention to the big city newspapers and TV stations. I'll be there later this morning. Ask for Captain Johnson. He'll be expecting you. I've made it clear to him that you are a special assistant to me and to give you anything you need."

"I'll call you if I learn anything worthwhile," John told Drake.

The call was politely ended. John turned to complete his task of making coffee to find his wife leaning on the kitchen counter listening to his end of the telephone conversation.

"What's up?"

"Another head has been found on the ice. Gretchen called first. That was Drake on the second call. He wants me to go down there and start poking around."

"John, are you sure you want to do this?"

"No, but I promised, and maybe I can be of some help. Better than having heads turn once a week every week like some sort of planned event."

"Please be careful. I don't want you to get wrapped up in anything that will cause trouble… and I don't want you to get dead."

"Kristin, my love, I've been dodging dying most of my life. If you'll remember, I've gotten pretty good at it. And I promise I won't do anything to speed up the process."

They shared a quick breakfast together before John climbed into their new Jeep and headed toward town. To no one's surprise, it was snowing. Seemed like a daily event up here in the North Country. And it was cold. Temperatures were hovering at close to ten degrees below zero, promising to reach a blistering ten above sometime later in the day. Again, not surprising. However, the combination of new snow and frigid temperatures would make the investigative job very difficult.

He reached the south end of the lake and walked up to the yellow police crime scene tape. He flashed the new badge that Superintendent Drake had given him at dinner the night before and asked for Captain Johnson. He was directed to a uniformed officer who greeted him warmly and respectfully. Superintendent Drake had obviously paved the way.

"Superintendent says I'm to treat you like I would treat him," he said with a broad smile. "So, how much crap can you endure," he asked jokingly.

"All you got, Captain," John replied with an equally broad grin.

Johnson led him out onto the ice to where the fourth head still rested. A team of forensic techs from the crime lab surrounded the head, gathering whatever clues they could. Cameras clicked all around the scene as other techs searched for telltale signs on the ice. The new snowfall was rapidly obscuring any discernible signs that might have been left in the old snow during the night and early morning hours. The head itself was now capped off with a crown of new snow.

"Mind if I just wander around a little?" John asked the captain.

"Be my guest. If you need anything, I'll be right here."

John meandered through the various pods of police officers from the different forces represented. He listened to the chatter of each group, trying to pick up anything meaningful from their conversations. There wasn't much. He heard everything from theories of international agents staking out the area to the hot chick that one officer bedded while his wife was visiting her mother in New Jersey.

He decided to add to his newfound wealth of useless information by wandering up the sidewalk toward town. Maybe he would hear some intelligent crime-solving theory from one of the locals hanging around the area. Across the street from the lakefront, he walked past all the shops that were closed for the winter season.

When he came to the top of the sloop near the main highway running through town, he turned back to get an elevated view of the entire scene. He stood directly across the street from the terrace he and Kristin stood on a week or so earlier. And right there, in front of him, close to the boat slip, stood four men dressed all in black with scarves pulled up to conceal their faces.

The sight of the four men slapped all his senses to full alert. He immediately looked all around him until he spotted what he was looking for. Parked at the top of the hill, he saw a white Ford Econoline van. He turned back toward the four men to see one of them staring directly at him. Their eye contact lasted only a fraction of a second, but in that time, volumes were communicated.

John quickly crossed the street and started to make his way through the crowd toward the men in black. Before he got halfway to them, the tallest of the four said something to the other three, and they simultaneously turned away from John and walked toward the closed stores. They entered a narrow alley between two of the buildings. John followed but he lost sight of the men as the narrow alley swallowed them.

By the time he entered the ally, the men had already cleared the far end. John ran to try to catch up. When he reached the end, he looked to his left and right. To his left was a small municipal park offering no cover. He saw nothing. There were no fresh tracks in the newly fallen snow.

To the right, a paved surface used for deliveries led back up toward the main street. He ran toward the upper end, knowing what he would see. Just as he cleared the last building, he saw the white van pull away from the curb, picking up speed as it dashed toward the edge of town.

The van was too far away for him to see the license plate number. All he could make out was the distinctive orange and black colors of the New York State license plates. For the first time in over a year, his stomach hurt. The ache way down below his navel was his warning signal. He might not have gotten the license plate number, but he was now convinced in his own mind that he was on the trail of those responsible for the recent murders.

Once the van totally disappeared, John ran back to the center of the police activity near the crime scene. He found Captain Johnson.

"How can I reach Drake?" he asked, grasping the officer by the arm.

"He's in the I.C. truck, right over there. He just arrived a couple of minutes ago."

John left the confused scene commander and sprinted toward the Incident Command trailer that acted as the mobile command post from which all activities concerning the crime scene were coordinated. He showed his badge to the officer guarding the doorway and was permitted to enter the trailer.

The interior of the I.C. truck was narrow and crowded. It was jammed with communications equipment along with five people blocking the aisle. He spotted Drake standing halfway toward the front. Drake's attention was drawn to the commotion as John entered and began making his way toward his new consultant.

"What's up, John?"

"I think I have identified your suspects," he answered calmly.

"What? Where? How the hell did you do that?" the amazed and puzzled Superintendent shouted. All other heads inside the I.C. truck turned quickly toward the exchange.

"Over by the boat slip. I spotted them from where I was up high, overlooking the area. I've seen them before. Kristin and I saw them twice when we were in town, trying to find out what was going on with the whole situation. I tried to approach them and when they saw me coming, they ran off. They ran behind the building across the street from the lake and, got into a white van, and sped out of town. We saw them get into the same van last time we were in town."

"That's it?" the commandeered asked.

"There are four of them. They are all dressed in identical clothing. All black from head to toe with a black scarf concealing the lower half of their faces."

"Four men, dressed in black, get into a white van and blast out of town ...... and you think they're our killers?"

"Yes!"

All eyes were on John.

"Yes!" he repeated forcefully.

Superintendent Drake realized everyone inside the truck was now staring at John, wondering who this stranger was and why he was nearly shouting into the face of their commanding officer. Drake took his new assistant gently by the arm.

"Let's step outside," he said, leading John toward the door. Once outside, they move around to the opposite side of the I.C. truck, out of sight and hearing of any of the other officers working close by.

"Okay, John. Tell me everything."

"I just did," John replied.

"Did you get a license plate number off the van?" Drake asked.

"No."

"Did you see any weapons?"

"No."

"Did they make any threatening moves toward you or anyone else?"

"No."

"But you think these four men dressed in black are our murder suspects? Why?"

"My stomach hurts!"

Drake fought back his immediate reaction, not wanting to laugh.

"Your stomach hurts?"

"Yes," was John's totally serious reply to the question.

"I'm sorry, John, but I need more than that. Unlike your experience, we need facts and evidence, not an aching stomach."

"You asked for my help. You said you wanted to utilize my experience. Well, I'm giving it to you. I doubt you'll be finding another head anytime soon. These guys will go to the ground now that they suspect that I spotted them. They'll go quiet for a while at least."

"Yeah, but John…".

"If you don't want to accept what I'm telling you, at least put out an APB or BOLO or whatever the hell you call it these days. Try to locate the van."

"Do you know how many white vans there are in this state? Thousands John. We would be stopping more than half the vans on the road. And we are right next to a major interstate highway with a ton of international traffic coming down from Canada."

"But how many of them have four men all dressed in black inside them?"

"Good point," Drake replied as he triggered the radio dangling from his belt. In less than five minutes, an alert was issued to look for an unmarked white Ford Econoline van bearing New York license plates and with four passengers dressed in black. All passengers were to be considered armed and dangerous.

"Happy now?" Drake sarcastically turned to John N. Anderson.

"Extremely!"

Chapter 9

"I need a gun!"

"Yeah, and I need a three-day weekend on the beach with last month's Playboy centerfold," Superintendent Drake responded to John's request.

"I'm sure if I tell your wife you said that, she'll see to it that she gets a gun," John teased. "You said you would issue me a badge and a weapon. I have the badge, and now I need the weapon."

Drake ignored him and pulled a file folder from the top drawer of his desk.

"Let's review what's happened in the last few days," he said to John.

"I'm not going to let you forget about the weapon."

"I know, but first, let's take a look at the file."

Fifty-eight white vans had been pulled over within a twenty-five-mile radius of the crime scene in the ten days since John last saw the four men dressed in black. Many had been pulled over more than once, accounting for a total of well over a hundred vehicle stops questioning drivers ranging in age from twenty to eighty years old. One old codger from Glens Falls delivering flowers had been pulled over eight times, five by female officers. He threatened to file a sexual harassment complaint against the last one. He was an eighty-six-year-old man and accused the female officer of trying to hit on him.

None of the vans pulled over were driven by nor had four men dressed in black as occupants. However, since John's pursuit of the four men, there have been no additional human heads found lying on the icy surface of Lake George. It was also determined that all of those that had been found belonged to clergy from the surrounding area. All but one were men. All but one were Christian, the other being a Jewish rabbi from Schenectady.

John and Superintendent Drake moved to the conference room located within the headquarters building of the New York State Police near the state capitol in Albany. Waiting for them when they arrived were half a dozen of the force's top officials as well as the heads of the Forest Rangers, Washington County Sheriff's office and finally, the Lake George police department.

The meeting had been called to review all existing evidence and information concerning the case. John's presence was justified by the Superintendent because of his status as a special assistant and the only person who had a theory of who the culprits might be.

"Why do you need a gun?" Drake whispered to John as they took their seats at the conference table.

"For two reasons," John answered. "First, the four men I believe responsible saw me just as clearly as I saw them. Second, I never go hunting without a gun."

"Hunting?" Drake injected.

"Yes. If these guys aren't going to reveal themselves, it's time to go looking for them. And since no one else is prepared to commit the manpower to do it, I guess I'll have to do it myself."

"John, you're not authorized to…"

"I know. I also know that you can change that in a heartbeat."

"Yeah, but…"

"No buts. Either you want me to help you or you don't. You told me you would swear me in and give me a badge and gun. I'm sworn, and I have a badge. Now, I need the gun."

The conversation was now isolated to only these two men. All the others in attendance watched the banter being exchanged between the two men, leaving them to wonder who was in charge.

No one else in the room had enough information about John to qualify what the hell they were talking about.

"You know what I can do," John continued, locking his glare on Drake. "I saw them. I know what I'm looking for. You came to me asking for my assistance. I didn't come looking for you. You asked me to use my instincts and my experience. Well, I'm telling you that these are the guys you're looking for.

"I don't wear a uniform, so I won't stick out. You gave me a badge, and now you have exposed me and my wife to what I believe to be the men responsible for these murders. So, do whatever you have to do to authorize me to carry a weapon and get me a gun."

"Are you telling me that you don't own a gun?"

"I didn't say that," John replied. "I know the whacky gun laws in this state, so I need to be permitted to legally carry a weapon. I don't want to get arrested for carrying a concealed weapon while trying to assist in solving a crime."

Superintendent Drake returned John's stare. After a very long twenty seconds, "Stand up," he ordered.

John stood.

"Raise your right hand. Do you solemnly…".

"Yes," John said, cutting him off.

"… You are now a fully authorized law enforcement officer of the New York State Police. You'll have a weapon issued to you before you leave the building. John…... if you fuck this up, I will personally cut your balls off on the steps of your front porch and hand them to your wife on a plate. Got it?"

"Got it," he replied. "And you had better kill me in the process, or I'll return the favor with a gift you, your wife."

"And your salary is zero, and you have no arrest authority!" Drake added

"You just said I was a fully authorized officer!"

"I changed my mind."

"Good! Don't want either one," John responded.

"What are you going to do?" one of the other men asked.

John hesitated. "Nothing illegal," was his only reply.

The rest of the personnel in the room remained totally silent as these two titans verbally sparred, oblivious to their presence.

Finally, the meeting got underway, lasting a mere thirty minutes. John exited the building carrying a service weapon and a supply of ammunition. Before he left, Drake dragged John into his office to deliver a final warning. John promised he would do nothing against the law, but he did not reveal his plan to his new boss.

"Let me warn you, John. We draw our weapons to defend and apprehend. We don't go hunting, as you put it during the meeting, and we don't assassinate suspects. We collect information and evidence, and we arrest the bad guys. We don't eliminate them. You violate these procedures, and I'll slap your ass in jail faster than you can spit. Got it?!"

"Charles, like I said, I've got it!" John replied.

He drove directly home and told Kristin about the meeting and what took place.

"So, now you're a cop."

"Yeah, I guess you might be able to say that...... I guess! Not completely, but quite a transition, don't you think?"

"John, are you sure you want to get involved in all of this? It could be dangerous, and what if…....".

"Don't worry, pretty lady. I'm not out looking for trouble, and I'm not concerned about my past surfacing. But those guys need to be found before there are any more heads found popping up on the lake. One thing I've learned for sure, cops don't think correctly. They don't understand people who think as the bad guys do. They don't understand their mentality and certainly not their view of death. These four guys, whoever they are, are trying to send some sort of a signal, a message. And I think I know how to find out what their message is and how it will lead me to them."

"John, you can't… solve this in the same way you did in the past. This isn't the same thing. You can't play by the same set of rules as you once did. These guys aren't targets you've been assigned to eliminate. This a normal law enforcement case where they're innocent until proven guilty."

"I know what the law says, sweetheart. I'm not some wild-ass cowboy riding the range looking for someone to string up to the nearest Cottonwood tree. But I also know that sometimes the law gets in its own way. That's why guys like me, and the agencies we worked for are necessary. I promise you I won't do anything to put myself in jeopardy physically or legally, but I also know that I can solve this problem faster than our newfound friends in Albany.

"Police forces around the world work in the same way. They collect and analysis every bit of evidence they can hope that it will lead them to their target. Sometimes, it's faster and easier to get the bad guys to come to you. I'll let the cops do their thing. I'm going to get our four guys dressed in black to come looking for me. And when they do, I'll be waiting."

"Okay, so what are you going to do next?"

"Not me, little lady. We! I'm going to need your help."

"Really?"

"Yes. We made a great team for a long time. I think we can do it again."

Kristin thought about it for a moment before saying a word. She could feel the excitement growing within her, anticipating what her husband might say next.

"I'm in! What do we do first?"

"We call our buddy Bruce! Better yet, I think maybe we should hop in the car and take a trip to D.C. and talk to him face to face. What do you think?"

Chapter 10

Bruce LaBue, formerly Kristin's superior, continued in his position within the Department of Homeland Security after the events surrounding the death of the president over a year ago. He played only a minor role in the incident, but he collaborated enough with John and Kristin to put him in prison for the rest of his life if it became known to law enforcement.

Originally having an adversarial relationship with John, the two men worked together in the events leading up to the president's death and, as a result, became allies and friends. Bruce also credited John with saving his life and probably those of his wife and children.

After having been placed in a no-win situation by the late president's chief of staff, John helped him to temporarily disappear from his job and from Washington, D.C. He arranged to get his family away from their home and took up residence within the safety and security of the Lake George compound.

Once the turmoil of the president's assassination began to settle, and following conversations with John and Kristin, Bruce decided to return to his home and job as if he had no part in what had taken place. John presented him with an open-ended offer to return to the compound should he ever feel he or his family were threatened or if he simply wanted a change in his career.

Over a year and a half have since slipped by, and Bruce has firmly re-established himself within the department and the Washington intelligence community. In addition, he had managed to remove John's personnel file from the government's computer records effectively erasing the fact that he ever existed. The only trace of John N. Anderson now rested in the memories of those few with whom he had contact during his fifteen years as a covert agent. It was impossible to erase memories, but because of his role as a covert agent, knowledge of him and his activities was tightly restricted to only a hand full of people.

Bruce also attempted to do the same with Kristin's file but was only partially successful. However, her job, although vital and sensitive, was one that would not attract the attention of anyone trying to pry into the agency or into John's past. Her was a job shared by a number of other federal government employees and did not present any sort of threat, nor was it seen as a gateway to the inner workings of any of the intelligence networks.

Since the shake-up following the president's death and the establishment of the administration of the new president, Bruce's position and responsibilities within Homeland Security have grown considerably. He was now the head of the department he had formerly worked in giving him greater access to information exactly what John needed.

"Hello!"

It was Sunday afternoon, and he was at home watching the Washington Redskins getting their butts kicked by the New York Football Giants.

"Bruce, it's Sally."

He paused before responding. His mind tried to sort out who and why he was receiving this call from. It took a moment for his mind to put the scattered pieces together.

"Hey, Sally! How are you?" he finally answered, fighting the alarm he felt, realizing who was calling him. He hardly knew the woman calling talking to him as if they were old friends and that he should immediately know who was calling and why.

"I'm fine. But I need to ask you for a tiny favor."

"Sure, what is it?"

"Well, do you remember that flag I sent to your wife to mount on the light pole at the end of your walkway?"

He hesitated for a moment, trying to grasp the meaning of what Sally was saying. There was no gift sent. There was no flag, but there was a pole at the street side end of his front walkway.

"Yeah, what about it?"

"Bob and I want to buy one for another friend of ours, a newly married couple. But I can't remember the size of the one I sent you guys. Could you possibly go outside and measure it for me?"

Bob! John Anderson's close friend. Sally, his wife. The couple who were the caretakers of the compound on Lake George who he and his wife met last winter while avoiding Washington, D.C., during the turmoil of the president's assassination. 'Newly married couple'. Was she referring to John and Kristin?

"I'd be happy to," he answered as he peeped out through his front window. "I can see it there now. How about I go out and measure it for you and give you a callback?"

"That would be great, Bruce. Thank you so much. I'll wait for you to call back."

"Okay, Sally. I'll do it right now and call you back. Give my best to your husband."

"Will do and thanks again, Bruce."

He slipped on his winter coat and walked out his front door. Parked at the end of his front walkway, there was a white Jeep Grand Cherokee with New York license plates waiting for him at the curb. He opened the rear door and got in. He was greeted by a warm smile and handshake from his former fellow government employee and her new husband and former government-paid and sanctioned assassin.

"What brings you two to D.C.?" he asked.

John pulled away from the curb and drove slowly through the neighborhood. He and Kristin brought Bruce up to date on the events that had taken place back in Lake George, as well as with Superintendent Drake.

"Yeah, he called me a couple of times. Seemed to be a straight shooter. Is everything okay with him?"

"You won't believe this," Kristin began. "He and our mutual pal here," pointing to John, "are now buddies. Drake has sworn John in as his special assistant. He even gave him a gun and a badge."

"Really? Don't you think that might be a bit risky, John?"

"Trust me, I'm taking it slow and easy," he replied to Bruce. "Besides, if you took care of my file as you've told me, I should be okay. And Drake had his old contacts at NSA snoop around and they found nothing on me and very little on Kristin. He got just enough information to make him curious, but if he hadn't had those contacts and prior experience, I don't think he would have been able to put two and two together. A total outsider wouldn't have a prayer of turning up anything."

"Good point," Bruce answered. "Just be careful, my friend. I don't want anything to bite you in the ass."

"Thanks, pal, but I think we're okay. So, what's happening back here in D.C.? We are a bit isolated up in the North Country, as you well know."

"Same crap, different day. Seems as if the whole world hates us, and half of the countries in the Middle East want to kill all of us. Other than that, nothing much."

"What about the presidential thing?"

"You mean the investigation into the assassination?"

"Yeah, that!"

"Let me see if I can make it simple. On one side, the late president's political party has found out all about his early life, the death of his roommate's girlfriend, the home confinement that was hidden by his father, his further indiscretions when he finally returned to college, and the trumped-up plans to assassinate the

Prime Minister of Canada. So, on the surface, they make just enough noise so the press thinks they are really concerned with solving the case.

"On the other side, there is a high level of glee that the bastard is dead and out of the way. The loyal opposition is using the late president's personal history as a hammer over the heads of their opponents to gain political advantages. So, there's no complaining coming from them either. Lots of behind-locked-door stuff is going on out of the public's eyes.

"Then comes our friends in the F.B.I. Not only have they confirmed all the crap about the late president's personal history, but they have also confirmed the plot against the Canadian prime minister. Plus, they now know that the plot included the killing of a valuable member of the intelligence community, namely you.

"So, the combination of being embarrassed by not having properly vetted the president as a candidate and the plot to kill one of their own sort of has them in a 'we don't give a crap' position. Like the pile of dog shit won't smell if you don't kick it.

"The press is being kept at bay by statements every now and then telling them that the investigation continues and that progress is being made. Neither is true. Sometime in the next month or so, a statement will be made by the F.B.I. and sanctioned by the C.I.A. as well as the leadership of both political parties, saying that the assassin was from a Middle Eastern country who escaped the U.S. through our porous southern border. Shortly after that, a second statement will be issued stating that one of our crack Navy Seal teams has located, attacked and killed the man in question and that his body was lost in the massive explosion that killed him, leaving no trace.

"That will be the end of it. A complete conspiratorial cover-up of gigantic proportion, providing all the JFK conspiracy theorists a new bone to chew on. The whole investigation has evolved into a huge C.Y.A. project. Everybody is approaching this in the same way, cover your ass!"

"WOW! Just what this town needs," Kristin said.

"How much did you have to do with this?" John asked Bruce.

Oh, let's just say that I was interviewed a number of times by the right people who accepted everything I had to say," he replied. "Now, what brings you two to my doorstep while I'm watching the Redskins get their asses kicked?"

"We need some information."

"Figured that. What do you need?"

"This thing Superintendent Drake called you about," John began. "There have been a series of murders around Lake George. The only part of the victims found are their heads. Each victim has been decapitated, and their head placed on the ice about a hundred yards off the town's beach. No bodies has turned up anywhere.

"Kristin and I have driven to town a couple of times to see what was going on. And now, I have this new status thanks to our new mutual friend, Charles Drake. Each time we have been near the crime scene, or at least where the heads are being found, I have seen the same thing.

"I've seen four men oddly dressed exactly alike. They are wearing nothing but black clothes, including a black scarf pulled up to cover the lower half of their faces. Each time I have tried to approach them, they take off and climb into a white Ford van and drive off as if their butts were on fire."

Bruce interrupted John. "Wouldn't the cold temperatures justify them covering their faces? Don't most people do that in your part of the world?"

"Yes," John agreed. "Or maybe they're smarter than the average onlooker and know that law enforcement might be scanning the crowd with facial recognition software looking for a hit.

"And not many are dressed identically and not many in all black. It looks almost like they're wearing a uniform of some sort. And when they move in unison. A little signal from one of them and they move in lockstep as if attached at the hip."

"Good point. All black uniforms like you're describing bring I.S.I.S. to mind. Those fanatics dress totally in black and cover their faces," Bruce said.

"Yeah, exactly. We've thought of that too," John said. "That's part of the reason we came here to see you."

"Okay, what's the rest?"

"I tried to get the state cops to buy into our thoughts. Got nowhere. All they keep saying is that they need more hard evidence before they will launch an investigation. We think they are being overly politically correct, especially considering we might be dealing with a group of sensitive minorities.

"In the meantime, heads keep popping up on the ice. What I'd like to know is if you can search your files to see if anything similar has been reported anywhere else in the country. Or, has anyone reported a suspicious group of men dressed in black traveling around in a white Ford van."

"That shouldn't be too difficult. What else can you tell me," Bruce asked.

"Not much. Only one of the four is considerably taller than the others. I'm guessing he's about six-three or so. Somewhat unusual for a man from the Middle East. A lot like Osama bin Laden. And, although I didn't get close enough to the van to get the license plate number, I could see that it was orange and black. Given that, I have to assume the vehicle is registered in New York State."

"Well, that's something. Okay, let me get to work on this and see what I can come up with. What are you guys going to do after you return me to my game?"

"Don't know," John said. "Hadn't thought much about it. Why?"

"Well, why don't you relax and hang around for a day or two? By then, I should have something for you, and we can meet again."

"Relax!?," John reacted. "In D.C.? Are you kidding me?"

"I didn't say in D.C.," Bruce replied. "Just somewhere nearby so you can get back to me in short order."

"Sounds good to me," Kristin added. "I'm not looking forward to the long drive back quite yet. My butt is numb, and I need a good dinner."

"Good! Give me a couple of days to see what I can come up with. Kick back and relax, and let me get to work," Bruce said to his two friends.

"Okay," John addressed Kristin. "But, I'm not staying in town. I hate it here."

"Got it!" she replied.

After dropping Bruce at his house, John headed southwest toward Manassas. He knew of a beautiful bed and breakfast in the area where they would be comfortable for a couple of days. In addition, if they needed to keep themselves occupied while Bruce stirred things up, they could spend the day visiting the Civil War monument at the battleground.

He had stayed at the B&B a couple of times when recalled to Washington for meetings or training. He also knew that it was the off-season for tourism in the area, and there should be no problem with availability. When he was checking in, he requested a room with a Jacuzzi. Fortunately, one was available. By the time they got settled in their room, it was time for dinner. Kristin found a directory in the desk drawer and selected a nearby steakhouse.

"I want one of those deep-fried onion things with lots of grease and dipping sauce," she told John. "And I want the best steak they have on the menu."

"Oh, really! And what do you think you did to deserve all of this?" John asked playfully.

"Uhmmmm! Nothing … yet! But, there might be dessert on your menu made specifically for you."

They spent the remainder of the evening enjoying the quiet countryside and a great steak dinner together. Kristin got her deep-fried onion plus a great big piece of cheesecake for dessert. When they returned to their room, John was rewarded with his own dessert in the form of a tender night of lovemaking with the woman he absolutely adored. He felt sure that he got the better end of the deal.

The following morning, after breakfast, they drove to the Manassas – Bull Run battlefield, where they roamed the grounds and visitor's center. The historical informational value of the day proved to be fascinating. The number of men fighting and dying in such a concentrated area was an eye-opener for John, and not once, but three battles on this same site during the course of the war. His more modern concept of war and battle made it difficult to comprehend what he learned from walking the grounds.

Kristin marveled at how a simple split rail fence or a ditch alongside a road could be considered a major defensive feature and how up close and personal the killing really was. For the first time in her life, she came to realize the futility of war and the cruelty and slaughter that were a natural part of the killing. She saw pictures of massive piles of amputated arms and legs stacked like firewood. Young men walking with the aid of tree branches because their own limbs now rotted away in a pile abandoned in a cow pasture.

When they returned to their room late that afternoon, a sense of depression hung over them. Neither couldn't shake the sights and images of the day. This heavy air prevailed until they watched thirty minutes of the nightly news on television to realize that the same senselessness continued to this very day in Africa and the Middle East.

"How will it all end?" she asked her husband.

He pondered his answer for a moment. "I think we'll end up killing ourselves long before the sun explodes to do the job!"

They spent a quiet night lying in bed, holding one another, reflecting on their day. There was little room for purpose or need for conversation. Their unspoken words brought a new perspective to the events taking place in Lake George.

Shortly after the noon hour the following day, John's telephone rang.

"John, it's Bruce."

"Hey, Bruce. Do you have anything for us?"

"Yeah, I sure do. We need to meet."

"You name the time and place, and we'll be there."

They agreed to meet on the top level of a public parking garage attached to Union Station in the center of Washington, D.C. and within sight of the capitol building. Bruce approached John's vehicle carrying a file folder in one hand. He opened the rear door and got in.

"Hey, guys. I think I've got something for you," he said as he passed the file folder over the seat to Kristin. "

"What have you got?" John asked.

"Well, I ran the information you gave me through our database, and it seems that there are a couple of possibilities. One is in southern California, and another is in central Texas. The California case took place about five years ago, and the one in Texas about two years ago. Both took place in small tourist towns during the offseason, and both towns were near a lake. However, neither town is far enough north so that the lake would freeze over in the winter.

"The victims were decapitated, just like in your case. However, with no frozen lake, the heads were found on golf courses near the towns. They were placed atop one of the holes, and when the golfers approached the green to putt their balls, there were the heads waiting for them.

"This information sort of tripped my trigger with interest, so I kept looking. A third case popped up. This one took place in central Michigan. A little town called Houghton right next to a lake of the same name. Pretty much the same story as you gave me. Decapitated human heads found on the frozen lake in the middle of the winter. And, like your story, nobodies to go with them."

"How many?" John asked.

"Total of six," Bruce answered. "John, they were all clergymen, all men and all from towns within fifty miles of the lake."

"Any suspects?"

"No. However, the wife of one of the missing clergymen remembered seeing a white van cruising by their house the day before her husband went missing."

"How come no one has heard anything about this?"

"Mainly because Houghton is four miles on the wrong side of nowhere. It is a tiny little town in the middle of central Michigan farm country. The lake is the only attraction. When the summer boating season is over, the town dries up until the following summer. Once the heads stopped appearing on the ice, everything got quiet again. With no suspects and no motive other than all the victims being members of the church, after a couple of months, the cops pulled up stakes and moved on to the next problem."

"When did all of this happen?" John asked.

"Exactly one year ago," Bruce answered. "These murders took place last winter.

Chapter 11

"What now?" Kristin asked.

The meeting with Bruce had ended with his promise to provide additional information should anything of related potential interest come his way.

John handed her his cell phone as he drove west on Interstate 66.

"Go into my contacts and find Charles Drake's number. Please get him on the Bluetooth hands-free speaker for me."

Drake answered on the second ring.

"Charles, it's John."

"John! Where are you?"

"Kristin and I are on Interstate 66, and we just passed Dulles International outside of Washington, D.C."

"Okay, first, what are you doing down there and second, why are you calling me?"

"I'm sure you remember Bruce LaBue."

"Yes, I do."

"We left him about an hour ago. I asked him to do a little research for us."

"Don't tell me. He found another case," Drake interrupted.

"Not one, three. However, two don't offer much, but the third one appears to be right on the money."

"Where?"

"Michigan."

"Michigan!?"

"Yes."

"What are you going to do?"

"What do you think? We're going to Michigan. I need you to get one of your people to make a couple of telephone calls for us. The murders took place in the town of Houghton, Michigan. That's H-O-U-G-H-T-O-N. Please determine what county that town is in and, call the sheriff, and tell him we're on our way. Be sure to inform him what my official status is with your department. It's Tuesday….," John paused, thinking through the trip he and Kristin had ahead of them. "Tell him we would like to meet with him Thursday morning at the Houghton town hall."

"What about the Michigan State Police?" Drake asked.

"I'm not sure this case got up to them. But, if you need to include them because of protocol, be my guest. And give them and the sheriff my cell telephone number should he want to contact me between now and the time we meet."

"John, if your friend in D.C. has info about the case, I would think the state police do as well."

"Good point. Okay, then, go ahead and let them know we're coming."

"Can you give me any details?" Drake asked.

"I'll let Kristin fill you in while I deal with this D.C. traffic. But please don't share our info concerning the Lake George case with either the sheriff or state guys in Michigan. I don't want to taint their thinking before we get there."

"Understood," replied Drake.

Kristin took over the conversation filling Superintendent Drake in on what was in the file Bruce had provided. By the time she finished and disconnected the call, they had cleared a substantial amount of the traffic on the busy interstate and were making good progress deeper into the Virginia countryside.

Later that night, John found a motel on the outskirts of Pittsburgh, Pennsylvania. After a gourmet $17.95 dinner at a nearby

Cracker Barrel chain restaurant, they fell into bed and called it a day. Neither slept well. The information and details Bruce provided kept them both tossing throughout the night. Both were out of bed, showered and dressed by seven thirty the next morning.

After what John called a 'lobby load' breakfast of cold cereal, cold Styrofoam eggs left over from World War II, cold sausage patties provided by the W.V. D.O.T. roadkill clean up team and coffee capable of cleaning grease spots off those same roads all served with a glorious selection of plastic utensils and complimenting Styrofoam dishes and cups, they were back in their Jeep and on the road headed north with a lifetime supply of methane gas brewing in their stomachs enough to propel an LP driving golf cart completely across the country. But….. it was free!

By late afternoon, they were approaching Houghton, Michigan. They drove through town, finding no hotels or motels open for business. When the season ended here, most local business owners became snowbirds and headed to the sunny south to escape the cold and snow. However, they did find a bed and breakfast displaying a small neon sign in its front window announcing that it was open for business.

After meeting and talking to the proprietor, they were secure for the night. Then, Kristin asked the magic question.

"Anywhere in town, might we be able to get some dinner?"

"Huh, this time of year?" the owner said. "You might be able to scrounge up a couple of two-day-old packaged sandwiches at the service station up the road. But he closes in about … three minutes. Or, if you ask real nice, I might be able to whip up something for you," she said, smiling.

"Please! Please! Pretty please!" Kristin begged mockingly.

"Okay, you two go up to your room and get settled in. Let me see what I can put together. My husband is pretty good at improvising a meal from stuff we have in the pantry. Might even make it a dinner for four and join you ourselves."

Forty-five minutes later, Kristin, John and the two owners, Joan and Bryan Olsen, of what turned out to be an extremely comfortable B&B, were all seated at the kitchen table sharing a bowl of pasta topped with Joan's home-made sauce, chicken parmesan, salad with bleu cheese dressing, garlic bread and a two-liter bottle of Chianti.

The conversation was light and friendly. Joan and Bryan shared stories about their lives in the boonies of central Michigan while Kristin added bits and pieces of her own contrasting young life growing up as a city girl. For the most part, John remained quiet, restricting his part of the conversation to taking jabs at the others when the opportunity presented itself. All laughed heartily over the meal, lasting for over an hour, genuinely enjoying each other's company.

"This has been fantastic," Kristin injected. "We can't thank you enough. The meal was great and the company even better," directing her thanks to both of their hosts.

"Music to our ears," replied the wife. "We're so glad to have you. Things get pretty quiet and lonely around here this time of year. How about we clear the table and sit in the living room by the fire for a while before we call it a night."

"Sounds great," Kristin added.

The men pitched in on the clean-up, and soon, all four were seated around the fireplace sipping the last of the wine.

"So, what brings you two to our greater metropolitan area?" Bryan asked sarcastically.

"Business," Kristin answered a little too curtly.

John sensed this might be a good opportunity to get a little local knowledge concerning past events.

"Kristin is being a bit protective," he began. "Actually, we are special advisors to the Superintendent of the New York State Police. We are here to talk to your sheriff about..."

"The lake murders," Bryan interrupted.

"Yes," John answered. "Is there anything you can tell us about what happened?"

Joan and Bryan glanced at each other before dropping their eyes toward the floor. Bryan finally broke the silence.

"Those murders scared the crap out of the local folks. Our pastor was among those killed. We helped identify his… remains. He was the second one found. The whole thing went on for weeks. Everybody took to locking their doors, something we don't normally have to do in these parts. Worst still is that the sheriff and state police never did find who killed all those people.

"And they never did find the bodies of those poor souls. Not to this very day. Killings just stopped, and all the gawkers finally left and went home. All the locals quickly put it behind them as best they could, and life went on. Accept the town is still a bundle of nerves. A couple of families left for permanently they were so scared."

"We couldn't escape," Joan added grimly. "We couldn't leave. This is our home. We stayed and kept our doors locked, with Bryan and lots of the other men in the area putting a loaded shotgun next to our bed. The whole town has been on edge ever since. Been a little over a year now, and folks are still uptight about it. Their not being caught leaves some folks wondering if there isn't a killer living among us. Once it gets dark outside, folks lock themselves in their homes. Never seen anything like it, and I've lived here all my life."

"Sure, hope you two aren't going to get things all stirred up again?" Bryan said.

"No," Kristin answered. "Ever hear of Lake George, New York?" she asked the two hosts.

"Yeah, vaguely," Joan said.

"That's where we live," Kristin continued. She went on to tell them of the events taking place back in New York and how she and John had followed the trail to Houghton. She told them they would be meeting with the sheriff in the morning to compare the two cases to determine if there were any links and if they could help lead them to the killers.

"We're not here to stir anything up," John added. "We're here because we're dealing with exactly the same thing you guys dealt with a year ago. Innocent men, and in our case, a woman, are being killed in this gross beheading manner. All are members of the clergy, just like here, and all mutilated in the same way. On top of the killings, like here, we haven't found any of the bodies. We need to get to the bottom of these killings and stop any more from happening."

"We also need to find the killers and bring them to justice one way or another," Kristin added.

"One thing we can tell you," John added. "I strongly believe that the people responsible for the murders in New York are the same people who committed the crimes here. The good thing is, I think they are long gone from your town and have moved on to our area."

Before anyone could add anything further, Bryan stood and made the rounds of the nearly empty wine glasses, pouring out the last of the two-liter bottle.

"Hate to ruin a good buzz with this conversation," Bryan said. "I'm not sure what you'll find out tomorrow. The county sheriff and state cops were totally baffled. Heads just appeared on the ice; nobody saw anything, and no tracks or evidence was left behind. Nothing! The damnedest thing you ever saw. It was like they levitated out over the ice and just dropped their heads out of the sky.

"One day, we had a nice peaceful community, and the next day the whole damn town is scared to death. Some suspecting their neighbors of committing crimes affects relationships that are generations old. Most folks are just as baffled and confused as the police. Not a damn clue as to who killed those poor people … and no dead bodies! To this very day, no bodies have been found."

John asked the one question he really wanted an answer to.

"A wife of one of the victims said she saw a white van cruising by their house the day before her husband disappeared. Is there anything you can tell us about that?"

"That would be Mary Hamilton. She's the wife of our pastor. We identified her husband, or I should say his head, to spare her from having to go through that mess. She lives about two miles from here. If you want to talk to her, I can give her a call."

"No, not until we talk to the sheriff first. We don't want to step on his toes, and it's important to follow protocol right now. Maybe tomorrow."

Chapter 12

Tomorrow came early for the entire Olsen household. John was up and heard stirrings in the kitchen telling him that someone was else up even earlier to make coffee. He could smell the fresh brew wafting up the stairs, engulfing the room he and Kristin occupied on the second floor.

Kristin was in the shower when he descended the stairs to find both Joan and Bryan seated at the kitchen table, sipping a mug of hot coffee.

"Good morning," Joan stood to greet him. "Hope you slept well," she tossed out as an obligatory jester.

"Not really," John answered honestly as he took a seat with a mug in hand. "I'm afraid our visit has upset you two, and we're sorry for that. I couldn't get it off my mind all night."

"Well," Bryan began. "We did have a rather difficult night as well. The entire situation concerning the local murders is kind of upsetting and unnerving to us. This is a very quiet rural area, and we're just not accustomed to this kind of thing. A big deal to us is when a farmer's cow dies, or some city slicker from Detroit comes up this way and shoots a goat, thinking it was a deer. Like I said, we're just not accustomed to this kind of thing."

"Understood," John replied. Just then, Kristin entered the room.

"Good morning, everyone," she said to all. "Am I intruding on anything?"

"No, no," Joan answered. "Bryan was just telling John how upsetting this whole mess has been to us and our entire community. The biggest things we have around here are the 4th of July fireworks and the Labor Day clambake. Murders, bodies missing, their heads appearing on our lake are a bit unusual, to say the least."

"What's your schedule for the day?" Bryan asked.

"We will first meet with the sheriff. After that, we'll have to see what he can tell us and go from there. Don't know how willing he's going to be to share information with us," John concluded.

"He'll be very open with you. I just talked to him a while ago. Told him you spent the night here and that we had a very enjoyable evening with you. He's anxious to meet you and share everything he has on the case."

"You just spoke to him?" Kristin asked in amazement.

"Yeah, he's my brother," Bryan answered. "Told him you weren't the typical smart-ass New York know-it-alls that are so near and dear to the hearts of folks out this way," he added sarcastically.

They all had a solid, tension-breaking laugh over Bryan's remark. Joan proceeded to place dishes of food on the table and the four new friends enjoyed breakfast together. Throughout the meal, the conversation was light, with nothing further about the case discussed.

"When do you intend to start your trip home?" Bryan asked.

"Probably as soon as we're done talking with the Sher… your brother."

"Think you might have a hard time doing that. I was watching the Weather Channel before you came down. We're about to get whacked with a snowstorm coming in off the Great Lakes. They're calling for maybe ten inches or better. I believe it's already started."

"Why don't you plan on staying with us again tonight?" Joan said. "No need fighting your way through a snowstorm. When it snows up here, and the wind gets too blowing, it can be very difficult driving. Can hardly see the front of your car. We get whiteouts when the snow blows across the flat country. Besides, where in the world would you go? There isn't very much in the way of accommodations for at least fifty miles. You can just leave your things in your room for the day."

"Sounds like a great idea to me," Kristin said gleefully. "I'd like to not have to sit in the car for a while. It's been a long couple of days."

It was settled. Kristin and John would have their meeting with Bryan's brother and then return to the B&B for the evening. John insisted that they all go out to dinner on him in return for their hospitality. Following the directions Bryan provided, they left for their meeting.

When they reached the town hall, they found Sheriff Michael Olsen waiting for them. Sheriff Olsen led them to a small conference room near the town clerk's office. Waiting for them in the room was a detective from the Michigan State Police, Jim Brown. He immediately made it clear that he was not the famous Jim Brown, a former professional football player. His joking approach to the subject eliminated any tension that might have been present in the room of strangers.

"You've come a long way," Sheriff Olsen began. "We received a call from Superintendent Drake. He asked us to please cooperate with the two of you and that you might have some information for us as well. So, how can we be of assistance?"

"Seems as if we might have a very similar series of murders taking place back home as you had here about a year ago," John said. He went on to tell the two men everything currently known about the Lake George case. The two Michigan lawmen listened intently to what John had to say, taking notes the entire time.

Detective Brown spoke first after John had finished.

"We've purposely kept this case as quiet as possible. Do you mind telling me where your information came from?"

"Kristin and I once worked for a federal intelligence agency," John said. "We still have a few contacts in D.C. We asked them to check their files for any similar cases, and they came up with yours. There were also a couple of others in other parts of the country that we ruled out for one reason or another."

"Can you tell me what agency that was?" Brown asked.

"I'm sorry, we can't," Kristin answered. "However, I can tell you that both John and I have considerable experience dealing with murders," she added without further detail indicating which side of the issue they might have been on.

Detective Brown and Sheriff Olsen alternately provided John and Kristin with the information concerning the local murders. They shared the frustration both the county and state authorities felt concerning the unsolved status of the case and the apparent dead end they have reached.

There was also a considerable level of frustration concerning the missing bodies. The only good news was that it appeared that the culprits had moved on since there hadn't been any additional heads appearing on the ice for well over a year.

"We weren't able to find any trace of the people responsible, not even a damn footprint in the snow. And what frustrates us even more is how they did all of this without being seen by anybody. The only thing I can think of is when it's snowing and, the wind is blowing, and we can't even see beyond the end of our driveways. The wind blows snow that can cover up all traces of footprints in a minute or two and would easily hide anyone walking out on the lake. Besides, none of the locals would be dumb enough to be out in that kind of weather anyway. The perfect combination to do something without being seen. We call them 'white-outs,' and it is during those times that we experience most of our traffic accidents. Visibility is limited to feet, not even yards. It would be easy to walk across an open area without being seen."

"The exact same type of thing taking place back on Lake George. A combination of wind and snow and few people out and about leaves little chance of being seen. The broad lake surface would be just like one of your open fields with the wind and snow blowing," Kristin added.

"One of the reasons we're here, Sheriff," John resumed. "It seems that someone might have seen your suspects."

"Really!? Who?" Detective Brown jumped in.

"The wife of one of your victims. I believe he was your second victim. If it's possible, we would like to talk to her."

"That would be Marie Paterson, preacher's wife," Detective Brown said.

"Yes, I believe that's the name we have," Kristin added.

Sheriff Olsen hesitated a moment before reaching for his cell phone, contemplating what was being asked. After a few moments of thought and consideration, he punched in a number from his contact list and waited. A moment later, he said, "Barb, call Marie Paterson and see if she's available for us to stop by. Tell her I've got a couple of people who need to ask her a few questions. I'll hold while you get her."

He paused before continuing. "Okay, good. Tell her that we'll be there in about fifteen minutes…... and tell her thanks." He turned to the others and said, "Hope you have boots to put on. It's snowing like the dickens out there."

John and Kristin followed the sheriff in their four-wheel drive Jeep Grand Cherokee. Detective Brown rode with the sheriff leaving John and Kristin a few minutes alone to compare notes on the meeting with the two law enforcement officers. They agreed that thus far, both men were being very open and that all was proceeding well.

Sheriff Olsen pulled into the driveway of a prototypical early 1960s one-story, three-bedroom, brick ranch-style home. It sat on a lot about five miles outside of town amid a dozen or so other homes that were all the same. It was one of those small roadside developments that, if you lost track of where you were for more than a minute, you might pull into the wrong driveway.

They were met at the door by an attractive woman Kristin judged to be in her early forties. She invited them all in, and once Sheriff Olsen finished the introductions, everyone sat in the modest den offering a warming fire in a wood-burning stove. Sheriff Olsen provided the necessary introductions.

"Marie," Olsen began. "These folks traveled here from Upstate New York. They're here looking into a case back there that is very similar to … to…., well, to what happened here last year. They'd like to ask you a few questions."

"I'll do whatever I can," she answered, addressing John and Kristin.

"Mrs. Paterson," John began. "I'm not going to burden you with the details of what's happening back in New York. The main thing I'd like to ask you is if you noticed anything different in the days prior to your husband's death?"

"Different? Different how?" she asked.

Kristin sensed the woman's nervous tension, trying to address John's question. She injected herself in hopes that a woman-on-woman exchange might calm the pastor's wife.

"Anything," Kristin said. "Anything in his daily routine or in his demeanor. Was he nervous about anything? Did he make any unexpected changes in his schedule? Did he talk about anyone you didn't know?" She was careful not to lead Mrs. Paterson to the one issue that she and John wanted foremost to address.

"Well," Marie began. "These folks, the sheriff and the state police asked me the same questions."

"We realize that," Kristin continued. "However, it's been a year since this all happened, and we're wondering if you might have thought of anything new since they last spoke with you?"

The woman pondered her thoughts for a moment before again making eye contact with Kristin.

"No, nothing that I can think of. My husband was a creature of habit. He liked to stick to his routine and schedule. I can't think of anything that he did or said that was different."

"How about you," John injected. "Do you remember seeing or hearing anything different, anything unusual?"

"Well," she continued. "As I told the sheriff, the day before my husband was … was… the day before he disappeared, I saw a van drive by the house a couple of times. It's really slow like I didn't recognize it, and in these parts, everybody knows just about every vehicle and who is driving it."

"A van," John continued. "What made it stick out to you?"

"A couple of things. First of all, I don't recall ever seeing it in the area before and then I noticed the license plates."

"The license plates?" John asked.

"Yes, sir. Michigan plates are blue and white. The ones on the van were a different color."

"Do you remember what color they were?"

"I do. They were orange and black… just like the ones on your Jeep out there."

John and Kristin looked at each other in surprise.

"Is there anything else you remember?" John asked.

"No, not that I recall. Oh, yes. One more thing that made me wonder about it. It was moving very slowly, like whoever was in it was looking at our house. Like trying to determine if anyone was at home Made me a bit nervous. That's why it stuck in my mind."

"How about the color of the van?" Kristin asked.

"Oh, it was white. A white van."

John leaned forward in his chair.

"Mrs. Paterson, I'm going to ask you to do me a favor. I'd like you to close your eyes and think of nothing but that van driving by the front of your house. I want you to concentrate on who was inside the van. Will you do that for me?"

"Sure!"

"Okay, close your eyes and picture the van. Try to remember the very first instant you saw it. What made you look at it? Try to picture the driver. Was he alone? Was there anything written on the side of the van?"

"No! I saw it slow down. That's what made me look at it. It slowed down right out front of our house. Right by our mailbox. But there was nothing on the van. No writing or anything. Just plain white."

"And the driver?" John asked. "Is there anything you can tell me about the driver?"

"He was black… no, I mean, he was all in black. Both of them were."

"Both of them?"

"Yes, the driver and the man in the passenger seat. All I could see was black. They must have been dressed in some sort of uniform. All black. Like delivery drivers. That's all I can remember. Even their faces were partly covered in black. That's what made me look at them. I thought it was very odd for them to have their faces covered. Lots of folks around here cover their faces in the wintertime. Protects them from the wind. But not while they're driving… not inside their vehicle. That didn't make much sense to me."

"You could see two men. Could you tell if there was anyone else in the van?"

"No, sir. It didn't have any windows on the sides. You know, it was one of those vans with solid sides, like a delivery van. No windows, but it did have a door. One of those sliding doors on the side. That's all."

"That's a lot," Kristin acknowledged to the woman. "That's a big help to us, Mrs. Paterson. You've been a very big help to us."

They left the widow with the promise that they would be sure to inform her if they caught her husband's killers. Kristin gave Mrs. Paterson a warm and sincere hug before leaving, trying to understand the depth of the woman's grief.

Once the four visitors were outside, John asked if the sheriff would show him where the heads were found on the local lake. It took less than ten minutes for them to drive to the scene. When they arrived, the sheriff and Detective Brown showed them the general area surrounding the lakeshore as well as walking them out on the ice to the approximate location of where the heads had been left.

The lake was surrounded by flat, open fields with no trees or structures to conceal anything. There were no crops evident at this time of year that might be used to cover an approach to the ice, further confusing how the heads appeared without anyone seeing anything, just like back in Lake George.

The snowfall had increased substantially. At least three or four inches had already fallen since John and Kristin had left the B&B earlier in the morning. The road conditions were getting worse by the minute.

"What can you tell us," Sheriff Olsen asked.

"Not much," John answered. "Very similar area to where we come from, except Lake George is surrounded by mountains instead of open crop fields. The proximity to your beach area and the distance offshore are very similar. What puzzles me is that your lake is surrounded by wide-open fields. There's no place for them to hide. No way to conceal their approach. How did they get out here on the ice and then get off without being seen?"

"Well," Olsen answered. "During the winter months, the lake is pretty well abandoned. If you parked here all day, you might see two or three cars go by. During the night, I doubt you'd see any. And then you add in the wind and snow and the white-out conditions. Makes it a lot easier to understand how they did it."

"Okay, but these guys put the heads on the lake to be found. We think they're trying to send some sort of a message. Killing only members of the clergy and then leaving their heads on the ice, there's got to be a reason. I don't think they would put them out here and risk them not being found."

"The only thing I can tell you," Olsen added. "The lakeshore road is on one of our daily patrol routes. At least one of my deputies is required to patrol this route no less than once a day. Maybe that's what they were counting on."

"Could be," John agreed. "From what Mrs. Patterson told us, we know they scouted out her house. I can see them doing the same thing out here and that they knew you guys would be driving by."

"Risky, but it all connects," Detective Brown added.

John paused. "One more thing, sheriff, do you remember what the weather was like on the day the heads were found or, even more importantly, the night before?"

Sheriff Olsen paused while thinking back. "I don't remember exactly. Hadn't given it any thought, but that won't be hard to find out. Do you think it might be important?"

"Don't know," John answered. "Just popped into my head. It might explain some things. I was interested to know if it was snowing and windy. It could be they timed their activities to the weather to avoid being seen. We could potentially match that up with the information back in Lake George and see what it tells us. Might explain the mystery of them not being seen depositing the heads on the ice."

"I'll be happy to check and let you know," the sheriff replied.

They wrapped up their meeting, standing in the snowfall. The two Michigan law enforcement officers promised to stay in touch with John and Kristin and to get the information they requested. John, in turn, promised to provide them with all the developments back in New York. They exchanged contact information and drove off.

John and Kristin found a local diner where they shared a light lunch. They discussed what they saw and learned during their morning of investigating the local crimes. They agreed that the information Mrs. Paterson provided concerning the van's license plates and, the black clothing and the covered faces sealed the deal in their minds that they were now looking for the same set of criminals.

"I'd like to take another look at the lake here," John said.

"Okay. Do you think you can find your way out there and back in this weather?" his wife asked.

"I think I can handle it," he answered.

They returned to the Olsen's bed and breakfast by mid-afternoon. By that time, at least eight inches of new snow had fallen with no sign of it letting up. Bryan assured John that by the next morning, the snow would stop, and the roads would be plowed and clear to travel.

"Snowfall like this was a routine event easily handled by the local snowplows. It's amazing how those guys keep the roads open and passable. Got to get those school buses out to pick up the kids and get them home safely".

"Same with us in New York. A couple of inches doesn't even warrant much in the way of conversation. When a foot or more piles up in a twenty-four-hour period, then the local people will pay attention," John added.

That evening, instead of risking going out for dinner, they all stayed at the B&B and all shared in another glorious meal prepared by Joan Olsen. Following dinner, the four sat around the fireplace and shared a warm evening of conversation and good company. In the morning, John and Kristin got up early and, after breakfast, bid a very fond farewell to their new midwestern friends.

In addition to the payment for their room, John left a one-hundred-dollar bill and a warm note of thanks for the warm hospitality, fantastic home-cooked meals and a great new relationship. Kristin got Joan to promise an exchange visit to the shores of Lake George in the springtime when the weather was more welcoming.

By the time John entered Interstate 75, the snowplows had done their job just as Bryan had promised. They made good time driving south to I-69, where he turned toward the east. In Port Huron, they crossed the border into Canada. Continuing east on Route 402, then blending into the 401. Slowed by the snowfall of the previous evening, it took almost all day for them to reach Buffalo, New York and cross back into the U.S.

They discussed stopping for the night but deciding to push on toward home. It was a very long day of driving made more tiring dealing with the snowy roads and creeping traffic. From Buffalo to Lake George took them another six and a half hours, and by the time they pulled into the lakeside compound, it was almost two o'clock in the morning. They were exhausted! When they entered their warm cabin, they made their way to the bedroom, practically ripped off their clothes and fell into bed. Sleep overtook them before the sheets were warm.

Chapter 13

By 8:30 the following morning, they were sitting out on their deck wrapped in a down quilt overlooking the ice-covered surface of Lake George, well-rested and enjoying the peace and quiet of their mountain home. The snow atop the ice glistened and sparkled in the early morning sun coming up over Buck Mountain on the east side of the lake.

Small talk, hot coffee and warm cuddling snuggle under the quilt were shared over breakfast of English muffins covered in melted butter until Kristin addressed the elephant sitting on the deck with them.

"What do we do now?" she asked her husband.

"We go hunting! John announced to his beautiful wife. "We're going to bait our trap and lay a trail. I want our four friends dressed in black to know that we're out there looking for them. I want them to get nervous. They will either come to us or get nervous and make a mistake. When they do either, we'll be waiting for them."

Right after he finished his second mug of hot coffee, John placed a call to Superintendent Drake. In a few short minutes, he brought New York State's top cop up to date on what he and Kristin learned in Michigan. He told Drake that he was convinced that they were dealing with the same group of men. Everything matched. The black clothing and covered faces. The white Ford van. The method of killing their victims and that all were clergy.

He further told Drake of his conversation with the wife of the number two victim and how he and Kristin had gently probed her without leading her to the answers she provided. He described the lake and the surrounding area where the heads were placed and that there were no eyewitnesses nor tracks leading to or from the lake.

"It's all too coincidental not to be the same guys," he said to Drake.

"I agree, John. But, why there and now here?"

"I don't know. There's no apparent connection between the two communities. Maybe they were just practicing and moved here when they were satisfied."

"Maybe," Drake replied.

"Besides Charles, I'm not sure Michigan was their first run at this. I told you Bruce uncovered very similar crimes in a couple of other states. Either these guys are jumping from state to state until they get it just the way they want, or other similar groups are committing similar crimes for similar reasons. Maybe we're dealing with something bigger than just our local situation. This may be a cell working under a larger network."

"God, I hope not," Drake responded. "These are some sick dudes, and I would hate to think they are part of a larger organized group. If these crimes are connected and if there's more than one group, this would qualify as an act of interstate terrorism and fall into the lap of Homeland Security."

"I hear what you're saying, Charles. And I know you would be obligated to report it as such. You do what you have to on a bigger scale, and I'll continue to deal with what we have right here in our backyard.

"One more thing, Charles," John continued. "Can you get me a weather report for the night preceding each morning a head was found on the ice?"

"Sure. Why?"

"Got an idea taking shape in my head. Oh, and I think it's time for a story to leak to the press that we have information about the culprits and that we are following some firm leads. I think we need to make them feel a little uncomfortable. I think a little pressure will help at this point. I think it might help draw them out."

"Got it. I'll get the leak working."

"Be sure it includes all the newspapers up in this area, Albany, Saratoga, Glens Falls, Warrensburg, even Bolton Landing if they have a paper."

They ended their conversation. Drake would contemplate everything John had told him, and he would also put in a call to the Michigan State Police to develop an official link. His first call, however, would be to Bruce LaBue to get information about similar cases in other states. He would also arrange for a "leak" to the press, including radio, TV and all the local papers.

Simultaneously, John and Kristin proceeded to dress in their warm winter clothing. They drove out of the compound in their Jeep Grand Cherokee, along with a cooler loaded with drinks and snacks. They had two cameras with telescopic lenses and two pairs of binoculars. Kristin also held a portfolio in her lap containing a couple of pens and a lined tablet for taking notes, along with maps of every county surrounding Lake George.

John first drove to the center of the Village of Lake George. The police activity on the lake shore was almost totally gone. It had been almost two weeks since the last incident. Things were quieting down with some degree of normalcy returning to the tiny village. The tension was still prevalent in the community, and there has been a noticeable decrease in pedestrian traffic in the local shops and restaurants throughout the daytime hours and particularly at night.

Events like this were a boom and bust for the local merchants. Boom when all the commotion was taking place, and all the flashing light vehicles created turmoil. Bust when the lights went out, and the local citizens began to think about the potential danger they might face.

John pulled their vehicle up to the same parking place where he had last seen the white van. He told Kristin that this was the spot from which the four men in black loaded into the van and sped out of town. They decided they would follow the same route to begin their search.

The roadway came to a broad "Y" at the north end of the village, with one branch leading north, following the lake shoreline toward Bolton Landing and Hague and ultimately to Ticonderoga. The other branch leads northwest toward the town of Warrensburg and North Creek.

It was a toss-up. There was no way for them to know which way the van had gone. Finally, and for no specific reason, they agreed they would take the branch leading to Warrensburg as their first search leg. The plan was to cruise through the town to see if they might get lucky and spot a white van or someone walking the streets all dressed in black.

The next decision confronted them almost immediately. Less than a mile from where the "Y" split the roadway, there was an entrance ramp to the interstate highway. Now what? Both ways would lead them to Warrensburg in only slightly different ways. John pulled off the road into a broad storefront parking area just before reaching the entrance ramp to the highway.

"What are you thinking, John," Kristin asked.

"I'm not focused. I've been out of the game too long, and for the last year and a half, I've tried my damndest to forget the past. To forget my old ways. Now, I need to have it fresh in my mind all over again, and everything is all jumbled up."

"How can I help?"

He thought for a moment. "Play devil's advocate for me. For the moment, try to go back and be my control agent again. Make believe we're running a mission again. I need you to think like a bad guy. Think like someone who knew I was after their butts.

The four guys saw me in the village. They knew I was headed in their direction. They saw me chase after them in the alley and behind the stores. They knew I was trying to catch up to them. So, don't leave anything out. I need you to help get my brain back on the right track."

"Okay," she replied. "The first question is, which way would you go? The interstate is the fast-high speedway out of town. If they took the interstate, they could go either north or south. I don't know where the road would lead them if they went straight."

"It leads into Warrensburg. It's a two-lane road that leads into the town and then goes up into the Adirondacks. Lots of places to hide. Lots of hunting camps and seasonal homes most of which would be empty this time of year or the camps used primarily on weekends."

"But lots of potential to get slowed down and stuck in traffic when driving through the village."

"Yes."

"Lots of time lost for you to catch up to them….. to see them lined up along the main street in town?"

"Yes," John replied.

They sat silent for a couple of minutes before Kristin came up with another thought. "John, when we saw those men the first time, their van was parked facing north. When you chased after them, it was facing north again. If you were them, would you drive into town and park facing the direction you came from… or would you face the way you wanted to leave?"

"I love you, baby!" he said to her with a big grin on his face. "I would want to be facing in the direction I wanted to make a quick and direct exit. I would be facing north because that's the direction I wanted to go the fastest way I could."

"And you would be looking for a place to hide."

"Yes!"

"But first…"

"But first, we need to eliminate the obvious."

"That being the way they would not go?"

"Correct. That's the fastest way for us to reduce the area they would most likely be held up in."

"So?"

"Always wanted to show you greater downtown metropolitan one street-wide Warrensburg," he said sarcastically.

"Can't wait!" she answered in the same way.

John continued driving, passing beneath Interstate 87 and driving toward Warrensburg. From one end of town to the other, the town was only a little over a mile. They drove slowly, observing every vehicle parked along either side of the road. They entered half a dozen parking lots providing spaces for various retail businesses. When they reached the west end of town, they looped around and did it all over again.

They spotted only three white vans in the process of searching the village. Each time they saw one, they stopped and observed it until the owner appeared and drove off. None of the drivers were who they were looking for. In the center of town stood a gazebo. John drove around the structure and headed west toward the local airport.

At the edge of town, he drove past the regional headquarters for the D.E.C. This facility was a local district home base for all the Department of Environmental Conservation officers as well as the State Forest Rangers. All the uniformed men and women working for this agency were fully sworn law enforcement officers with the same arrest powers as a state patrol officer. They were cops! The only difference was they wore green uniforms and drove either green or red pickup trucks. Instead of patrolling highways, the vast forests of the state were their responsibility, and John knew that if something were to happen in the woods, these people would know about it. He would keep them in mind for future assistance.

It didn't take much to figure out that the area near these buildings would not be a good place to hide if you were trying to stay clear of the law. John decided to move on and take their search elsewhere. He returned to the main road passing through Warrensburg and headed northwest again. He was now on the same route he had driven to Canada a little over a year ago when he was involved in his last assignment for the government.

They drove for hours through every town, village, hamlet and wide spot on the road. By late afternoon, they had made a complete loop covering the southeastern sector of the Adirondack State Park. Had it not been for the four-wheel drive of their Jeep, they would never have been able to search all the back roads and hidden drives that they had covered. The further into the mountains they drove, the deeper the snow, the colder it got, and the less maintained the roads.

The snow aided their search to a degree. It was impossible for a vehicle of any kind to drive off-road or on any surface without leaving a clear track behind. A lightweight Ford van would not be a vehicle capable of dealing with much of this area.

If they saw tire tracks, they followed them, usually leading to a private home or seasonal cabin tucked into a hillside or a secluded patch of forest or to a small fishing lake. If there were no tracks, they skipped it and moved on to the next turn-off.

John knew one thing for certain. The four men he sought were living somewhere in a house or cabin. It was far too cold and wild for them to be camping out in a tent as they might have done in the spring or summer season. These mountains are too wild, with nighttime temperatures falling well below zero, for anyone to be living for weeks or months in anything less than a sturdy house or cabin capable of being heated.

They arrived back at their cabin shortly after eight o'clock that evening. They were both exhausted from the intense day they had spent searching. After a quick snack and a hot shower, they fell into bed.

John knew that the chances of spotting either the white van or any of the men in black were extremely slim. But, he felt like he had to illuminate the area they covered today and spending a day hunting and pecking around the fantastically beautiful Adirondacks with his wife wasn't the worst way of spending a day.

"First thing in the morning, we've got to call Superintendent Drake," John thought he heard himself say aloud.

Kristin thought she heard herself say, "Uh huh!"

Chapter 14

When Kristin awoke, she didn't find John in his usual place out on the deck, sipping a hot cup of coffee in the freezing cold air. This morning, he was lying next to her, all curled up and snuggling in their warm bed. The sun was up, and the trees sparkled and twinkled in the clear, cold air. She could hear the wind blowing across the lake and pushing its way through the trees surrounding their cabin. Winter was truly a breathtaking magic time of year in the vast crystal palace surrounding them.

She tried to remain still so as not to disturb her husband, but nature called, and the message was that she needed to use the bathroom. When she returned, she found John sitting up waiting for her. He wasn't fully awake yet. He was trying to rub the sleep from his eyes as she crawled back under the covers and wrapped herself around him.

"Good morning," she said warmly.

"Morning!" he answered.

"Are you okay?"

"I feel like every muscle in my legs, back and butt are screaming at me. I'm as stiff as a board. I must be getting soft and old."

"I can't do anything about the getting old part, but I can work on the getting stiff thing if you want," she said, half joking. "That was a long drive yesterday without much of a break from our trip to D.C. and then all the way to Michigan and back here."

"You got that right," he answered her. "I need to take a hot shower and move around a bit. I'll put the coffee on."

"Okay, I'll wait here for you."

He returned twenty minutes later, holding two mugs of coffee, to find his wife sound asleep. He looked at her and marveled at what he saw.

She was beautiful!

In his mind, he thought of her as an actress who could tantalize and charm any man alive or as a model whose picture appeared on the cover of some fashion magazine. But, he couldn't come up with a single face or body that fit her. It wasn't only her facial beauty; and it was a combination of all of her physical assets enhanced by her warm and loving personality. The way she carried herself. She appeared to be taller than she really was by virtue of the way she stood and moved. The ease of her demeanor with others and mostly with him. Her posture signaled self-confidence and inner strength that made her even more attractive. She had a shapely body with full, firm breasts and a thin, curvy waistline.

To him, she was the complete and total package.

It was at moments like this that he fully realized how lucky he was to have her in his life. He also realized how different his life had become and how much of that difference he owed to her.

The memory of all the years that he spent alone traveling the world as a salesman and secret government assassin flashed by in an instant. It was the moments like this that he now made every attempt to slow down… to absorb and to appreciate his new life with this woman. It was these moments that he had learned were the real reason for being alive.

She stirred as he sat on the bed next to her.

"Good morning again," he said playfully.

"Hi. I must have dozed off again."

"Really! Could have fooled me. And, here I thought you were ready to take a jog around the lake in your pj's," he jabbed at her.

"Can we wait just a little while? My running shoes are still a little wet from our last jog," she returned his sarcasm as she stretched her aching muscles.

"Yeah, I guess. Why don't you hop in the shower while I give Drake a call?"

With her fresh clothing draped over her arm, Kristin walked into the bathroom to shower and dress for the day. John sat on the couch in their den and dialed his phone.

"Hello!"

"Charles, it's John Anderson."

"John! How did your day go yesterday?"

"Not well," he confessed. "More miles and lots of nothing. We made sure we left an impression everywhere we stopped. Told everyone we talked with that we were looking for four men driving a white van and if they came across them, to let them know."

"Think it will do any good?" Drake asked.

"I doubt it, but you never know."

"I hear a big 'but' somewhere in there."

"Well, quite frankly, I think we're spinning our wheels, no pun intended, just driving around hoping that by chance we bump into these guys. I don't think it was a total waste of time. I think we needed to eliminate the area we covered. But, I also think I've got to re-think what I'm going to do next.."

"Well, I think you'll like what you see on the front page of the Albany Times Union this morning. I had my press secretary drop a few bits of information in just the right places, and the paper ran with it. I'm also told that the Saratogian and Saratoga Today papers have also been put on their front pages. I haven't seen the Glens Falls paper yet.

"On top of that, I received a call yesterday from Detective Brown's boss," Drake continued. "He said that Brown gave him a very positive report about your meeting, and as a result, the Michigan

State Police are formally requesting that we cooperate with each other concerning these two cases."

"I think that's a good idea," John added.

"There's more to it than that, John. He and I are mandated to report our interstate case sharing to the F.B.I. I got word late yesterday afternoon that the Bureau has already reported the case to Homeland Security. DHS decided that even with what little existing evidence we have indicates, and we could very well be dealing with a potential terrorist situation. They will be sending a team up here within the next day or two to take a look at things."

There was a pause in Drake's sharing of this new information. John sensed there was more he wanted to say.

"What are you holding back, Charles?"

"Well, I'm afraid they're going to want to talk to you. I had to include in my report that it was you who traveled to Michigan on behalf of this department, and I know Brown's boss also included your name in his report, " Drake added.

"Hummm! That could be a problem," John added.

"I realize that. I don't want to put you at risk in any way, but you know better than I do how those DHS guys can be. I'll do everything I can to keep you out of it, but…"

"I know. Lucas Martin, not John Anderson, will just have to deal with it when it happens…... if it happens."

"Understood. But you introduced yourself in Michigan as John Anderson. What do you think we should do next?" Drake asked.

"I'm not sure, Charles. Right now, I think Kristin and I need to take today and catch up a bit. I need to sort some things out. We're a little bleary-eyed from driving all day and all night to get back from Michigan to get home and then spending all day yesterday in the car again. Besides, we need to digest everything we learned in D.C. and Michigan, as well as what you just told me about the DHS. How about we plan on getting our heads together sometime late tomorrow?"

"Sounds good to me. Give me a call in the morning when you're ready and we'll see what's going on here in Albany and go from there."

"Okay. By the way, did anything interesting happen while we were gone?"

"Fortunately, not!" Drake answered. "We still have a C.S.I. lab team in the village, but nothing new has popped up."

"Good!" John replied. "I'll give you a call in the morning."

The call ended, and John knew immediately that he would not be sharing the DHS news with Kristin. He knew that she would worry herself to death over the potential exposure that might result. He heard her come out of the bathroom following her morning shower. He decided to make another phone call.

"Be right back, Kristin."

"Where are you going?"

"Need to talk to Bob for a minute," he lied.

Slipping on his warm winter jacket, he grabbed his cell phone and walked out into their front yard. He continued walking toward Bob's house just in case his wife should be watching from their front window. Once he was out of sight of his cabin, he pulled his phone from his pocket and dialed a new number.

"Bruce LaBue," the voice answered.

"Bruce, it's John."

"Well, good morning. How was your trip to the Midwest?"

"Very informative. Listen, I have a problem." He explained the results of the visit to Michigan and his telephone conversation only minutes ago with Superintendent Charles Drake. Bruce recognized at once the potential damage to not only John's new life but to his very existence. Exposure to his past could lead to a host of very unpleasant repercussions.

"Sit tight," Bruce responded. "Let me make a couple of phone calls and see what I can do."

"Okay, if Kristin answers the phone when you call back, don't let her know what this is about. I'm not going to tell her unless I have to."

"Don't blame you. Give me a couple of hours. I'll get back to you one way or another before the day is over."

He disconnected the call and walked back toward their cabin. When he turned toward his front porch, his friend and confidant Bob Herman was standing only a few yards away.

"I overheard your part of that. Is everything okay?"

"Just another little wrinkle in my everyday mundane life," he joked. He went on to share the past few days with Bob, including the potential problem with DHS. There was almost nothing in his life that he withheld from Bob. He trusted the man, literally, as much or more than he trusted his wife.

"I have two thoughts," Bob injected. "First, I could always fake it for you and take your place at the meeting. I've stood in for you in other situations. Secondly, you could always hop in the motorhome and take off on a vacation and simply not be available for a meeting."

"You're right. I thought of that when talking to Drake. You are almost as creative as I am, even when you're being a smart ass. But I won't let you fill in for me on this. I would never expose you like that. If anything happened, as a result, I'd have to deal with Sally, and that scares the crap out of me more than anyone coming after me with a gun."

"You know you love me because I'm a smart ass, but you have a valid point. I'm not sure I'd want to mess with Sally, either. I've been married to the woman for years, and she still scares the crap out of me."

"Yeah, I love you both, but don't let it go to your head. Let's just stand by and see what Bruce can do."

"Okay, let me know."

"Please don't say anything to Sally. I'm not telling Kristin about this unless I have to."

"Got it!" Bob replied as he turned to walk away.

"One more thing, Bob. Maybe we should run a check on all of our electronic security equipment. I want to be prepared should these newspaper articles stir up any interest that resulted in an unexpected visit from our black-clad friends."

"Got it! I'll start on that right away."

When John re-entered his cabin, he found Kristin seated at the kitchen table sipping a hot cup of coffee.

"I heard you talking to Superintendent Drake before you went outside. What did he have to say?"

"I brought him up to speed on our little tour yesterday. Seems like he got a telephone call from his counterpart out in Michigan. After Detective Brown reported in, his boss decided that they wanted to cross-reference their case with ours."

"Sounds reasonable," she commented.

"It does, but Drake also informed me that by the two states working the same case, it automatically brought in the F.B.I. who then had to report it to Homeland Security who has now designated the case as a possible terrorist act. I think all the feds have been super sensitive since 9/11 with anything that even looks close to being a potential terrorist situation, particularly if it has anything to do with New York. And, on top of that, it seems the Lake George case has made front page news on all of the local papers after Drake leaked a few facts to the press."

"Wow! That's moving things along rather rapidly."

"Yeah! Drake also told me that DHS is sending a team up here to oversee what's going on," he blurted out without thinking. "He's going to try and keep me out of it and away from any D.C. people."

"John! Are they going to want to talk to you? Will this put you in jeopardy? Could this expose us? What if…"

"Hold on, baby girl. Don't get all bent out of shape. I wasn't going to tell you about this for this very reason.

"Why not?

"Because of the very reaction you are having right now. I knew this would get you all worried and cranked up."

"Yeah! Well?"

"Don't get yourself in a tizzy, and I'll handle it. Don't even know if they'll want to talk to me, so let's not get our blood pressure pumping, just jet," he said as he leaned over and wrapped his arms around her, trying to calm her and to disguise his own growing concern.

"What else did Drake say?"

"He said we should take the day off and recover from our marathon trip to D.C. and Michigan and our grand tour of yesterday. He ordered me to ravage your body for hours," he joked. "He also wants to meet tomorrow to talk about what's next. So, today is a chill day. We're going to do nothing by veg out. And spend the day running around naked."

"He did not say that!"

"Well, maybe that was my idea."

"Good, let's go shopping."

"I said, running around naked!"

"And I said shopping!"

An hour later, John had their Jeep splashing along through the snow melt, making Shelving Rock and Buttermilk Falls roads a slippery quagmire as they headed toward the mall in Glens Falls. The ride proved one issue conclusively: exactly who ran the household perched in the quiet cove on the shores of Lake George.

Chapter 15

They returned to their cabin shortly after four o'clock that afternoon. The sky had turned the color of pewter announcing yet another snowfall was approaching. It was late February, the final stretch of winter. This was the time of year of the heaviest snowfalls and the coldest temperatures. Mother Nature wanted to send a final message to let the world know who was in charge. The air was so cold that even sound froze. The quiet that surrounded the lake bordered on the unnatural.

John's cell phone buzzed, vibrating in his pocket. He took it out and looked at the display screen. It was Bruce LaBue calling from Washington, D.C. Kristin was in their bedroom emptying the bags she filled at the outlet stores. John walked into the kitchen, putting as much distance between himself and his wife as he could without leaving the house.

"Hey Bruce," he answered the phone.

"Hi, John. Well, I think we have a bit of a problem."

"How so?" John asked.

"I talked with a couple of my contacts at DHS. Seems like the Lake George case is attracting more interest than either of us thought it would. A team is being dispatched to Albany first thing in the morning. It's being headed up by an agent named Don Costa."

"Do you know him?"

"Oh, yeah! Do you remember Andrew?"

"Sure, I do. Your former assistant who was mysteriously killed by a hit and run."

"Right! Well, Costa was his replacement. I got saddled with him within a day or two of Andrew's death. He charged into the department like he owned the friggin' place. Pissed off everyone he came into contact with, including me."

"A real charmer!"

"That's one way of putting it. The thing I'm most concerned with is that by taking Andrew's spot in my office, he had access to all our files… including yours. He didn't have any part in your file disappearing, but he would or could have known that it was there one day and gone the next. He certainly knew you existed and that Kristin was a former employee and your controller.

"He also worked on the case involving the Canadian Prime Minister and the president's death until the file was closed. Long and short of it is he knows of the existence of Agent John Anderson.

"But, I never met him!?"

"No, when I say he knows John Anderson, what I mean is that he knows who John Anderson was and what he did. He also knows that John Anderson has dropped out of existence and that his control agent left the agency immediately after a potentially explosive international case."

"Can you stop him from coming up here?"

"No. He managed to get himself promoted over a lot of other people ahead of him, including me. His arrogant personality caught the attention of all the right people, and he played it like a fiddle. He got transferred to a different department out of my area of authority. I lost contact and control of him. He's a real prick and is ready to climb up anybody's back to get ahead.

"So now, as a result, his orders now come from someone too far above my pay grade for me to have any influence. I tried but got told in no uncertain terms to back off. There's one more thing John, he knows Kristin by sight as well as reputation. He worked in the same department as her while she was still here, so he knows her first hand."

"That won't be a problem. I'll keep her away from the meeting."

"Okay," Bruce continued. "There is a little good news. He doesn't know Lucas Martin. I almost completely positive of that."

"Okay! Got it. But I don't think that will work."

"Why's that?"

"Because I identified myself as John Anderson when we were in Michigan, and both their report and the one file from New York with the F.B.I. refer to me by that name. So, I can't appear in any meetings calling myself by my real name."

"That sucks. Just be careful John, watch your step. Remember what I said? This guy is a real prick. He's out to make a name for himself and he doesn't care who he steps on doing it. He won't step on toes, he'll step on the whole damn foot. And if there happens to be a neck or two in the way, he'll step on them as well. He worked for me for only a few months and tried to cut my balls off to get promoted. Luckily, he got out of here before he did me any damage."

"Like I said, a real charmer." To lighten the atmosphere, John jokingly asked Bruce, "Can I kill him?"

"If you can figure a way, be my guest. Might even get you a medal of some sort with the blessing of a whole bunch of people I know."

The two men laughed and bantered between themselves before ending their call. John walked into the bedroom to inform Kristin of the conversation. The DHS team's involvement had gotten beyond the point of trying to keep it from her. She had to know, and he needed to share it with her. The presence of Don Costa was a threat they would both have to be aware of and deal with.

While he was bringing his wife up to date, his telephone vibrated a second time, signaling the receipt of a text message. He looked at it to see that Superintendent Drake had scheduled a meeting in Albany for two o'clock the next day and requested that John be there. He acknowledged receipt of the message and confirmed that the schedule worked for him.

"This worries me, John," Kristin said after he finished bringing her completely up to speed. "I know this guy, and I don't like him. He's a sneaky glory-seeking backstabbing status, seeking son-of-a-bitch who will climb over dead bodies to get where he wants to be."

"WOW!" John exclaimed. "Why don't you tell me how you really feel about this guy."

"Don't turn your back on him, John. He could be dangerous."

"Yeah, well! I asked Bruce if I could kill him," he said, trying to get her to lighten up a bit. Her facial expression did not change. "He didn't think it was funny either," he added, not getting the hoped-for response.

At precisely one forty-five the next afternoon, John walked into the conference room located next to Superintendent Drake's office. He arrived early in hopes of talking to Drake to fill him in on his conversation with Bruce concerning Agent Don Costa. It was too late. When he walked in, Drake was already seated at the table, talking to a new face. It didn't take long for John to find out who the new face belonged to.

"Ah, good. You're here," Drake said as John entered the room. "Let me introduce you to Agent Don Costa. Agent Costa is with Homeland Security. Agent Costa, this is………".

"Lucas Martin," John said, cutting Drake off and extending his hand to Costa. "I'm Superintendent Drake's special assistant working the case you're here to talk about."

John decided to take the risk of introducing himself as Lucas Martin instead of John Anderson in hopes that DeCosta didn't know or had forgotten the name in the two-state police files. If DeCosta really knew John Anderson, there was nothing to lose and it was worth the risk of finding out.

"Uh, yeah," Drake fumbled. "… Lucas has, uh, he has just returned from Michigan, where he talked to the folks out there."

"Great!" Costa replied, taking John's hand. "You can fill us in on everything you've learned."

For the next hour, the three men discussed and shared information concerning the murders in Michigan as well as Lake George. They also briefly reviewed the similar cases Bruce had uncovered. The exchange was both cordial and respectful. Each man was interested in sharing and learning all the known facts concerning the horrible beheadings that had taken place in the two states.

"Well, gentlemen," Costa began. "I've been sent here to oversee and coordinate the efforts concerning these two cases and to offer whatever support you might need. However, it's easy to see that, on this end, it would be counterproductive for me to interfere with the way things are being handled.

So, Superintendent Drake, if you have no objections, I will defer the operation to you and your staff and stand by to lend assistance if needed. Please know that I have the authority to call in whatever asset and resources you might request, so don't be bashful."

"No objections at all, and don't worry about our being bashful," Drake responded. "At this point in the case, your department standing by would be the smoothest way to proceed."

"Good," Costa replied. "I'm confident that you, with the assistance of Mr… Martin, will do just fine. However, I want to reassure you that if there is anything that I can contribute, my entire department will be available at a moment's notice. And, to keep my bosses happy, I'd like to be briefed a couple of times a day so I can let them know that everything is moving forward and that progress is being made."

"Sounds good to me," Drake said.

The three men stood as the meeting reached its conclusion. Costa firmly shook the Superintendent's hand as he prepared to leave the conference room. Just before he exited, he turned back, extending his hand once again toward John.

"And thank you for your assistance in this case. I look forward to working with you to its final resolution. Look forward to seeing you both very soon. I have just one question, Mr. Martin: how do you know Bruce LaBue?"

John's alert systems peaked. He looked at the new member of their team, trying to read every expression his face might reveal.

"Oh, my wife once worked with Bruce, and we would occasionally bump into one another at social events," he said, hoping that his explanation would be accepted.

"Ah, yes!" Costa replied. He turned toward the door with one last farewell jester before leaving the room. He turned his back and walked out of the room. With his back to both men, he dropped his last comment, saying, "Thank you, Superintendent Drake! Mr. Anderson! Oh! And please tell your wife that she is very much missed in the office."

"Well, I guess there's a reason why he's in the intelligence field. He obviously knows more than he's willing to reveal."

John remained silent, wondering if Costa would do the same, or… would he really give John reason to have to kill him? Or by using 'Anderson' in his departure, was this just a way of letting John know who held the cards. The tossing out of 'Anderson' and the comment concerning Kristin's time in D.C. came at John as a challenge… a threat… one to which he would have a measured response.

"What now?" Drake said, trying to get John's mind back on the case and of the revelation that had just smacked him in the face.

"I think we need to pick up where we left off. I still don't see these killers coming out of their hiding places and walking in here with their hands over their heads. They're out there somewhere, and they're not coming to us

… we've got to dig them out.

"Something you need to understand about DHS, Charles. They're not like the F.B.I., they don't take the lead in cases like this. All they will do is sit back and monitor what other people do. Then, they will criticize and attack the process to make themselves look good. They will take all the credit for what goes right and somehow avoid being around when something goes wrong. It's still going to be up to us to solve this case and watch the pissing contest between the two agencies.

"I'm a firm believer that nothing happens unless you make it happen," John added. "That's where we are now. We've got to make something happen. Somehow get our men in black to show themselves or screw up and lead us to wherever they're held up. Somehow, we've got to make something happen. To start with, I think Kristin and I need to resume what we were doing before DHS stuck its ugly face into this."

"I couldn't agree more," Superintendent Drake injected. "But roaming the back roads isn't working. There's got to be another way."

"You're right. I've got to do something different. Give me a while to think it out and discuss it with Kristin."

Drake paused for a moment before speaking to the back of John's head. John hadn't moved since Costa left the room. He continued to stare at the doorway, processing what he had heard.

"John," Drake began. "I know this guy coming on the scene tosses you a curveball, but don't let it get to you. I know he has a reputation for being a real shit, but he seemed like a pretty decent guy to me. Don't panic over this."

"I don't panic!"

"Just don't do anything stupid!"

John answered, still holding his stare. "Charles, if this guy knows me, he also knows what I did when I worked for the government, and if he knows that, he knows that threatening me is not a very good idea. And, if he's as smart as he wants us to believe he is, well, let's just hope I don't have to … take any drastic steps to protect my wife and me."

"John!" Drake said in a warning tone. "Don't get foolish. Don't put the two of us at odds with each other."

"Don't worry, Charles. If I did anything … you'd never know it."

Just then, a voice came from the telephone on the superintendent's desk. "Superintendent Drake, Mr. Anderson has an urgent call. I tried to tell the man that you were in a conference, but he insisted. Said it was a matter of great importance concerning Mrs. Anderson."

The two men looked at each other. Drake gestured to John to take the call at his desk.

"Hello!"

"John, it's Bob. You better get back here. There's been a shooting!"

"Shooting!? What's happening? Are you alright?"

"I took one in the leg."

"Kristin!! What about Kristin?"

"…Get here as fast as you can, John!"

Chapter 16

"I want my car and two cruisers out front before I get there," Superintendent Drake shouted at his aide. He overheard John's end of the telephone conversation and could hear Bob's voice as he reported what had taken place back at the Lake George compound.

"My car is parked a block away," John said.

"Leave it! You won't be able to keep up with us. We'll make much better time if we take state cars with lights and sirens."

The two men immediately ran from the conference room and headed toward the elevator. By the time they reached the main floor, there were three cars waiting at the main entrance to the building. One was a black unmarked sedan in addition to a State Highway Patrol car in front of it and a second behind. All three had red, blue and white lights flashing from bumper to bumper.

Superintendent Drake jumped into the front passenger seat of the black sedan and John into the rear. Drake immediately grabbed the radio mic and started barking orders. To his driver, he ordered for him to drive north toward Lake George by the quickest route and to have all emergency devices in full operation. His driver relayed the instructions via his lapel mic to the drivers of the other two cruisers. All three vehicles sped toward the I-87 Northway that would take them north toward Lake George.

Superintendent Drake continued talking on his car radio. "Who's on the scene?" he asked of whoever was on the other end. He was given the name of the officers already within John's lakeside compound. Drake immediately contacted those officers directly exchanging the latest details.

He then turned to his driver and instructed him to proceed to Glens Falls Hospital after learning that is where Kristin and Bob had been transported. The three cars screamed their way along the interstate highway, bullying every car and truck out of their path.

John sat passively in the rear seat, only half hearing what was going on around him. His mind was numb with the thoughts of his wife lying in a hospital, shot and possibly near death. He couldn't think. Wouldn't allow himself to think. Somewhere in the distance, he thought he heard sirens. Maybe even a voice shouting orders of some kind. A blur rushed in front of his eyes out of the reach of his brain. He felt as if he were inside of a big bubble.

He felt fear... anxiety... love... hatred... confusion... all blended together, filling his body, flooding his mind, and pumping through him as thick and slow as catsup from a bottle.

Fear of what was ahead. Anxious not knowing what was going on around him. Love for the woman beyond his reach to protect. Hatred for whoever hurt the one person he knew he could not live without. Confusion about what had happened, what will happen, and why it had all happened.

In what seemed somewhere between a heartbeat and a lifetime, John sensed the car he was in coming to a sudden stop in front of a large building. The rear door nearest him opened and he felt a hand grip his arm and forcefully but gently tug him off of the seat to stand outside on the sidewalk. A blast of cold air reawakened him. Shocking him back to the moment at hand.

"John, are you okay?" a distant friendly voice asked him.

It took him a moment to regain his composure before recognizing and acknowledging the voice of his friend Charles Drake. It had taken a little over half an hour for the convoy of police cars to reach the emergency entrance to the Glens Falls Hospital.

"Yeah! Yeah, I'm okay. Where do we go?"

"Come on. Let's go inside and find out what we can," Drake encouraged gently, knowing that John was in some sort of shock. They proceeded inside to be met by an entourage of uniformed police officers, both state and local. A state officer wearing sergeant stripes on his sleeve greeted Superintendent Drake.

"This way, sir. Mr. Herman is in the ICU. Mrs. Herman is with him. The medical staff is waiting for Mr. Anderson's arrival."

"What about my wife?" John managed to squeeze out of his tight throat.

"She's still in surgery, sir. Doctors are waiting to tell you what's going on. This way, please."

A short elevator ride and a few paces later, John was greeted by the embrace of his long-time friend Sally Herman. She leapt from the chair next to a bed filled with her prone husband, who looked up at John, passing unspoken communications between them that only very old and trusted friends would understand.

Sally finally released him and led him to Bob's bedside.

"Hey bud, how are you doing?"

"I'm good, John. Don't know why they insisted on keeping me here. I'm okay. Took one in the upper leg, but nothing major was hit. No bone and no artery. I'll be as good as new in a few days."

"What…" John stammered, trying to control his emotions and voice.

"She took three hits. One in her right leg just below the knee. A second in her right arm a couple of inches above the elbow." He paused.

"And the third?" John asked tentatively.

"…She took the third in the chest. Upper left, just below the collarbone. That's what they're working on now in the O.R."

John paused to collect and organize the thoughts racing through his mind. He knew immediately from his own experience that bullet wounds, as Bob was describing, were not fatal and that his wife would recover.

"What happened?"

"I was working in the yard right in front of your cabin. I was clearing the new snow and spreading some rock salt on the icy areas. Had been out there for about ten or fifteen minutes. Kristin came out on the porch with a mug of hot coffee for me. That's when it all started. I was walking toward the porch to take a mug from her. I'm almost to the bottom step of your when suddenly I heard gunshots coming from behind me. I turned to see what was going on, and I got hit in the leg. When I got hit, I spun around, and that's when I saw Kristin falling and sliding down the steps toward me. She was bleeding pretty badly, but she was conscious. I crawled on top of her, but the shooting had already stopped. Then Sally came running up to us."

"Did you see the shooter?"

"No. The shots came from the lake. But, when I was on the ground, I was too low to see anything. Couldn't even see the ice."

"Did you see anything, Sally?" John turned and asked gently.

"By the time I got to Bob and Kristin, the shooting had stopped. I looked out toward the lake and saw two snow machines. One was already moving, but the other was sitting still on the ice. A man was getting on it just as I looked."

"What do you remember about the riders?"

"The guy trying to mount the second snowmobile was dressed entirely in black. When I saw that, I looked again at the other guy, the one that was already in motion on the other machine. He was dressed the same way, John. From head to toe in black."

The three friends were quiet for a moment, knowing the importance of what Sally had just reported.

"Thanks, Sally." Then he turned back to Bob.

Bob reached out with his free hand and took John by the forearm. "John, I was working in the yard for at least half an hour before getting close to your house. Kristin came out only after I got close to your porch. These guys could have shot me anytime they wanted. But they didn't. I think they were waiting. I think they were waiting for someone to come out of your cabin. I think they were gunning for you or Kristin or both."

John grew quiet. His face changed to stone. His body hardened, and his voice became all business, a monotone Bob had heard many times before. Bob knew this man. The man John had become in the last few seconds. He knew him, and he was afraid of him. This man was not his friend. This man… this version of his friend, scared him.

All the while the conversation among the three friends was taking place, Superintendent Charles Drake stood only a couple of feet behind John, taking in every word. He didn't know John Anderson the way his friends did, but he, too sensed the change.

"John, we need to talk."

"Not now. I need to know what's going on with my wife first."

He left the cubical encompassing his friend and went looking for a doctor or a nurse who could tell him what was going on in the O.R. with his wife. It took only a few minutes. He was finally approached by a doctor who had been in surgery attending to Kristin.

"Mr. Anderson?"

"Yes."

"I'm Doctor Reed. I've been attending to your wife."

"What can you tell me?"

"Well, she's a lucky lady. Had it not been for your friends, she would probably bleed to death before she got to any medical facility. She has incurred three gunshot wounds. One here on her leg." Doctor Reed pointed to the area on his own leg. "A second to her arm about here," pointing to his own arm. "These two, although painful, were not life-threatening, and we managed to control the bleeding very quickly. Both were through and through wounds.

"The third wound was far more severe and could easily have been fatal. A bullet entered here" he pointed to a spot on his chest just above his heart and, below his collarbone and to the left of his throat. The location was different than John had expected and he knew it was far more dangerous.

"The bullet passed completely through and exited from her upper rear shoulder. An inch to the right or lower on her body, and she would have died within seconds. Fortunately, your two friends applied enough pressure to stem the bleeding long enough for us to get her into surgery."

"What is her condition?" John asked anxiously.

"Stable by very serious. Yes, to your next question. She will survive and will recover completely. She might have a slight limp for a while until she regains all of the muscle tone in her leg. Her arm will be fine. She will require a good bit of time to recover from her chest wound. You're looking at a couple of months of quiet recovery."

"When can I see her?"

"Shortly," Doctor Reed replied. "She is being prepared to be moved to the I.C.U. Right now. It will take the nurses a little while to get her down here. We will keep her sedated for the next day or two to keep her calm and quiet. You can talk with her, but I'm afraid she's going to be pretty drugged up, so we can control the pain. She's not going to remember much for the next few days."

"How long will she have to stay here?" John asked.

"I'd say at least a week. She's in very serious condition, Mr. Anderson. Three GSWs are enough to kill just about anybody. But your wife is a strong, healthy young woman and should recover nicely. Right now, she just needs some time and attention. I'll be checking in on her regularly."

"Thank you, Doctor Reed."

"You're very welcome. I'll talk with you soon."

And with that report, the doctor turned and left John standing in the hallway with Charles Drake there with him. Drake placed his hand on John's shoulder to comfort him and to assure him that he was not alone.

"John, we need to talk."

"No, we don't!" John answered.

"What do you want to do now?" Drake asked.

"What do you think!"

"John, standing here right now, I'm your friend. If you do what I think you're thinking about, I'll be a cop. Do you get my drift?'

"Don't worry, Charles. Like I've told you before, you'll never know."

Chapter 17

An hour later, John was sitting next to his wife's hospital bed, holding her hand and talking to her. She was not aware of his presence or the warm words of love and encouragement that he uttered softly to her. Sally was there waiting with him when Kristin was first brought into the I.C.W. unit. She wanted to greet Kristin and to let John know she was there to support both of them, as well as her wounded husband, whose bed was only a few feet away.

John remained at his wife's bedside for the rest of the afternoon. Sally returned about six o'clock.

"John, why don't you go get something to eat? I'll stay with Kristin while you do."

"I'm good, Sally. Thank you. Besides, you need to stay close to Bob."

Just as he said those words, Bob came hobbling into Kristin's cubical on a set of crutches.

"What are you doing out of bed?" John asked as his old friend approached and wrapped an arm around John's shoulders.

"I'm fine. Doc says I can go home first thing in the morning. Just want to keep me overnight for safety's sake."

"Sally can't go home by herself tonight," John said.

"Have no intentions of sending her back to the compound alone. She's going to stay here in town. Already got her a room at the hotel down the street. I talked to Drake while you were waiting for Kristin. He's got the entire compound wrapped up in a nice yellow crime scene ribbon anyway. We can't go back in until his people finish their check of the entire area, including the ice where Sally saw the two snowmobiles. Might be a couple of days."

Bob could easily detect the cold detachment of his friend's behavior. He knew it well. He had been at John's side when he prepared for many of his 'assignments' over the years. He knew how to read John's demeanor and behavior.

"John, what are you thinking?" Bob asked. "You're not going to try to take these guys on all by yourself, are you?"

John didn't answer.

Sally spoke next. She reached out and took John's hands in hers and turned him in his chair so he had no choice but to look directly into her eyes.

"John," she began. "Listen to me and listen good. I've known you for a lot of years. Bob has never told me what you did for the government. But I knew. I've known all along. I stood with you when you returned home, needing time to decompress, as well as times when you needed to heal from your unspecified injuries.

"I knew then, and I know now what's going on inside your head. And for the very first time, it's my turn to talk."

"Sally…" he interrupted.

"Shut up and listen," she demanded. "A year ago, you brought this woman home. You brought her into our lives. We have accepted her and learned to love her. She's special. She has changed our lives… all of our lives… especially yours.

"So, listen to me real good. DON'T FUCK IT UP!"

John had to drop Sally's hands as he and Bob simultaneously busted into a roaring laughing spell. Neither had either ever heard Sally use anything close to this language and even under these dire conditions, neither of them could control their shock.

Once they regained their self-control, Sally had a bit more to say.

"This woman loves you. And you love her. She will recover from these wounds, but if you go out and do something stupid like…

like…...killing people, you will kill her in the process. If you go back to that life, you will destroy this one. The one you have with her. The life both of you deserve."

John hesitated for a moment, looking directly into Sally's eyes. Then, he reached out and embraced her, pulling her to him and holding her tight. And suddenly, he dropped his head to his chest and burst into tears.

It took him a couple of minutes to regain his composure. Sally and Bob sat on either side of their close friend, each with a hand on one of his shoulders to comfort and support him and to silently signal that they were there with him and for him. The cold-hearted, cold-blooded, detached and unemotional assassin, for the first time in any of their memories, became completely human.

His wife, the first and only person he ever allowed to get close to him and the very first he ever allowed himself to get close to, lay critically wounded in a hospital bed. His fear of her dying, driven by his love for her and the vulnerability that this love created, exposed and revealed him for the first time in his life.

"I'm okay," he finally managed to say to Sally and Bob. He took Sally's hand and lifted it to his lips. He gently kissed the back of her hand in a gesture of thanks and sincere gratitude for her presence and her friendship and for her stern words.

"Yes, you are," Sally replied. "You'll be just fine. And so will Kristin. She will need some time to heal, but she is a strong woman who won't let a couple of bullets get in the way of having that family she keeps talking about."

"What!?" John exclaimed.

"You heard me. She wants to have a family. She wants to have children with you. So, do you think this bump in the road will stop her? I don't think so."

"Children?"

"Yeah, John. Children. Kids. You know, those little humans that pop out of the most mysterious place in the world. And she wants them with you. So, if you go off and screw things up......!"

"She wants children?"

He sat with her for four days. He never left her side. He slept in a chair next to her bed holding her hand, waiting. Waiting for the doctors to bring her out of her chemical-induced coma, they decided to put her in to assist in her healing. He waited with the thoughts of her and her wanting children.

Him? A father? He couldn't quite grasp the idea much less the reality of it. Never in his life had he ever imagined being a father. Never had there been anyone in his life who would connect that possibility to him until Kristin.

She completed him. The same as if she were his heart or his lungs or his arms and legs. She was as much a part of him and his own body. Watching her lay in her hospital bed with her eyes closed and her chest rising and falling with silent breaths, he came to realize how much she meant to him. He knew he loved her. But, for the first time, he had come to realize want love was. How deep and strong and broad his feelings for her had become. How she had awakened him.

He held her hand while resting his forehead on her bed. He cried again. For the second time in his adult life, he cried.

He felt a hand caress the back of his head. He was jolted upright by the touch.

"Don't cry, my love. I'm right here," Kristin mumbled through dry drug thickened lips.

Doctors and nurses hovered over her for the next hour while John, Sally, and Bob paced nervously in the hallway outside of her room. He had alerted the medical staff the moment he recovered from the shock of his wife's touch. White coats and dresses rushed to Kristin's bedside while Bob and Sally came from their hotel room only a couple of blocks away. All the comments made by the medical personnel passing in and out included broad smiles reassuring the waiting trio that good news was coming their way.

Finally, the lead doctor approached John with the news. "Your wife is a real trooper, Mr. Martin. If I didn't know better, I would think she just came back from the hair salon to get her fingernails buffed and polished. She is doing great, but she'll need a couple of weeks of quiet rest and a bit of pampering before she's back on her feet."

"She'll get all of that and more," Sally said when she sensed John choking up and not able to respond to the doctor.

"When can we see her?" Bob asked.

"Right now!" the doctor replied. "Just don't overwhelm her for too long. She needs rest, and she'll probably doze off every few minutes. She still has a lot of drugs in her."

"When can I take her home?" John was finally able to ask.

"Don't get too carried away, Mr. Martin. Your wife was damn near killed. She's going to need some time to heal. I'd say give her a couple more days here for us to look after her and monitor all her signs. Once I'm sure she's stable, we'll release her."

John approached her bed from one side while Sally and Bob approached from the other. They took each of her hands and held her tightly but gently. John leaned over and kissed his wife as he fought for control of his emotions.

"Hi, baby!" he said.

"Hi back to you," Kristin answered with a huge sleepy grin on her face.

Sally and Bob leaned over and gave her a hug. The usual exchange of words took place for the next few minutes when Sally finally took Bob by the hand and led him toward the door.

"Time for us to leave these two alone," she announced to Bob.

Once they were out of the room and John was alone with his wife, he sat on the bed next to her to get as close as he could. He could see she was fighting to stay awake.

"Go to sleep, sweetheart. I'll be right here with you."

"John?" Kristin tried to speak. Each knew what the question was.

"Not now, baby. Not now. You're going to be fine. We'll talk after you rest. Sleep now."

She dozed off immediately. John remained at her side, holding her hand, afraid to leave her for fear that she might evaporate and that he would find that all of this was just a dream. That this beautiful woman and all the emotion he felt for her wasn't real. He didn't deserve her. He didn't deserve this new life she created for him.

The months with her seemed like a dream. So different! So new! So strange had his life become. From the violent world of death and killing and being alone to the tenderness and love this woman had brought to him, how she found and released emotions within him that he never knew he had, never knew existed in him. She touched places within him that didn't exist before her. He exposed places he had never been in touch with before.

Now, she lay here wounded. Shot three times, jerking him back to his old world… to his old life. Sally was right, and he couldn't allow himself to revert to his former life and destroy all of this. But, neither would he… neither could he allow this to go unfinished. Neither could he allow this to go… unavenged!

Chapter 18

Kristin was released from the hospital on the morning of the fourth day following her coming out of the chemically induced coma. John was with her in her room, helping her get ready to leave the hospital.

"I can't wait to get out of here," she said. "I want to be home with you."

"Well, my love, you'll be with me, but we won't be going home just yet. I'm afraid the police kept the house off-limits to us for longer than we expected."

"Are they gone now?"

"Yes!"

"Well then, why can't we go home?"

"There's a matter of repairs that are needed. Seems someone shot out a few windows and left a bunch of bullet holes in our front door and porch."

"Oh, that!"

"Yeah, that. So, I rented a suite up in Gore Mountain ski lodge for a few days until the repairs were done. Bob has already contacted a couple of guys who will start first thing in the morning. Once they are done and the place is all cleaned up, we'll go home."

"Okay," she replied, squirming down into the wheelchair.

A little more than an hour later, they were settled in their room in Gore Mountain. Kristin fought to keep her eyes open. She tired very quickly after expending the energy to leave the hospital. John helped her into the plush king-sized bed and tucked her in for a nap. As he turned to leave the room, Kristin grabbed his arm. He sat on the bed next to her.

"John," she began. "Promise me." He knew immediately what she was referring to.

"I can't!"

"John, please. You can't go after them. You can't go back. Please, John."

"Kristin, they almost killed you! How do you expect me to let that go? Every bone in my body is aching to make them pay for that."

"I know… I know, but you can't. You can't go after them the way you used to do. You can't! Please, John… for me, for us. Please. Promise me you won't hunt them down and kill them."

He was silent. He was afraid to look into her eyes. He knew if he did, he could never refuse her, and he could never lie to her. He knew he was trapped. Trapped between his love for this woman and his years of training to kill any and all threats to himself and now to the woman he loved. He also knew she was right. He couldn't go after them in the way he was trained. But he also knew he couldn't stand by and do nothing.

"John!"

"…I promise."

She threw herself at him, wrapping her one good arm around his neck and pulling him tightly to herself, yelping in pain from her wounds. He was finally able to settle her down and left her to rest. He left the bedroom closing the door as he stepped into the living room of the suite. He flopped down onto the couch, exhausted and trying to absorb the impact of the promise he just made to his wife. His cell phone vibrated in his pocket.

"Hello!"

"John, it's Charles Drake. We need to meet and have a conversation ASAP. How's Kristin doing?"

"She's doing okay. I just got her settled. She's napping right now."

"Good! Where are you?"

"Gore Mountain."

"Can you be here in the morning for a meeting?"

"I think so. Let me get ahold of Sally and see if she can come up and stay with Kristin. I'll get back to you in a little while."

At ten o'clock the next morning, John entered the office of the Superintendent of New York State Police in the state capital of Albany. He was led to the conference room adjoining Charles Drake's office. In addition to Drake waiting for him was Agent Don Costa of the Department of Homeland Security.

"Good morning, gentlemen," John said, extending his hand first to one man and then he other.

Drake took the lead. "Good morning, Lucas. Agent Costa and I wanted to bring you up to date on what we have learned from the shooting at your house, and we want to discuss future activities.

John knew exactly where this was going.

"Don't worry, I've already promised my wife that I would behave myself."

"Good to hear," Costa answered. "Look, we don't have to get into the nitty-gritty of your history. We know where you came from and what you are capable of doing."

John N. Anderson, the assassin, turned stone-faced toward the man in front of him. "No, agent Costa. No! You might think you do," the assassin continued. "But you don't. You don't have the slightest idea what I'm capable of. And you don't want to find out.

"However, you're right, we don't need to go there. It would be better left that way," he said to both men across the table in a way both would understand that he had just issued a warning. His voice and his stare were as cold as the water beneath the ice covering Lake George.

Drake picked up the conversation attempting to calm the tension that existed between John and Agent Costa.

"Here's what we know, which is very little. Sally was the only witness and she didn't see very much. My CSI people recovered four slugs from your front door and porch railing. They pulled three additional slugs from inside your house that apparently went through one of your front windows. Plus, they recovered a dozen shell casings from the snow-covered island about two hundred yards out in the lake directly in front of your compound. They are all .223 caliber bullets. So far, no ballistic match on file. We suspect the weapon was not American-made."

"What makes you think that?" John asked.

"Well, as you know, every gun made in the U.S. must have a round fired through it, and that round is then put on file with the feds before the gun is sold. So far, nothing matches in the federal files. That would indicate the gun is probably foreign-made. Sally's description of the men she saw indicates they were dressed in all-black garments just like the guys you have been looking for."

"And I'll bet the gun came into the country with them from somewhere in the Middle East," John said.

"We don't know that for certain, but I would tend to think you are correct. But, the question is why?" Costa asked.

Drake continued. "Clearly, they came after you as a result of the story in all the local papers. Don't know how they linked you to the story, but maybe we'll find that out soon. Kristin, unluckily, just happened to be the person who stepped out through your front door. Bob told us that he had been working in front of your house for at about thirty minutes before she came out and the shooting started. So, if they wanted to kill Bob, there would have been plenty of time. But the gunman waited. Our guess is he was waiting for you."

"That makes it personal," John said.

"Don't get carried away just yet," Costa injected. "We have to approach this problem objectively."

"Fuck you, Agent Costa! If I was the target, and seeing as it's my wife with three bullet holes in her body, screw logic, it's personal. When somebody tries to kill me and almost takes out the one person in the world that I care about, it's personal. Real personal! And I have every intention of dealing with this 'problem', and I'll do it 'objectively'".

"Calm down!" Drake injected, grabbing John by the arm. We're all on the same side here, so let's focus on what we know and not what we feel."

The three men continued to review the current status of what they knew and didn't know about the mysterious men in black, as well as the murders and the situation at the compound on Lake George. Another hour slipped by in a tense environment before the meeting broke up with the departure of Agent Costa.

Once he had cleared the room, leaving John and Superintendent Drake alone for the first time since the shooting that put Kristin in the hospital, The room fell silent.

"I don't trust that guy," John finally said, breaking the silence.

"Don't trust him or don't like him?" Drake asked

"Both!"

"He's a fed," Drake replied. "They don't have a federal charm school anywhere in D.C. that I know of."

"Maybe not. But there's more to it."

"What do you mean, John?"

"My stomach hurts!"

"Your stomach hurts!"

"Yeah. It's the best scientific gadget I have. It's worked for me for a lot of years."

"Okay," Drake replied. "Your stomach hurts. But what are you going to do now?"

"What do you mean?"

"Just that. After you leave my office, what do you plan on doing?"

"First, I'm going back to the hotel where my wife is resting to be sure she is in good hands. Sally is with her."

"And then?" Drake continued pressing.

"And then I'm going hunting."

"John, remember something. I swore you in as a police officer. There are rules. Rules you're not accustomed to following. You have to follow them now. You can't go after these guys like… like you went after your… assignments when you worked for the feds. It's different now."

"Different?! They almost killed my wife."

"I know. But now I'm warning you. Don't go out there and leave a bunch of dead bodies for me to find. If you do… I'll come after you just as I intend to go after these guys. Do you understand?"

"…Yeah, I got it."

John left Superintendent Drake standing in his own conference room. He didn't add anything to his final comment. There was no explanation or qualification needed. Both men knew exactly what the thought process was racing through John's mind. Drake knew he would have to hold the reins on John real tight. He didn't want him or his actions to get out of control. He warned John and again reminded him that he was currently a sworn officer of the New York State Police and needed to conduct himself accordingly. He only hoped that once he cooled down a bit and had time to think, the message would sink into John's head.

John drove back to the lodge at Gore Mountain, trying to convince himself that everything would be okay, that he and Kristin were secure, and that Don Costa would not risk exposing them in any way. However, he knew he had to share this information with his wife. She had to know. She had to be prepared to deal with this man whom she would surely encounter while this case was still in progress. And, he had promised to keep her involved.

When he entered their suite, Kristin was waiting for him. She knew immediately from the expression on his face that there was something amiss. She put her good arm around him when he sat next to her on their bed, and she pulled him close to her.

"What's wrong, John?"

"There's something I have to fill you in on."

He gave her a thorough briefing on the meeting with Drake and Costa, covering all the case-related information. When he finished with that, he then told her word for word what followed. He told her how Costa addressed him and Mr Anderson in their meeting the day she was shot and what he said about her being missed in her old office.

"What are you thinking?" Kristin asked after a short pause.

"Well, I don't like the guy, but he didn't come across as a bad guy. So, if Bruce is right and he really is a bastard looking to make a name for himself, he's one hell of a good actor. Either way, he took the opportunity to send me a signal. Loud and clear, he wants me to know who's in charge."

"Why would he do that?" she asked.

"I would have done the exact same thing if I were in his shoes," John replied. "I would play that chip in the same way he did for the exact same reason: control. Except for one thing."

"What's that," Kristin asked her husband.

"He tripped over his own arrogance. He exposed himself to me by dragging you into the conversation. He's either a total amateur at this game, or he's extremely clever and confident and has an ulterior motive. It can only be one or the other, or he would never have mentioned you. He thinks he knows my background, and he should know by bringing you into the conversation, he has put himself at risk. He should have known by exposing you that I would not hesitate to react to protect you."

"John!"

"Relax, sweetheart. I didn't say I was going to go out and kill him, and I just said that he should have known that I could and would if necessary. By playing that card, he put the game back in my control. I'll deal with Mr. Costa… and I promise I won't hurt him… unless I have to."

"John!"

"Kristin, I promise. But you've got to accept that he has his reasons, and those reasons could be dangerous. This was not a casual comment. He dropped this bomb for a reason, and I've got to find out what that reason is."

"What do we do now?" she asked.

"Now, you rest and get better. I need my beautiful wife and my partner back in one piece."

"And you?"

"… You rest."

Chapter 19

Rest is exactly what she did under the watchful eyes of John, Gretchen, and Sally. Kristin rested and enjoyed the pampering she was receiving until a week had slipped by. Then, the restlessness caught up to her, and she wanted to go home.

"Okay! Okay!" John exclaimed in response to her demands. "Let me check with Drake to see if his crime techs are finished and if they have released the site. Our repair guys have been held up waiting for them to clear out so we could start the repairs."

He already knew the answer. The crime scene technicians had finished their work days ago. Superintendent Drake had informed him that he and Kristin, as well as Bob and Sally, could return to their homes and begin the necessary clean-up and repairs. Bob had already returned and begun working on the cabin, patching and repairing the bullet holes and the shot-up front door.

John was stalling. He needed to make one last visit to the compound before Kristin's return. He needed to retrieve some … items. Items were necessary for him to proceed in the search for the men who almost killed his wife.

He left Kristin in the suite they had been occupying at the Gore Mountain Lodge and drove back to Lake George. He drove through the village to see what activities were taking place both on the ice and on the streets. He found both areas to be extremely quiet. The local citizens, as well as the out-of-town gawkers, seemed to have had their fill and gone home or were keeping to themselves in their homes. The police presence on the ice where the heads had been found had also packed up all their gear and headed back to their nice, warm patrol cars and offices.

He then drove home to his cabin tucked in the private compound on the east shore of Lake George. When he got there, he found Bob working on the final bits of repairs that needed fixing before they could return. The cabin looked as if nothing had ever happened.

"Hey Bob," he greeted his old friend.

"Hi, John. Everything okay?"

"Yeah, everything's fine. Just need to pick up a few things I might need."

"Anything I can help you with?"

"No. I need to go down into my locker for a few minutes."

"John! Are you talking about the locker I think you're talking about?"

"Yes."

"Why are you going in there? What do you need from there?" he pressed. "The stuff in that locker is a part of your old life, not this one."

"They almost killed my wife, Bob!"

"Yeah, I know. You keep telling me that. So, you're going to go back to your old life and finish the job for them?! You're going to strap on your six guns and go shooting up the countryside looking for the bad guys?"

"Bob…"

"Don't Bob me, John. And don't hand me a line of shit about only you can do the job. You're the only guy who can save the world. That's bull shit, and you know it. I've stood by and watched you for too many years. Sally and I have stood by knowing what your job was and waited for you to return, reading the headlines in the papers or listening to the news on TV, knowing damn well where you had been and waiting here to patch you up. For years, we fixed our bodies and our minds.

"So, don't fucking Bob me, okay! We are not going to stand by and say nothing and watch you strap on your six guns and go off and kill somebody or a whole fucking mob of somebodies. Not this time, John. If you do, you will also kill the woman you love. The one person in the world you have allowed in your life and, I might add, brought into ours. We love her, too. And, you pig-headed ass hole, in case you haven't figured it out yet, we love you too.

"You go off gunning for these guys, and Superintendent Drake will come down on you like stink on shit, and you won't have anywhere to go. He knows all about you, and even if you leave no trace behind, he'll know it was you, and he'll come after you.

You might hide, but you'll be all alone. Totally alone. You'll never be able to come back here and she'll never be able to go to wherever the hell you might be. Kristin will no longer be a part of your life. You will have destroyed her and your life together."

Both men stood there staring at each other. The only thing around them was silence. Ever sound frozen by the sub-zero cold surrounding them. Neither spoke. Neither moved. Until finally, John broke the tension.

"WOW! How long have you been holding that in?" he asked his closest friend.

"Long enough!"

"Obviously."

"John, don't fuck this up, bud. You've got too much going for you. Besides, Drake made you a cop. Do it the right way. Do it his way. Just this once, do it his way and do it right."

John looked out over the lake he loved so much. He found peace here. The lake. The forest. The wind. The warmth of summer and the white cold of winter. The log cabin was the only home he had known in his entire adult life. Peace! Bob and Sally and Gretchen… and Kristin.

"I've made both Kristin and Drake a promise. I'll make the same promise to you and Sally. I won't go gunning, as you put it, for these guys. But, I can't just sit by and do nothing. I've got to find them, and I need to be prepared to protect myself and my wife. That's why I need to go into the locker. And, I might need your help," he said finally.

"You know I'm right here with you, bud."

"… Okay. Let me get Kristin home tomorrow, and then we'll put this together."

"Where do you want to start?" Bob asked.

"I don't know. Let me take care of my wife first and then… and then I'll need a little time to think."

"Okay, by me."

He left his friend and went to his secret locker buried beneath his cabin. It was totally encased within a solid cement room with its own environmental control systems to protect his equipment, along with room for at least four people to survive for a week or more should the need arise. He looked around, hearing Bob's words echo inside his head. And the promise he made to Kristin.

After a couple of minutes, standing there alone in the quiet of the locker, surrounded by tools of his former life, he turned and left, locking the door behind him. He took nothing with him.

He returned to the hotel suite and had a quiet dinner with his wife. Although not pain-free, she was finally off all pain medications, so they were able to enjoy a good bottle of wine with their room service meal.

In the morning, John insisted on wheeling Kristin out through the lobby in a wheelchair. She had an escort of four fully uniformed state troopers supplied by Superintendent Drake. The entire party made quite a departing impression on the hotel staff and guests.

Following the drive home, John, with Sally's help, got Kristin settled back in her home. Bob and the local carpenters had done a fantastic job on the repairs, erasing any and all signs of the incident that took place what seemed like a hundred years ago.

Gretchen showed up later that afternoon with a fully prepared dinner for five. John, Kristin, Bob, Sally, and Gretchen relaxed as best they could, avoiding the topic of recent events. By eight-thirty, Kristin was fighting to stay awake. Everyone excused themselves, and John put her to bed for the night.

"Bob," John called out. "Meet me after breakfast. We have some business to attend to."

"I'll see you in the morning," Bob replied.

By eight o'clock the following morning, John was up and ready to go. He had prepared a hot breakfast for Kristin and had her all set up to spend a comfortable day in their den. Gretchen had promised to come by later in the morning to check up on her and to prepare lunch for the recovering patient.

Bob met John outside. "I'll drive," John announced.

The two men climbed into John's Jeep Grand Cherokee and headed south on Shelving Rock Road toward state route 149. It was a slow fifteen-mile drive along the wet and icy dirt road. By the time John turned right toward the outlet mall, it was damn near impossible to determine the true color of his vehicle. It was covered with mud and dirty slush.

"What are you planning on doing today?" Bob asked.

"Think! I need to back my brain up to before Kristin was shot. She's all I've been able to think of since then, and I need to go back and put all the pieces of this case together. I need to figure out how these guys are thinking and get ahead of their next move."

"Okay, how do we do that?"

"Right now .... just drive around the village to see if I can figure things out. I need to put myself in their place. Get in their heads. Determine where they came from and where they're going."

"Sounds like fun," Bob said sarcastically.

"Not much, buddy, but it works. I've done it dozens of times on dozens of missions in all parts of the world and been successful with it. People may speak different languages, eat different foods and have different customs, but they all basically think the same. Just give me some time."

"Like someone once said, everybody puts their pants on the same way," Bob added.

"You got it, Bob!"

They drove into the village of Lake George, where John parked his Jeep. He got out and walked onto the ice to the spot where the heads had been found. He didn't say a word. He just walked and looked and studied the area from one side of the lake to the other. He absorbed everything. Bob would later say he thought John could place every snowflake on the ice exactly the way he found them.

Later, they returned to the Jeep and drove to the south end of town near exit 21 off I-87. John sat in the miniature golf parking lot and observed the area for almost half an hour.

Then, he drove to the north end of town and did the same near exit 22. After another thirty minutes, he drove back toward the village and turned left on Route 9, headed north toward Diamond Point, where he repeated his road watch from the parking lot of a motel closed up for the winter.

"How about some lunch?" he suddenly asked Bob.

"Good by me. How about pizza?"

"Done!"

They drove to the center of the village of Lake George and entered their favorite pizza joint, where they ordered a large pepperoni pizza cooked well done with two small side salads and two cold beers.

"Are you ready to tell me what you learned this morning? I've been bored to shit watching you without saying a word to disturb your thought process," Bob asked.

"Not yet. Not sure yet. Need to think it through for a while."

"Okay. What's next?"

"Pizza, beer and then I need to go for a long walk......alone. I'll take you back home so you can have the rest of the day with Sally. And, thanks for being with me today."

"John, I didn't do a damn thing except sit and watch you."

"That's all I needed you to do. I just needed you there. Now, I need to call Drake."

Chapter 20

John returned to his cabin to spend a little time with Kristin and to bounce some of his thoughts off her. She was an experienced government agent in her own right and he valued her input all the years they worked together while she was his control agent. He needed to have her input now as much as any time in their past. She was his sounding board who, through many assignments, had listened and helped him refine his plans. He needed her to do it again.

"Hi, baby. How are you feeling?"

"Much better. Feels like I've been shot only once instead of three times."

"Well, that's progress. Sure am glad one of those bullets didn't hit you in your sense of humor."

John fell silent. "What's on your mind, John? All I have to do is look at your face to see that you're brain is broadcasting. Something's buzzing around inside your head."

"I've tried to reconstruct what little we know about this group. Pieces just aren't fitting together. There just isn't much to work with."

"How so?"

"Well, let's review what we do know. There have been five murders here, and they are most likely connected in one way or another to those in Michigan. All were clergy of the Christian or Jewish faith. If we're right about the perps being the guys we saw dressed all in black, along with what little we could see of their facial features, everything would suggest that they are from the Middle East. So, I'm guessing this is more than likely some sort of a religious matter."

"That makes sense; I'm with you so far," Kristin said.

"Okay, but why here?"

"Well, Lake George is a well-known tourist area in the northeast."

"No, I mean, why here in the U.S.? There is Christian clergy all over the world. For example, why not in Rome, Italy? The place is crawling with priests. Five decapitations, there would be world news. Here it's a blip on the evening news broadcast and for only as long as the next hot topic pops up. Next guy that runs for two touchdowns in a game steals the headlines."

"What are you trying to say, John? Do you think there is something more to this than delivering a religious message to the West from some Middle Eastern Muslim group?" She paused to study his face and body language. "Your gut is talking to you, isn't it?"

"Yeah, and I don't like what it's telling me."

"You've lived and operated for years listening to your gut. So, tell me what's going on, and we can talk it out."

"...I have a strong feeling that these guys are being run by someone in the U.S. The message, whatever it is, is directed at us because whoever is behind this is right here in our country."

"WOW! Now I can see why your gut hurts. What makes you think that?"

"For starters, we know that this is at least the second place these types of murders have taken place. First Michigan, and now here. There might be others we don't yet know about and haven't connected to what we now know."

"Okay, what else?"

"The attack on our compound...... you being shot."

"What?!"

"Think about this. Question number one: who knew we were working on this case? The New York State Police and the Department of Homeland Security."

"Okay."

"Question number two. How quickly after we got involved did the shooting take place? Do you really think that this group would first find out who we are and second get word to their chief halfway around the world and third get word back approving a hit on us right here in our home and right in the area they are operating in?"

"Go on!"

"Next, the shooting. Drake's lab says they used .223 caliber rounds. That's a small bullet primarily used in rifles designed for close-quarter fighting. They are meant to inflict maximum damage in tight, crowded areas. These guns are not long-distance weapons. Particularly in wide open windy environments like we have here. Shooting from across the ice in the wind would be totally unfavorable conditions for an assault-type weapon."

"Keep going, John."

"If these guys wanted to kill you or me or both of us, they would have sent in someone who is a trained marksman who would be equipped with a sniper rifle using .300 or .308. My personal favorite is the .270 caliber rounds. It's what we call a flat shooter with a high velocity. More stable in the wind. There would be no missing at this range. You would be dead, and there would be no spent cartridges left behind. Or the shooter would have waited for me to show up to do us both."

"They're amateurs!," Kristin blurted out.

"They're amateurs," John agreed. And they're being run from within the United States."

"WOW! You've got to stop driving the backroads all by yourself. Your brain is in overdrive. No wonder your gut hurts. So, what now?"

"I need to talk to Drake."

John placed a call to the Superintendent of the New York State Police. His call was put through immediately.

"John, what's up?"

"I need to talk with you."

"Go right ahead."

"No, not on the phone. I need to meet with you as soon as possible."

"Is it important?"

"I think so."

"Sound like you've got something eating at you. I'm wide open this afternoon. Wait, hold one." John could hear Drake talking to someone in his office before he came back on the line. "John, I've got a chopper sitting outside. I can have it up there in thirty minutes to pick you up. Save you driving on those icy roads."

"Great! I'll be waiting on the ice."

Thirty minutes later, the state-owned helicopter landed just a few yards from the shoreline in a cloud of blowing snow. John boarded the aircraft and was immediately whisked off toward the state capital. Within half an hour of being picked up, he had entered Superintendent Drake's office and reported everything that he had discussed with his wife.

"Have you shared this with Costa?," Drake asked.

"No!"

"I think we should."

"I don't!"

"Why not?"

"Charles, how many people knew about my involvement with this case?"

"Maybe a half dozen in my office. I don't know about Costa's side of it."

"Of all the people who know of my being involved, how many are aware of my previous... employment experiences?"

Drake was speechless. John continued.

"Either you or someone on your staff or..."

"...or someone in Costa's office!"

"Exactly! There's a leak somewhere, and the only person I trust is sitting right here with me, and if I'm wrong about that, then I'd have to kill you, too."

"Shit!" Drake exclaimed as he stood up, looking as if he was about to punch the next person who crossed his path. "Are you accusing Costa of being the culprit?"

"I don't know Charles. That's my point. I don't know, and not knowing can be deadly."

"Shit!" Drake repeated, stomping around the room.

"Did you share my history with anyone on your staff?"

"No! No one. I was going to talk to my Chief of Security about it, but after meeting you and getting to know you, I decided to keep what I know to myself."

"Could anyone gain access to the same source or method you used to learn about me?"

"No. I used a totally secured line restricted solely to me. The only person who could override my authorization codes would be the Governor, and he doesn't know you exist."

"What's all this tell you?"

"Costa??"

"Or one of his people. I'm not saying it's him. I'm just trying to narrow down the possibilities," John added.

"But, he's a Fed, John! They're all feds. Why would......?"

"Like I said, Charles. I'm not accusing him. All I'm saying is that I believe we have a leak somewhere, and if it isn't you, then who can it be? If it's not Costa, then it's got to be someone in his office or one of the agents traveling with him. The only other person involved is Bruce, back in D.C., and I trust him.

"Think about this, Charles. You're telling me no one on your staff knows anything about my past. You've also told me that there has been a total media lock on me and my participation in this case or any relationship I have with your office. So, if my name didn't appear in the press at any time, how did these guys know who they were after, and how did they know where to come looking for me? How did they know precisely where to go on a thirty-mile-long lake to sit and take pop shots at my wife or me?"

"God damn it, John," Drake huffed as he paced around his office, trying to figure out what was going on. "I can't believe there's a leak in my office!"

He stops behind his desk and presses a button on his phone.

"Yes, sir," a female voice responds.

"Get Captain Hughes to come in here right away."

"Yes, sir."

"Who's Captain Hughes?" John asks.

"He's my chief of security. I'm going to get him to dig into the background of every man who has worked on this case."

"No, you're not!" John screamed at him.

Drake blanched from John's onslaught. "What do you mean? I... we need to get to the bottom of this and determine if there's a leak and who it is."

"Charles! You start poking around, and you'll tip off whoever it might be, and that will be the end of it. You'll drive the leaker so far underground that we'll never find out who it is.

"This is my ball game, and we'll play by my rules," John continued.

"Just a damn minute, John. First of all, you work for me, and secondly, you don't bark orders at me and tell me what to do or not to do."

"You're forgetting that it was my wife that was shot, and it was me they were after."

The two men challenged each other from across Drake's desk, staring into each other's eyes with the intensity of two wild beasts measuring for an attack. John reached into his pocket and removed the badge Drake had given him weeks ago. He tossed it onto Drake's desk and turned toward the door.

"What are you doing?" Drake shouted at him.

"I don't work for you anymore, Charles. Never really did. I'll leave my handgun with the guard in the lobby."

"John, hold on a minute."

"No! And let me warn you, Charles. If you or any of your men get in my way or threaten me or put me or Kristin in any danger, I'll put them down without blinking."

Drake's face flushed with anger. "John, you've just threatened a police officer, and I could have you arrested right here right now. Let me warn you. If you harm one of my men, I'll put you down like any other criminal."

"And let me warn you, Charles, I've put down forty-two men in my life. So don't think for a second that I would hesitate on number forty-three? Threatening me is not a healthy way of planning your future."

He turned his back on Drake and walked out of the office without another word. A moment later, Captain Hughes appeared in the same doorway.

"You wanted to see me, sir?"

Drake hesitated. "Never mind, Captain. I've already taken care of the matter.

Chapter 21

The moment John walked into their cabin, Kristin, once again, knew something was wrong. A distance expression had reappeared on John's face. One she hadn't seen in over a year. It scared her.

"John? What happened, baby?"

He took her by the hand and led her to the couch. Sitting next to her, holding both her hands in his, he relayed the entire meeting he had with Superintendent Drake. He explained how he told Drake about the potential leak and the shooter finding them. He also told her what he had come to realize about his behavior of late, and how he needed to regain his professional composure.

She took in all he was saying, wondering where it would all lead.

"John, why?"

"Why what?" he asked.

"Why do you need to regain anything? This isn't a mission that has been assigned to you. This in not anything you need to deal with. Let Drake and the state police take care of it. Let DHS deal with it. Why don't we just get in our motorhome and leave for a while? We can move from campground to campground as often as we want, and nobody will ever know. We could travel for months and get away from all of this."

"That all sounds great and easy, Kristin. It would be the smart thing to do until now. It was true until someone attacked this compound and put three bullets into my wife's body. That changed everything and makes this whole thing personal... very personal."

"You're scaring me, John. I don't want to go back to that life. I don't want that to be a part of our new life. I love what we have found here, what we have put together and what the future holds for us. For the first time in my life, I'm excited about what's ahead. And, you big jerk, in case you don't know, I happen to love you. I love you a lot!"

He held her hands in silence. For what felt like hours, he held her while wrestling with his thoughts.

"Kristin, if we were locked up here in our cabin and someone came onto this property, broke into Bob's house and harmed he and Sally, would you want me to sit idly by and do nothing? Would it not affect our lives, and wouldn't you want me to do something about it?"

"No! Yes! Of course, it would affect us, and I would want you to do something."

"If the same thing were to happen to Gretchen, would you want me to sit here and say that it's not my business because she lives ten miles away, so we'll leave it up to the local cops to take care of?"

"No."

"If you had a rotten board on your deck and had a toolbox filled with carpenter's tools, wouldn't you expect me to fix it?"

"I have tools, Kristin. And I know how to use them to fix certain things. If..."

"Stop!" she said. Now, it was her turn to sit silently and hold John's hands.

"I get it," she finally said. "I don't like it, but I get it. I get it!"

"Good! I need you on my side. We have certain experiences together and I need both of us to put them back in motion. You are a valuable asset to me, and you've kept me alive for a long time. We were a great team."

"Okay! I agree. You said 'we' have certain experience. If you're going to get involved, then so am I. Yes, we were a team. And yes, we have been a very effective team. So, if we do this, we continue to do it as a team."

It was clear to John that she was talking to herself as much as to him. She was flushing the situation out of her system convincing herself while rationalizing the entire situation.

"Deal!" he said, wrapping her in a tight embrace. "I love you," he whispered in her ear.

"And I love you… you royal pain in the ass," she playfully whispered with equal love and tenderness as she nibbled on his ear lobe.

They both laughed their way through her sarcastic jab. Then they sat back, knowing what their next step needed to be. They needed to plan.

The rest of the afternoon and early evening were spent on their couch discussing and rehashing all the limited information they currently had. Human heads severed from their bodies found on the ice-covered lake. No bodies were found. No evidence is left behind. Four men dressed in black were seen multiple times leaving the area in a white Ford van. A similar case in Michigan. Possibly two others. That's it! Nothing more.

Then, they discussed and added everything they had learned about the murders in Michigan. Six victims. All members of the clergy. All Christian. The same execution style of beheadings and, again, no bodies. The same ice-covered frozen lake with no sign of the killers except for the potential sighting of a white van with two men dressed in black.

Why were the heads being left on a surface of a frozen lake? Was there a reason? Was there some significance, or was it just a convenient place to expose the heads to be sure they were found and seen by local residents? Where were the bodies? Why were they not being displayed by the killers?

Too many questions… to few answers!

The culprits seemed to have disappeared in both states, except for one big fact. Since John chased after the four men on foot in Lake

George Village, there have been no additional murders. For law enforcement who needed hard facts, this was not an acceptable basis to move forward. Not enough to pursue, to launch a full-fledged investigation or to arrest anyone. Nowhere to begin.

In John's world, however, this was enough to seal the deal. In his world, guilt was determined just as much by actions and innuendo as by facts. He had what he needed. He didn't need to see the four men whack off the next head to know who did it. He knew, and it was time for him to act.

The two former government agents, now a husband and wife team, agreed that the four men had more than likely 'gone to ground' as the mob would call it. They suspended their activities in fear of being caught. They knew John had seen them. They knew that they were now at risk. And then, there was the attack on their compound, resulting in the wounding of both Kristin and Bob. By now, they knew they had missed and had to assume that there was a search going on trying to find them.

But John and Kristin agreed that there was more to come. They agreed that this was probably a temporary lull that would last only until the murderers once again felt secure enough to continue killing. They were just waiting for things to cool down a bit before getting back to business. Four clergymen had been killed thus far. A Catholic priest, an Episcopalian priest, a Jewish rabbi and the latest, a Presbyterian minister.

What, or who was next? There were numerous religions, and all were represented in the local area. Which would be the next target? Who would be the innocent clergy killed because he or she chose to preach the word of God?

"That's it", John blurted out.

"What?" Kristin asked.

"It's obvious that these guys are trying to send a message and that it is against religion. So far, we have ten victims if we combine the two states, Michigan and New York. Of the ten, nine are Christian, and one is a Jewish Rabbi. But none are Muslim. That's their message.

"So, let's give them a target. A target that gives them a reason to come out of hiding and justify their risk of taking action. One that's too tempting to resist. One that they will see as an attack on them. An affront to whatever the hell their message is."

"What are you thinking?"

"I'm going to become a member of the Cloth. I'm going to take a bible and use it to beat them. The very thing they seem to be trying to destroy will destroy them. I will loudly condemn their faith. Insult them and dare them to silence the devil."

"And just how do you intend to do that?"

He was pacing around their living room impatient with himself as he tried to piece together all the ideas swirling around inside of his head.

"Think for a minute, Kristin. What major religious group is not represented by one of the current victims? Consider both Michigan and New York. What major religious sect has not been victimized so far?"

"I don't know, John. There are so many."

"So far," he continued. "So far, they have killed only in the north. Without being able to connect the possibility of similar crimes in the other states that Bruce dug up, we are only dealing with two northern states. That leaves the south."

"Baptists!" Kristin blurted out.

"Exactly! I will impersonate a bible-thumping, loud-mouthed Southern Baptist preacher to come to save the world. I will bring fire and brimstone to Lake George. I will go out in public and berate the cowards who have committed these murders. I will challenge them to come after me. And when they do, we'll be waiting for them."

"Where?" Kristin asked.

"Right where they seem to like to show off. Out on the ice," he paused, pacing the room. "Oh, shit! I've got it!"

"What?"

"Kristin, you wouldn't know this, but just north of here is a town called Schroon Lake. It sits on the edge of a lake by the same name. Some years ago, a religious group known as the 'Word of Life Fellowship' moved in and bought up a ton of real estate and basically took over the town, making it into their worldwide headquarters.

"Some people compare them to the Church of Scientology, but they're not. They are a Christian group, very unlike Scientology, that is a very questionable church with no real God connection. They actually are closer to an organization formed by Billy Graham from North Carolina and the Youth for Christ movement."

"What's your point, John?"

"My point is Billy Graham is known around the world. And Billy Graham is a Baptist! I can easily take on the persona of a Baptist preacher and stir things up right here in town. It would be totally accepted by the locals and appear to them as just another activity by this well-known group headquartered just a few miles from here. But, to our four missing friends, it will be a thorn in their side.

"We'll rent one of those great big tents and pitch it out on the ice right on top of where the heads have been found. Kristin, we're going to have a meeting. We're going to have a revival meeting out on the ice."

John grabbed his phone and touched its screen. Within a few seconds, he said, "We need to talk!" followed almost immediately by "We'll be there."

At nine o'clock the following morning, he and Kristin entered the building housing the headquarters for the New York State Police. They were immediately ushered into the conference room adjacent to the office of Superintendent Drake. Awaiting them was Superintendent Drake, along with four of his top staff members.

"Okay, John, what's on your mind this morning?" Drake began.

"We have a plan."

"We? No, we don't have a plan. You have a plan. You stomped out of here yesterday, threatening me and my men. I should slap a set of cuffs on you right now and throw your ass in a cell."

"Yeah! Well, that was yesterday. Sorry about that, Charles, but you pissed me off, and I lost my temper for a minute."

"Please listen to what he's got to say before you slap him in irons," Kristin said sarcastically.

"For years, the two of us were an extremely effective team. We have an idea we think will work to bring our four guys out into the open. And we would like your support."

Drake looked at Kristin with a degree of surprise and skepticism. He knew she was formerly an employee of the same federal intelligence agency John worked for, but he wasn't aware that they had been a team.

"You two were a team? You mean...?"

"No, she was not a field agent. She was my control. She ran me for many years from her office in D.C. That's how Costa knows her."

Drake bounced his glaring eyes between the couple sitting across from him, trying to put all the new pieces of information together in his head. Only his imagination limited what he imagined these two people might have done in their past or what they might be capable of doing now.

"Okay, let's hear it."

John glanced at the other men in the room. Drake immediately picked up on what was going through John's mind.

"They stay," Drake barked. "I'm not going to allow a repeat of yesterday, and I have full trust and confidence in my staff. You threaten me again like you did yesterday, and these guys will drag you out of here in cuffs. So, either keep talking or leave; I'm good either way," his anger from the previous day surfacing once again.

"Okay!" John said, returning Drake's glaring look.

Together, John and Kristin laid out their conversation of the previous evening. She outlined the what, when and where, setting the stage for the operation. John laid out the how. He would disguise himself as a loud-mouthed, bible-thumping Baptist minister to bait the trap. He would walk into every public building the targets the targeted men could visit. Gas stations, grocery, convenience, hardware and every other kind of store he could think of. He would preach out loud and, leave pamphlets behind and make a general pest of himself, so people would talk about him and what he was doing long after he had departed the establishment. And, all the while, he would be telling everyone within earshot about the tent revival meeting to be held on the ice.

If the four mysterious men dressed in black dared to poke their heads up taking the bait, the State Police would swoop in and take them into custody.

"That simple?" Drake said.

"Yeah!" John replied.

Drake contemplated what he had just heard. He glanced around the room at his staff members. Heads hanging down, studying the tabletop, none of them chose to make eye contact with their boss. Their body language distanced them from any reaction to the plan just presented, not knowing how their boss would react. Drake leaned forward, putting both elbows on the conference table.

"John, you're forgetting a couple of the points I made to you concerning these men and, now, your idea."

"What?" John demanded.

"Well, as I told you, we have no evidence that these men are guilty of the murders…"

"And?"

"And, other than your… gut-aching suspicious guess, we have nothing linking them with any crime…"

"And?"

"And you are ignoring the fact that you are a civilian and that I can't put you in harm's way. You quit yesterday, remember? You threw your badge at me and left your weapon with the lobby guard."

"So, even if these four suspects of yours came marching into that tent beating a drum, we couldn't arrest them."

"Bullshit," John reacted.

"John!" Kristin grabbed his arm, attempting to control and calm him.

"John, my ass!" He turned to Drake. "Have you got a better idea?"

"No," the Superintendent admitted.

"So, you're just going to sit around and wait for another head to pop up. Is that it?"

Drake didn't respond.

"If I bait the hook and they come after me, there's your proof! That will be the evidence you so sorely need. At the very least, you can take them in for questioning and do some background checking while you have them in custody, find out where they live and give it a good search. Scare the crap out of them," John added.

"John," Drake injected, trying to calm himself and the hot-tempered man before him. "We have a thing called 'probable cause'. We are bound by that. We can't just go around pulling people in off the street because one of us gets a pain in his gut. And your gut hurting doesn't qualify as probable cause. Don't you see what I'm getting at and the problem that would cause?"

John hesitated a moment before speaking. "Let me tell you what the problem is. You guys are the same as hundreds of law enforcement agencies I've dealt with all over the world. You think the only good idea is the ones you come up with. Well, let me tell you something, Mr. Superintendent. It's that attitude. It's that mindset that made my life so easy for over fifteen years. It was that 'know it all' approach, that weakness that I exploited repeatedly. You guys think you know it all, and you don't know jack shit!"

"You came to me, Superintendent. You came looking for me and in your big speech in our cabin, you said you wanted to take advantage of the way I think and how I could help you and your people understand the way the bad guy's minds worked. I came here today to live up to my part of the bargain. I promised I would share my thoughts and experiences with you. Well, here I am, and quite frankly, you're wasting my time."

He stood and headed for the door.

"Where are you going?" Drake demanded.

John turned back to face him.

"I'm going to catch a killer. No! Make that four killers."

"John, if you cross the line, I'll fry your ass!" Drake shouted.

"Not if you don't have any evidence, you won't. Don't forget, you'll need probable cause. You seem to forget, I've made a fortune out foxing guys like you in countries around the world. I've never left 'probable cause' behind, and I don't intend to start now. For your own good, Superintendent Drake, don't you or any of your people get in my way."

He stormed out to the conference room for the second day in a row and out of the building with his wife chasing close behind. She had to run to keep up with her husband. Once they were back in their car, she grabbed him by the arm.

"John, you just threatened the Superintendent of the New York State Police again. Are you crazy?!"

"Yeah! Well, I didn't exactly threaten him. It was just sort of a warning. He'll get over it."

"Where are we going?" she asked.

"Shopping!"

"Again?"

"Again!"

Chapter 22

By mid-afternoon, they returned to the compound. John carried half a dozen bags into the cabin. They contained all the necessary items he would need to carry out phase one of the plan he and Kristin had settled on to lure the unknown subjects into revealing themselves.

It had been more than three weeks since the last head was found on the ice at the south end of Lake George. Had the four mysterious men in black left the area? Had they moved on to a different part of the state or country to continue their murderous rampage? Had John's brief encounter with them scared them off? Or had they simply gone to ground as he previously thought they might?

There were only two ways to find out. Either wait around with your finger up your butt waiting for them to strike again… or to set the trap to entice them, bait the trap to draw them out and then spring the trap to snag them.

John was not built to sit around. He was not built to wait for another person to be killed. He was not built to react. He was built to act, to take control. He recalled what he was taught very early in his training, 'nothing happens until you make it happen.' And if you make it happen, you control the action. It was time to take control and make something happen.

The next morning, he began to implement his plan. From the shopping bags, he took out all the items he needed to disguise himself as a Baptist minister. He was dressed in a black suit. Over that, he wore a mid-calf-length black overcoat. To disguise his face, he applied a full-face short-haired beard and finished off with a pair of black-rimmed eyeglass frames holding a fake lens. Kristin added bushy false eyebrows to finish off the new look. Even the few local people who knew him would have a very difficult time recognizing who he really was.

His plan was to drive to the village and walk the sidewalk near the crime scene, waving his bible while loudly challenging the killers to come be saved by the Christian savior, the Lord Jesus. He knew there was still enough press presence nearby to get attention and hopefully get exposed on the local television news channels. If the killers were anywhere near the village or watched any of the local newscasts to check for any potential pursuit, they were apt to see John in action.

But it wouldn't happen! His plan ended before it ever got going. The best-laid plans of mice and men would come to a screeching halt before ever being put in motion. Kristin was helping him put on his overcoat when John's phone rang. When he saw the incoming number flash on the screen, he immediately knew who was calling. He pressed the appropriate button and curtly answered.

"What!"

"Good morning, John."

"What do you want? Why are you calling?"

Kristin stood next to him, listening, holding his arm, trying to calm and control him as best she could.

"Well, two things. First, I want to apologize for the way the meeting went yesterday..."

"And?"

"...There's been another head found," Superintendent Drake said sheepishly.

John held the phone without responding. A certain degree of satisfaction, a sort of 'I told you so' feeling flushing over him.

"So, you didn't call to apologize; you called to tell me there's been another murder?"

"Both."

"Both my ass," John said angrily.

"John, I'm sorry. You were right. We waited too long… I need your help."

John knew this was not the time to feel vindicated. Not at the expense of another human life. He knew that it took a lot for Drake to call him, and he respected that. He took a deep breath and agreed to meet the Superintendent at the scene. He and Kristin departed as soon as the telephone call was ended.

When they arrived in the village, the chaos was already in full bloom. John had driven their Jeep down the ice-covered lake to save time. It was a good thing that he did. The town was jammed with vehicles.

Police cars, fire trucks, ambulances, news trucks and all the invading gawkers were already in place, lining the lakefront and surrounding streets. It didn't matter that it was snowing, and the skies were dark grey, and the temperatures were near zero; the show must go on. This little village, normally sleeping through the winter and snuggled up against the most beautiful lake in the entire country, was now a mess.

Everything about the town has been tossed on its head. Most of the permanent year-round residents tried to hide. They wanted to avoid the unwelcome turmoil while all of this was raining down upon their lives.

The skiers, hunters, snowmobile crazies and hikers visiting the area to enjoy the winter sports loved every minute of the commotion and added to the turmoil. They saw it as free entertainment. Added value to their short-term visit. Law enforcement hated it. Frustrated and embarrassed by their inability to solve the crimes that were now receiving national news coverage, making everyone look bad.

After parking out on the ice well away from the center of the action, John and Kristin walked up to the police barrier. Both identified themselves and were permitted to cross the yellow tape.

They saw Drake conversing with a small group of officials and approached, only to be stopped by one of the senior staff members.

Drake looked at John with a puzzled expression painted on his face. He immediately recognized Kristin, but who was the strange man standing next to her.

"John?" he questioned, seeing this strange man with a full beard and bushy eyebrows.

"Yes."

"WOW! If it weren't for your wife standing next to you, I would have had you escorted out of here."

"Good! Now, what can you tell me?"

"Not much. The Head was found in the exact same place as all the others. It's a male. Looks to be in his mid-forties. That's about it for now. Too early for us to know much more. The medical examiner and the crime scene techs are still working in the area. It will be a few hours before we know anything more substantial. That said, I don't think we'll find anything more than what we did with the others."

"Anybody recognize him?"

"Not certain. One of the county sheriff's deputies thinks he knows who it is. We're trying to locate that person and any family members to see if he's okay or if he's missing, and this might be him. Someone who can give us a positive I.D. We'll know shortly."

"Can I take a look?"

"You can go as close as the M.E. will let you."

John turned to Kristin.

"Wait here, baby. I don't what you to hobbling across the ice. Your leg isn't totally healed yet. And, besides, you don't need to see this."

He walked to where the M.E. and crime scene techs were busy doing their thing. He looked over their shoulders to peek between the kneeling techs to see as best he could, but didn't see anything that struck him. It was an almost exact repeat of the previous crime scenes. A severed human head was placed upright on the ice, surrounded by a circle of pink blood-stained snow. No apparent trail of footsteps or vehicle tracks anywhere around the location. Just clear hard ice. A yard thick and thirty-two miles long.

He returned to where he had left Kristin waiting, taking her gently by the arm to lead her away. While walking toward the shoreline, he glanced toward the village and all the people straining their necks to catch a peek of the gruesome scene. He stopped dead in his tracks. He turned his back toward the crowd and grabbed Kristin by the shoulders, spinning her around so she was now face-to-face with him.

"John! What is it?" she said in response to his grabbing her by the arm.

"Look over my right shoulder. What do you see?" She raised herself up on her tiptoes to see over her husband's shoulder. She scanned the crowded sidewalk and hillside leading up toward the center of the village.

"What am I loo… Oh, my God. I see them!"

"Look up at the top of the slope, up toward the main street. Do you see the white van parked anywhere?"

"Yes!"

"Okay, here's what I want you to do. Nice and easy, don't show any sign of alarm. I want you to walk slowly back to our car. Then I want you to drive around all the emergency vehicles parked on the ice and drive off over by the beach. Go around the block and come up behind the van until you can find a spot to park as close to it as possible. If there are no spaces, double park in the street about fifty yards behind the van. Once you've done that, lay on the horn so I can hear you and know you are in place."

"John is one of those men, the one who shot me?" she stiffened.

"Can't answer that right now. Just do as I ask, and you'll be fine."

"What are you going to do?"

"When I hear the horn, I'm going to approach our four friends and start ranting at them. I'm going to be a preacher pounding on my bible just like we had planned. I'm betting that once they see me coming, they will bolt from where they are standing and head directly for the van. I'll follow behind, and once they pull away, I'm going to jump into our car, and we're going to follow them."

"John, won't that be dangerous? Are you going to tell Drake what you're doing?"

"No, and no. I don't intend to make any contact with them right now. I don't want them to think we are chasing them. I just want them to leave and head toward wherever they are staying. All I want to do is find out where they go. We'll follow at a distance to play it safe."

"Okay!" she said.

"Okay! Are you ready?" he asked her.

She nodded her head, stood on her toes again and kissed him on the cheek. She then turned and slowly walked across the ice toward their car, casually waving to people she didn't even know, trying to add to the normalcy of her movements.

John waited, not looking back at the four men. He didn't want to give them any reason to leave before he was ready. It took Kristin almost ten minutes to reach their car and drive around until she found a spot close enough to the white van. When she did, she lay into the horn, knowing that every head nearby would turn in her direction. So be it, she had to signal John.

A hundred and fifty yards away, standing on the ice, John heard the blare of the Jeep's horn. He immediately turned and started walking directly toward the four men dressed in black. A short distance from where they stood, he raised his arm and pointed at the bible he had taken from his coat pocket. He ranted as loudly as he could, shouting accusatory remarks in their direction. It took only a few of his loud words to attract the attention of the man John believed to be their leader. The tall one.

He and John glared into each other's eyes as John approached, getting closer and closer with each stride. The four men suddenly turned and started to walk up the slope toward their white van at a very rapid pace. John could have easily overtaken them, but that was not what he wanted to do. He wanted them to escape. He wanted them to lead him to their safe location.

It took less than a minute for them to reach the van, open the door and pile in. A moment later, the van shook as the engine sparked into life and only another few seconds before it began to move forward. John saw where Kristin had parked their Jeep and headed for it. She was sitting behind the steering wheel, waiting for him. He opened the passenger side door and got in.

"Okay, baby. Nice and easy, follow them, but don't get too close. Keep as far back as you can and still see where they're going."

She did as John instructed. The target van proceeded north on Route 9 through the downtown Lake George area. At the north end of town, it bore slightly to the left toward Warrensburg. However, at the intersection with Interstate 87, it slid up the ramp leading to I-87 headed north. Kristin had barely cleared the first bend in the road when she and John caught a glimpse of the van going up the ramp.

She followed their path, keeping a safe distance. Entering the interstate highway, they saw the van disappear as it rounded a semi-trailer truck that now separated them from their quarry.

"Stay behind the truck. It will block their view, and we'll still be able to see if they get off the highway."

She again followed his instructions. The van sped past the Warrensburg exit and continued north on the interstate highway. Approaching the next exit, John saw the red glow of brake lights.

"Slow down, Kristin; I think they're getting off at this exit."

Sure enough, that's what happened. John saw the van's brightly lit tail lights go out as it turned right at the top of the ramp. Kristin followed slowly, maximizing the distance between the two vehicles. She also turned right on what John knew was Bolton Landing Road.

Just as Kristin got on the road, they saw the van cross over the old steel bridge spanning the Schroon River and immediately turn left onto a dirt road.

"Don't turn," John shouted. "Keep going straight."

"Why don't we follow them?" Kristin asked excitedly.

"Because I know exactly where that road goes. It's a dead end. It parallels the river for a mile of two. It then curves off into the woods and comes to a dude ranch at the far end. That's got to be where they are held up. If we drive down there, they will spot us before we can get close to them. We'll spook them. I'll find another way. Keep going straight. This road will take us back to Lake George in the town of Bolton Landing. Turn right when we reach Route 9N, and we'll go home."

"Home?! Don't you want to go after them?"

"Yeah, but not before I figure out just how I'm going to do it. If I'm correct and that's where they are living, we know there are at least four men that will be there. But that place is big enough to hold a small army. I don't want to go blundering in there and be greeted by more people than I can handle. Let's go home."

Chapter 23

When they arrived back home, Kristin sat and elevated her leg for a while before she prepared one of John's favorite lunches. She made grilled sandwiches with Havarti cheese, thinly sliced apple and orange marmalade and heated both sides on a skillet until the cheese melted. She accompanied this tasty treat with a cup of hot Manhattan clam chowder and a glass of warm cider. The combination took the chill out of their bones from the long morning in the elements.

All the while she was resting and then preparing lunch, John paced the floor, thinking and planning. How and when he was going to approach the four men, he firmly believed to be the killers of now five local clergymen and what he would do when confronted by them. This was the task at hand. One that he would normally have days, if not weeks, to plan. But not now. Now, he had to move quickly.

His phone rang.

"Hello!"

"John, it's Charles. What happened to you? I saw you and Kristin walking the scene earlier, and the next thing I know, the two of you disappeared."

"We gave chase."

"What! What do you mean you gave chase? After who?"

"I'll give you three guesses, and the first two don't count."

"They were there?"

"Yes. And we were able to follow them." He went on to tell Drake the whole story of their morning's adventure. Drake finally cut him off.

"I'll see you shortly, and we'll discuss it further," and broke the connection. John returned to his lunch.

When they finished clearing lunch, Kristin found John sitting on their couch with a topographical map of the Adirondack area spread out in front of him. Included within the boundaries of the map was the area where they saw the van drive down the dirt road. At the far end of the road was located a dude ranch that catered to customers from New York City and Boston who wanted a wilderness experience in the mountains during the warmer months.

The forest and mountains surrounding the ranch stretched for miles, offering enough territory for a very realistic time in the woods. Most of the ranch's customers lived in the heavily populated areas of downstate New York, where wilderness was defined as a large potted plant stuck in the corner of their foyer.

The ranch was encompassed on the west by the Schroon River and on the east the upper reaches of Lake George. To the north and south lay thousands of acres of dense wild wilderness populated by deer, black bear, turkey and coyotes, along with many small game species. And very few, if any, people.

John knew the area. He had hunted in it as a young man and he had participated in many 'search and rescue' missions as a member of LASAR looking for people who wandered off and got lost in the woods. He recalled one very serious and important fact about these search and rescue efforts. It was an unspoken condition that rested in the backs of the minds of all the search team members. For the first three days of their effort, they operated with a mindset of "search." After that, it shifted in their minds switched to "recovery" mode.

These mountains were beautiful… but they were also deadly. If a person was not experienced in living in the wild and wasn't properly dressed and equipped, life expectancy was short. Even in the warmer spring, summer and early fall months, three days was all the time expected for survival. A twisted ankle, an injury from a fall, attack by an animal, lack of water, lack of food, rapid and severe changes in temperatures once the sun went down and, most dangerous of all… panic.

Hyperthermia was high on the list of killers. Daytime temperatures could reach into the nineties and fall into the mid-forties at night. John knew that most people believed that it had to be cold to suffer hyperthermia. He also knew that they were wrong. This killer can occur on a hot, sunny beach in the middle of the summer. If a person leaves the water and sits on a blanket in the hot sun with temperatures in the eighties or even nineties and begins to shiver and shake, he knows that is hyperthermia in its simplest form.

Any one or combination of these climatic conditions would kill the unprepared subject of the search effort. John knew this. He had experienced it many times. Even experienced woodsmen injured during a hunt perished before they could be located and rescued. Search for the first three days meant looking for a living person. Recovery from that point on meant hopefully finding the intact remains of the subject. After a week or two… nothing was left to find. Mother Nature, in her grand scheme, would see to it that the land and the wildlife would consume what was left.

During the cold winter months with deep snow and temperatures approaching minus thirty degrees below zero, the timetable changed… for the worst. Cold temperatures, wet feet from walking in the snow with improper footwear, wet clothing even if the moisture came from the person's own sweat. The disorientation caused by whiteout conditions. Snowfall causes everything in every direction to blend together as one totally encompassing cloud of white, filling in footprints and covering over a trail within minutes. It was like walking in a room filled with smoke.

Yes, John knew all of this. He studied the map. His mind is beginning to focus on how he would deal with the four murderers in black. A plan was coming together. He knew what the end would be. But first, he had to be sure. He was not an indiscriminate killer. He had no intention of becoming like one of the people he usually sought out to eliminate. And, he had made Charles Drake, as well as his wife, a promise. But he knew he had work to do.

Within an hour of returning to their cabin, John's phone rang. It was Bob.

"We have a visitor."

"Who?" John asked.

"Your friend, the top cop, just buzzed from the gate. Wanted to know if you were home and if I would open the gate for him."

John contemplated his answer for a moment.

"Sure, let him in and bring him here. We've been expecting him. I'm pretty sure I know what he has on his mind."

Within a few minutes, an unmarked car that a blind man could determine was an official government vehicle pulled up to John's cabin. Bob made a U-turn on his four-wheeler and disappeared toward his own home. John and Kristin both walked out onto their front porch to greet Superintendent Drake.

Once inside, the somewhat stiff formal greetings completed, the three of them sat in front of the glowing fireplace. The relationship between the two men had grown a little tense since the two recent meetings in Albany.

"What's up, Charles?" John asked.

"I want to continue with the discussion we had on the phone earlier. You took off rather quickly this morning. A couple of my men saw you barreling up the sidewalk, shouting like a madman for some reason. They didn't know it was you. They reported seeing some crazy-looking guy with a gray beard waving a bible.

"Then they reported seeing four men dressed in black seemingly trying to get away from you. I sent one of my guys to see what was going on, and he reported seeing a white van speeding out of town and a Jeep just like yours in pursuit. Any of this sound familiar?"

John studied the man who represented the established authority he once hated and avoided for years. But, he had gotten to know Charles Drake, and, although he wore the uniform and they recently had their differences, John liked and respected him as a man. He had grown to accept and trust him and knew that there was a second side to the man uncommon in most government officials.

"Sounds familiar. Confirms what I was telling you on the telephone," John responded.

"Care to tell me about what happened after you chased after them?"

"I spotted our four friends as Kristin and I were walking off the ice. We also saw the van parked up on the hill. I sent Kristin to get our car and park near the van. Then, I wanted to see what would happen if I approached them. I was shouting and slapping a bible to get their attention."

"And?"

"And as I expected," John continued. "They spooked. As soon as they realized I was coming at them, they took off, got in the van and drove away."

"And you got in your car and followed?"

"Yes."

"And?"

"…And, here we are back in our nice warm cabin talking to… a friend."

Drake gazed at John, trying to see into the man's head. He switched his eyes to Kristin, who immediately averted her eyes to the floor.

"You followed them where?" Drake asked.

Neither John nor Kristin responded.

"You found out where they have been hold-up, didn't you?" Drake asked.

Again, neither responded.

"John, if you're withholding evidence, that's a crime. I told you in my office the other day that if you step over the line, I'll burn you. Now, is there anything else you want to tell me?"

"Can't be a crime if you don't have any criminals, right? You keep telling me these guys are not on your radar until you have evidence, so as far as I'm concerned, my wife and I went for a ride in the country to look at the view."

John looked at his wife. They exchanged a conversation with their eyes and without words. He turned back toward Drake who was clearly fighting back his temper.

"Charles, you did your homework on me before you ever came here weeks ago. You know who I am, where I come from and what I did. Here's something you might not know.

"Not once in my entire career did I ever break the law. Not once did I ever stray from my assignment. Not once did I ever 'cross the line,' as you like to put it. Not once did I ever leave a trail that would lead anywhere. Not once did I ever discuss or divulge to anyone how I went about my business. And … not once did I ever fail. I stayed within the limits of what I was approved to do. The only person I've ever shared things concerning my job is sitting right here next to me."

Drake listened intently. His next question bordered on implicating all three people present in the cabin of either murder, treason or complicity.

"What about the president?"

"What president?"

"You know damn well what president. Do you think I didn't have that figured out before I ever came to meet you the very first time? Come on, John, give me a little more credit than that."

"What about him?" John replied.

"Was he the mission? Didn't you break the law when it came to him, and I presume you also had something to do with the death of his chief of staff?"

"They became the mission," John replied. "When a criminal asks that a crime be committed and then attempts to have it covered up with yet another crime… the rules change. They threatened my life and that of the person I love. My actions were in self-defense. What happened to the president was the result of his own doing."

Drake studied the man across the room. He looked at Kristin, who now returned his examining gaze with a steady, piercing look of her own. He knew that all the federal agencies that would normally hunt down the assassin of a president with all the energy and might at their disposal had not done so. He was told that the F.B.I. and others learned after the fact of the plot planned by the president to kill the Canadian prime minister and regarded that plan as treasonous. The former president had placed himself above the law and paid for his actions. Case closed!

"Anything you want to add to this conversation, Kristin?" She hesitated a long moment before answering.

"Charles, you've gotten to know me. Do you think I could love a murderer?"

"No."

She continued, "What John did as an agent, he did, as I have said before, as a soldier without a uniform. What he did, he was ordered to do. For years, I was a part of that life. I was his control. I ran his missions. I was just as much a part of each one as he was. If he's a murderer, I'm a murderer. I knew what the mission was and who the target was long before he did. So, if he is guilty of a crime… so am I. If the president's death wasn't justified, cuff both of us and drag us off to the nearest jail."

"But," she continued enthusiastically. "Remember this, the former president also ordered John's death. He ordered that John was to be killed to cover the illegal actions he was ordering. And then he added me to the list of those who needed to be silenced. So, in my mind, John acted in self-defense, and he acted to protect me.

"Any agent, any cop, you included, are trained to complete their mission and survive. To protect themselves. That's what John did. And if you want to put me in the middle of that, I'm glad to be there and make no apology for our actions.

"I'll say what John won't. Yes, we followed our four blackclad friends. Yes, we think we found where they are held up. And yes, we could have gone blasting our way in and killed some, if not all of them.

"But that's not the way this man operates. Nor do I. We are and have been a team. A professional team. All we have discussed since returning home is what's the next step. How do we find out for sure that these guys are the ones we're all looking for? How do we justify our next move? And what will our next move be? Not just go barging in and shooting up the landscape like some James Bond or Jack Reacher make-believe movie characters might do, killing anyone who might be anywhere near the scene. His intention is to find the proof you need to take these guys into custody, not add notches on his gun."

"Okay, I got that," Drake interrupted. "But, why haven't you come to me with all of this? Why haven't you reported all of this to me? I'm the police!"

"That's exactly why!" Kristin continued. "You think you know everything about John and his past life. You don't. He doesn't trust the police. He doesn't trust authority. He doesn't trust the way you operate. It has damn near gotten him killed more than once.

"He lived for years by his own instincts, avoiding you guys all over the world. And I might add, justifiably so. Each and every time he completed an assignment, the police did everything they could to find and kill him.

"I've witnessed him being set up. I've seen him fight his way out of situations where he was being attacked from both directions. It's not easy for him to suddenly accept you and your position. I can tell you that he, that both of us, have accepted you as a friend. But, he is accustomed to working alone. To survive on his own. To be successful, ON HIS OWN!"

The three sat quietly for a couple of minutes before John spoke up.

"Charles, as you can see, there's a lot more to why I love this woman than just her pretty face." He hesitated before continuing. "What she says is correct. Let me add this. First, I promised you… and I will repeat my pledge to you that I will not break the law. It's not my style to rush in with guns-a-blazing. Please try to understand and accept that your way of dealing with this situation and mine are very different.

"I know mine works. I know if I told you where we think these guys are located, you would call in the troops and surround the place that. You would use overwhelming force to bring them in. That's the way you have been trained. If I thought that would work in this situation, I'd be happy to be a part of it.

"But, I don't think it would. If I'm right about where they are, they would know you're coming and be gone before your first guys got within sight of the place. So, it will take different tactics. And, quite frankly Charles, I'm far better at those tactics than anyone you have have on your force or that you have ever met.

"So, I'm asking you. Please trust me. Trust us. Trust that if I'm wrong about where they are holed up and if I'm wrong about the way they need to be taken into custody, I'll be knocking on your door asking for help."

Once again, the three of them sat silently, wondering who would break the tension. Finally, Superintendent Drake spoke.

"Kristin, if I remember correctly, you make a mean cup of hot chocolate. What's the chance I might talk you into one before I have to go back out on that damn frozen lake?"

Chapter 24

It was mid-afternoon by the time Superintendent Charles Drake left Kristin and John's warm cabin on the lake. Their conversation over Kristin's excellent hot chocolate was much more friendly and far less tense. When he left, Kristin and John simultaneously took a deep breath, expelling almost two hours of nervous tension.

"Screw this hot chocolate; I need a glass of wine," Kristin said.

"I need to take a walk," John said as he reached for his jacket. "I'll be back shortly."

"Are you okay?" Kristin asked him.

"I'm fine, baby, just need a few minutes of cold air to clear my head and settle my nerves. I'll be back in a few minutes."

John left their cabin and slowly walked toward the lake. The sun was bright in the sky, and the trees sparkled as the sunbeams danced through the ice and snow-covered limbs. But additional heavy snow was forecasted for latter in the day, continuing well into the night and for the next couple of days. John could smell it in the air. He could see clouds building to the west. It looked like Mother Nature was building up a reminder to all the two-legged critters just who ran the show and who really was the boss of the wilderness.

He walked out on the ice. The only sounds he heard were the wind and the ice. A low hum rolled over the lake, coming from the swaying of the trees in the forest being pushed back and forth by the rush of air sweeping down out of the north. The unseen moving waves in the ice pushed by that same wind emitted deep baritone moans and groans as the vast frozen surface rolled and pushed against the shoreline. The combined sounds reminded him of radio, with its volume turned way down and the base tones way up. The booms and hisses coming from the moving ice played a symphony celebrating the beauty they enhanced.

A few minutes later, John saw Bob strolling toward him. Bob Herman, his long-time friend. One of only a handful of people within whom John had total trust. The two men had served in the military together. Fought together, bled together, and stood side by side in battle, building a bond like no other experience could build. After their military service, they trained together to become government agents. Only John would succeed. Bob would suffer an injury washing him out of the program.

However, Bob's experience and knowledge of what John was doing gave them a path to building a strange and dependent relationship stronger even than it was while serving in uniform together. Bob needed John to help him secure his current job as the caretaker of the compound. When he married Sally, the newlyweds moved into the home supplied by the owner's association as a portion of his compensation package, and they have been here ever since.

John relied on Bob as well. This was John's safe haven. His retreat it was where he came to rest and heal. Bob was his security. His confidant. His anchor is to be replaced in part only by Kristin Blake, now John's wife. Bob guarded and maintained the fortress within which John felt secure.

The other person John held close was Gretchen Black. Following the death of his adoptive parents, she raised him as if he were her own. She became his mother and trusted ally. She knew what he did while he worked as a government agent, but she never asked questions and didn't want to know any of the details. All she wanted was for him to be safe and happy. She acted as mother, nurse, housekeeper, personal assistant and anything else that she decided John might be in need of.

Bob, Sally, and Gretchen warmly and lovingly accepted Kristin into John's life. She was the missing element. She was the one person he needed to be rounded out. She was needed to fulfill him. To fill the huge void in his life created by what he did as well as who he was. She, for the first time in his life, brought him love and happiness. She returned the promise to his life.

A latecomer to the group was Bruce LaBue. Bruce was Kristin's former boss when she was also a government employee acting as John's control agent. Initially, Bruce was John's enemy because of his position over Kristin. John had threatened to kill more than once. However, things changed as John's last assignment revealed itself to be treasonous and illegal. Bruce proved his friendship and loyalty. Currently still holding his old position in Washington, D.C., he turned into a very valuable asset having access to information John might need from time to time.

"You okay?" Bob asked John as he approached him on the ice.

"Yeah! Just needed some air. Had a long meeting with Drake. Got a little tense, but we cleared up some things."

"Anything you want to talk about?"

The two men walked slowly toward one of the many islands scattered in this part of Lake George referred to as 'the narrows.' John brought Bob up to date on everything that had taken place during the past few days. He told him about seeing and pursuing the four men in black and following them to where he now thought they were hiding. Bob was familiar with the location.

He also shared the conversation that had just taken place in his cabin after Bob had escorted Drake into the compound a couple of hours earlier. He told Bob that he had not shared the location of the four men with Drake.

"You've been a busy boy lately," Bob said. "Anything you need me to do?"

"I might. The first thing I need to do is get into the dude ranch and see if I'm right about these guys. I'm willing to bet that I am, but I've got to confirm that before I do anything else. I promised both

Drake and Kristin that I wouldn't go blasting my way in without first confirming that I was right.

"Drake has threatened me a couple of times that if I do anything illegal, he'd fry my ass. He again explained that he couldn't go in there without reason, and he couldn't search the place without some sort of evidence or cause. And he can't send an officer in there to dig up anything. So, that's what I'm going to do. I'm going to get him the evidence he needs."

"Legal in his world or yours?"

"His, which I'm learning to live in. Remember, I'm not a sworn officer any longer. I'm just a nosy private citizen."

"How are you going to get into the dude ranch without being seen? The road leading in there is close to ten miles long. If you're right, I would imagine that they are watching it pretty damn closely."

"I think you're right. I'll have to find a different way in. I'll have to hike in cross country to avid the road leading into the ranch."

"WOW! John. Bushwhacking through virgin territory. That's a tall order this time of year. Shortest way in is probably from somewhere along the interstate and it's got to be at least three or four miles in from the highway. There's got to be more than two feet of snow in those woods. Going to make for a very difficult and dangerous hike."

"Yeah, I'll have to use either cross-country skis or snowshoes to get in there. But I don't see any other way. Right now, I'm planning on hiking in during the day and arriving to search after dark."

Bob jumped in. "Meaning you'll have to hike in during the afternoon. That's okay. But, then, you'll have to hike out during the night… or spend the night in the woods. Pretty tough this time of year. Temperatures are forecasted to fall well below zero every night for at least the next week."

"Damn it, Bob, shut the hell up. I hate it when you're right", John said, jabbing at his old friend. "I might need your help. I don't want to get Kristin involved too much and I don't want her worrying about what I'm doing."

"Got it! I can drop you off and stand by to pick you up when you come back out."

"That's going to be difficult. I checked the other day when we were up that way. There's very weak and spotty cell service north of Lake George. I might not be able to contact you."

"Ouch! That makes life a bit more difficult. Well, we'll just have to figure out how to get you home. Maybe we'll revert to using good ole Indian smoke signals", Bob joked.

They had a good laugh while walking back to the compound. When they reached the shoreline, they exchanged a warm hug like only two old friends can do.

"Thanks, Bob", John said. "I needed that. I feel a lot better after talking with you and bouncing things off you. Helps me get things sort of aired out."

"That's what I'm here for, ole buddy. Now, go give that beautiful lady of yours a big hug and a kiss and relax for the rest of the day. We can talk more in the morning."

John did just that. When he entered his cabin, he grabbed Kristin, lifted her in the air spinning her around as if she were a stuffed teddy bear. Lowering her to the floor, he planted a big, wet, juicy kiss on her lips.

"I love you," he said to her.

"WOW! I saw you hug Bob out by the lake. Did you tell him the same thing?" she asked jokingly.

"Not quite, but you can give him the credit for the kiss you just got. It was all his idea."

"Really? What else did he tell you to do?"

"He said that I should ravish your body until the sun comes up tomorrow."

"I love that man. He has such great ideas and gives such wonderful advice."

John lifted her in his arms and carried her to their bedroom where he followed the idea he credited on Bob's behalf. Neither he nor Kristin really cared whose idea it was. Being ravished by the person you loved was a great way to spend a cold, wintry afternoon in the mountains of Upstate New York, or anywhere else for that matter.

Later, while lying beneath the fluffy down, filled quilt that covered their bed, they quietly snuggled together two like igloo-bound Eskimos wrapped in a bear skin. The wind outside had kicked up and whistled through the trees, engulfing their cabin. It was snowing just as promised by the weatherman. The combination added to the magic of the moment they were sharing. Somehow, the isolation and ruggedness of where they lived added to the strength of their relationship just as it tempered the strength of those choosing to live here. The tough environment toughened those who lived in it and intensified their passions.

Holding his naked wife next to his bare chest, John filled her in on the real conversation he had with Bob earlier in the day. Sharing his thoughts with Bob and now with Kristin, his mind eased and the plan on what, when and how he was going to deal with the four strangers in black began to take shape and clarify.

He shared his thoughts with Kristin. She asked questions and made a couple of suggestions that helped him to hone the developing plan. Her value as a collaborator increased every day. Her intellect, instincts, and experience complemented his and helped grind off some of the rough edges of his ideas.

By the time they reluctantly crawled out of bed and showered together, it was time for dinner.

"Let's go into Saratoga for dinner tonight," he suggested. "I don't feel like cooking, and I'm in the mode for pasta."

"In this weather?"

"We'll be okay. We have four-wheel drive, and if it gets too bad, we'll just get a room and stay there for the night."

"Oh, dear God, let go of my arm before you twist it off."

John called ahead and made a last-minute reservation at Chianti's restaurant, one of his favorites. The drive into Saratoga Springs took over an hour and a half because of the snow-covered roads. But they made it safe and sound. Once there, they shared a wonderful authentic Italian meal and a bottle of dry red wine. Kristin enjoyed a wonderful meal of veal Marcella, and John stuffed himself with lasagna, splitting an antipasto salad between them.

"I'm too tired and a bit too tipsy to drive home. What do you say we stay in town tonight?" John suggested.

"There you go again, trying to hurt my arm," Kristin teased. "Sounds to me like you had this planned all along."

"You might be right, my darling woman."

John drove a few blocks to one of the largest hotels in Saratoga located on the north end of Broadway. He knew that during the off-season, reservations were not needed to book a room. He was right, and they were immediately ushered to a room overlooking the park at the rear of the hotel. They collapsed into bed, barely getting out of their clothes before falling sound asleep. The wine was working its wonders.

The following morning, Kristin ordered a hearty breakfast from the room service menu. They stuffed themselves again while sitting snugly wrapped up in the fluffy terry cloth robes provided by the hotel. Before showering and dressing for their forty-mile drive home, they tenderly and warmly took gave themself to each other once again. The two of them strongly sensing and cherished the magic that passed between them during these intimate moments.

On the way back to their cabin, John shared the final plan that he had formed in his mind. All the pieces seemed to fall into place once he relaxed, thanks to the great meals and wine and lovemaking with his wife. It was a slow drive home. The snow had continued to fall all through the night and the road into the compound had not yet been plowed.

"Are you going to share your plan with Superintendent Drake?" she asked him.

"No! If I do, he'll overrule me because he classifies me as a civilian. He would either come up with another idea or simply threaten me in some way to be sure I was a good boy."

"John, you promised him you would not kill these guys, at least until you had proof that they are really the bad guys."

"I have no intentions of killing anybody. Like I told you, this is a two-part plan. First, I'll hike in and scout out the entire area to see what I can find. If I don't find anything incriminating, we're done. I'll hike back out and report to him that I had the wrong guys, and you and I will be on the next flight to the Virgin Islands."

"And if you do find something?" she asked.

"Then I'll hike out, and we'll decide what the next step should be. I might find nothing, and then again, I might find a stash of weapons and terrorists. The four-to-one odds don't bother me, but given the location, I don't want to risk them slipping away. I'll tell Drake what I found and then he'll call in the cavalry. His guys can go in strong and overpower them."

"Okay! That makes me feel better. I don't want to see you…"

"Don't worry, baby, I'm not going to do anything stupid like getting killed."

"You damn well better not! I sure hope you don't find anything. The Virgin Islands sound too good to be true.

Chapter 25

Noon the following day, Bob pulled to the northbound shoulder of Interstate 87 just north of the Bolton Landing exit. It was not a random spot he chose. It was exactly where John had instructed him to make a quick stop, allowing John to exit the vehicle, reach into the rear seat area and take hold of his backpack and cold-weather survival gear.

After returning home from the previous night out with his wife, he had spent a good portion of the afternoon gathering and packing the equipment and supplies he thought he might need to carry out his plan. He packed enough warm insulating clothing and basic survival gear to hold him over should he have to spend a night in the near-zero temperatures.

This was not new to him. He had winter camped, hunted and hiked in these mountains for years as a boy and as a young man. He had also participated in several winter cold weather 'search & rescue' missions requiring preparation for extended stays in brutal conditions typical in the north country this time of year.

He learned early on that two extremely important pieces of equipment necessary for success and survival were, first, his footwear and, second, his gloves. It your feet froze, you die, and if your hands stiffen up from the cold, you lose the most important tools God gave to man.

Included in his gear, he had a high-quality Silva compass and a topographic map of the area encompassing the dude ranch. His two specialties, while a member of the L.A.S.A.R. team, were wilderness survival and cross-country navigation. He was very well trained in the use of a compass, GPS and topographic maps. This experience along with his equipment, gave him a high comfort level as he set out to complete his current plan.

He quickly jumped the metal guard rail that ran alongside the highway, allowing Bob to barely come to a stop before continuing toward the next exit, where he would turn around and head back home. John quickly crossed over the steel safety barrier; he did not want to draw attention from other vehicles zooming past. He took a few steps and disappeared into the trees adjacent to the roadway.

As he and Bob had anticipated, the snow was deep. The natural snowfall was added to by the accumulation thrown over by the passing plow trucks. He immediately sunk in up to his crotch. He sat on the first big rock he came to, un-lashed his snowshoes for the outside of his backpack and attached them to his boots. Once done, he looked at his compass to establish the exact heading he wanted to take and began his trek toward the suspected killers. In doing so, he also logged the back azimuth in his memory so he could find his way back to where he began his hike.

He had oriented his map before leaving home and knew the exact compass setting he wanted to follow. He had plotted the drop-off spot and the route into the dude ranch while studying his maps the night before, trying to find the easiest route in and out of his target area, avoiding the killer elevation changes he would encounter in this hilly country.

His first obstacle was the Schroon River. It was not a major deep-water river, but it was wide with rapid water flow. In the dead of winter, the runoff water that would normally fill the river was locked up upstream in the form of ice and snow. In the spring, when the thaw came, the water levels would increase dramatically, making this currently gentle flowing river into a raging torrent and crossing it much more difficult and dangerous, if not impossible. Right now, the primary concern was trying to keep his feet dry and not slip on the icy rocks and fall into the swift-moving shallow water. He was far more concerned with staying dry than being swept away by the current.

Even with the water levels being low, getting wet could be deadly. When he reached the river, he took his waders out of his pack and put them on. Reaching up to his chest, the waders would provide him with way more depth clearance than he would need to traverse the fifty or sixty-yard-wide river.

He gingerly placed one foot at a time, being sure that each was firmly in place on the bottom before lifting the other and taking the next step. He was being ultra-careful knowing that the pack on his back could upset his normal balance and could cause him to go tumbling into the icy water.

It seemed like an hour before he touched the opposite river bank. In fact, it had taken him less than five minutes to cross. When he was back on firm ground, he removed his waders, buckled them together, hung them over a tree branch and marked them with a piece of plastic Day-Glo orange tape so he could easily find them when he returned. They were too heavy to lug around, and he would not be needing them again on this hike.

He put his snowshoes back on, checked his compass, and set off again. It was tough going. The snow was deeper than he had expected. Even with snowshoes on his feet, the hiking was very slow through the cold powdery white stuff. The snow, because of the very low water content and frigid temperatures, was very light and fluffy and didn't hold any weight. With each step, he sunk almost up to his knees. It was like walking on feathers. He had to make frequent stops to rest and catch his breath. The effort was exhausting.

After an hour, he stopped to drink some of the hot tea that Kristin had filled his water bottle with. He also ate a protein bar to keep his energy level up. He knew that dehydration and lack of nourishment could be a major concern. Proper hydration was just as important in cold temperatures as in hot. Like any other mission he had ever planned, he knew he had to take care of himself to be successful.

He trudged on. He frequently referred to his topo map and compass to determine his location and the course of least resistance. This was a rough, hilly country, which only added to the difficulty of hiking through the deep snow. He changed his course several times to avoid the worst of the hills and gullies in his path. Ravines presented the most danger. When filled with snow, they appeared to be flat while able to swallow him in snow many feet deep. They were bottomless pits lined with rocks and boulders ready to break and swallow his body, leaving no trace. If he fell into one and were injured, his remains, what was left of them after the local scavengers finished with him, would not be found until spring.

By late afternoon, the winds died down, and the temperature plunged. The sun threatened to disappear behind the hills to the west. Darkness came early in the forest. He knew it would be more difficult and more dangerous to hike in the dark. He quickened his pace as much as conditions would allow. He needed to reach the outer limits of the dude ranch soon.

Suddenly, John heard a crashing sound off to his left. He stopped dead in his tracks. He knew what the sound was. The crashing was followed by a low groaning that confirmed his fears. A black bear! For some unexplained reason, it was out of its winter den cruising the forest. The crashing sound came from the bear pushing over a dead tree to get at the insects sleeping deep inside or hoping for some beechnuts or acorns to come tumbling down.

John had not crossed any tracks in the snow. That told him that the bear was either moving toward him or perpendicular to his path through the woods. Either way, it wasn't good. He was not carrying any kind of gun big enough to protect himself or to ward off the bear. If he tried to shoot the animal with the 9MM handgun he had in his pack, he would do nothing more than piss off a very dangerous foe.

He knew better than to try to outrun it should it come after him. Even without the deep snow, he could not outrun a bear. He also knew that you couldn't evade a black bear by climbing a tree. Either action would be a signed death warrant.

He heard a second crash. Another tree pushed over. This one sounded slightly closer. He had to decide and decide quickly what his next move would be. He had to evade the animal approaching him. Fortunately, the wind was blowing in his face, carrying his scent away from the bear.

He had only two ways to go. He could retrace his steps and move away from the animal, hoping he wouldn't be heard. Or he could hunker down and bury himself in the deep snow, hoping the bear would pass him by.

His heart was racing! Dealing with a wild animal was far more different than dealing with a human. He knew how humans would react in most situations. A wild animal, particularly a hungry pissed off bear roaming outside of its warm den, was a different matter altogether. Would it feel threatened and run for safety, or would it feel cornered and attacked? Would the bear see him as a threat and run away, or see him as lunch and come at him? He wasn't about to leave it up to the bear to decide. He slowly turned and quietly as he could, began to retrace his steps through the woods. He walked about fifty yards before he heard the third crashing sound. Definitely closer! Time to hide. John took off one of his snowshoes and lay down in the snow. Using the snowshoe as a shovel, he scooped snow from a drift within his reach and completely covered himself.

Within a minute or two, the only part of him exposed was his head, from his eyes to his crown. He set the snowshoe down and laid back, scooping snow with his arms until he was confident that he was totally buried. The snow would both conceal him and reduce his scent. He lay completely still. Breathing as shallowly as he could. Listening! His sense of hearing is enhanced by the adrenaline flow within him.

His heart was pumping so hard he was sure the bear could hear it. He lay completely still. He could hear the bear snorting. Another crash! Sound traveled differently in the cold and snow. It was extremely difficult to judge how far away it was. A yard or a mile. His senses played tricks on him. John imagined that he felt the bear's footfalls vibrating the ground approaching him. Minutes dragged by. Another crash. Further away, but not by much. Slightly to his right this time. Lay still!

More minutes!

Lay still!

Another crash. This time, definitely further away and to his right. The bear had passed by. It had crossed his path and was moving away from him.

Don't move!

Not yet!

Wait!

Minutes agonizingly dragged by.

Sweat ran down his back.

Another crash, this time barely within hearing.

Deep breath. Slowly, rise up. Take a look around. Quietly get to your feet.

Wait!

Wait!

Calm yourself!

He was wet from sweating.

From tension.

Okay, time to move on.

Carefully!

Quietly!

Quickly!

To the left. Move to the left. Circle away from the last sound. Open the distance between my path and the bear. Move forward toward the left.

He had been able to talk himself through the tense moment. He had learned this technique from his years of covert missions around the world, where he found himself totally alone with no chance of help coming to assist him. It had worked for him when he was attempting to avoid people wanting to kill him. It worked for him then. Would it work for him now? A bear was not a man. He knew how a man's mind functioned. Was a bear as predictable?

Within a couple of minutes or resuming his trek, John crossed the tracks of the bear. It had moved off toward the south and away from him and where he wanted to go.

One very positive effect of this run-in with the bear was the peaking of his senses. It was as if he had rubbed the tip of his nose with sandpaper. Everything became sharper, clearer, brighter, louder. He became aware of odors he hadn't noticed just a few minutes earlier. He knew he was getting close to the dude ranch. He could smell it. Humans had a way of manufacturing their own stink.

Within an hour of the bear encounter, he came to the edge of a clearing in the forest and into an area that was obviously maintained by humans. The underbrush had been cleared. He felt sure that he was now walking atop a mowed grassy area buried beneath the snow. But, he needed to stay within the tree line and remain hidden.

Darkness was rapidly approaching as he had hoped it would be. A few minutes later, he saw the first building that he guessed was a part of the dude ranch complex. Stepping back further into the tree line, he continued until he saw additional buildings, as well as a large clearing he presumed was used for either parking or recreational activities.

He saw additional buildings across the cleared area. These buildings were lined up in a semi-circle configuration with a large, flat, clear snow behind them. He knew there was a lake on the ranch and he assumed that's what he was looking at. All the buildings were dark and looked to be boarded up for the winter.

There was a mix of cabins and bunkhouse-looking buildings of various sizes, as well as a couple of three-story buildings that looked more like small motel units or dormitories. He saw no lights. No heat plumes from furnaces or wood-burning stoves. No signs of life.

To his left was a different story. He saw two structures making up what appeared to be the main central focal point of the ranch. One looked as if it housed the dining hall and kitchen facilities. The other looked more like it was a reception hall. A sign tacked to the outside wall announced that it was the 'office.' Above the office, a second floor consisted of what must be to be living quarters. Lights were on in the lower floor, and smoke came from the chimneys servicing each of the two buildings.

To the right of these two buildings was a flat, open white expanse of the lake frozen over and the ice covered with snow. He could see additional cabins way off in the distance across the lake. These appeared to be more like single-family homes. Had to be higher-priced upscale housing units on the waterfront or possibly for live-in staff, John deducted.

None had lights coming from them. Only the two buildings to his left showed promising signs of life. He moved to improve his line of sight. Bingo, there it was. A white Ford Econoline van pulled up slightly behind the building he believed to house the kitchen. It was parked half-hidden next to a dumpster unit, and there was a doorway that looked to lead into the rear of the kitchen. There were no other vehicles in sight.

Time to wait again. This time not for an angry bear to move away. This time, he needed to wait for darkness and to observe any movement within the compound area. He needed to position himself where he could observe the clearing and the occupied buildings without being detected. He also needed to stay warm for the next few hours while he waited. It was getting colder by the minute now that the sun had disappeared from the winter sky. The complex of buildings was now engulfed in a silvery glow, holding down the crisp white blanket to snow covering the ground.

He found a place where he could crawl between a stack of wood cut for either a stove or fireplace and a small shed. He took off his pack and wedged it up against the cut logs to make himself as comfortable as he could. Once he was settled in, he sprinkled snow over himself to break up his outline and help camouflage him against the white background.

He hadn't been sitting very long before three men exited the building that John believed to be the dining area. They, as expected, were dressed all in black. They were too far away, and the light had faded to where he could not clearly see their faces. However, he felt sure these were the men he was searching for.

The three men didn't seem to be going anywhere. They did not approach the van. Instead, stood looking across the clearing in the direction of the entrance road as if waiting for someone to arrive. Then, John heard a distant rumbling of an engine. It wasn't an automobile. It was… a snowmobile. The noise got louder and louder until, finally, a snow machine came speeding along the road and into the clearing. A fourth man dressed in black. He drove the snow machine to within a few yards of where his companions were waiting.

Then, another surprise presented itself. Another man emerged from the dining hall. He was much taller than the others. This was the man John believed to be the group's leader.

There were not four; there were five men. One must have been left behind to guard the area each time John and Kristin had seen the other four in the village. One additional man, John thought, didn't present much of a change to his plan. He would simply have to be a bit more watchful.

The five men stood outside the building, clearly having a discussion. John could hear voices, but he could not hear words. Once again, they were standing just a little too far away for him to understand what was being said. He did, however, know that they were not speaking English. It was a calm discussion. There was no panic or sense of urgency in their conversation. That was good, John judged. That signaled to him that nothing had happened to heighten their level of alertness.

It seemed that things were quiet and normal for them. Probably an update report from the man who entered in on the snow machine, most likely a guard watching the road approaching the ranch.

The discussion outside of the dining hall lasted for only a few minutes. The five began rubbing their arms and dancing around in the snow on cold feet. They re-entered the building, disappearing behind the closed door. John waited and watched to see what might happen next.

Nothing did. He sat in his concealed locations for two more hours. Watching! It was getting colder as the night deepened. He reached into his pack to find a couple of protein bars and a bottle of water. Dinner was served. Half-frozen Styrofoam-tasting nougat and nut bars washed down with ice-cold water. Delicious!

He was getting cold, and his legs were getting stiff from being immobile for so long in the frigid temperatures. He needed to move around and regain the circulation in his legs and butt. However, he had to be careful. He didn't know if one of the five men inside the building was assigned to keep watch over the clearing or if all five were sitting around a warm, cozy fire, planning their next beheading.

John stood up and slipped behind the shed he was sitting next to. There was an unlocked door on the side of the shed facing away from the dining hall. He decided to step into the shed to get out of the wind and elements for a few minutes and, hopefully, warm up a bit. He pushed the door open and stepped inside.

"Holy shit!" The sight struck him like a hammer. Inside the shed, the final confirmation he needed abruptly greeted him. Laying on the floor, neatly stacked and fully dressed, were four headless bodies. A fifth was propped up against the wall opposite the door. It was a bazar sight. Almost fake-looking. It appeared as if the fifth body was holding a class for the other four laying on the ground instructing them on how to lay there and be still. A room full of headless mannequins waiting for the teacher's approval to go play out in the snow.

They were frozen solid. Human bodies are supposed to have heads. These didn't. They looked… incomplete, laying there as if they were unfinished pieces of sculpture awaiting the final strokes of the artist's hammer to be finished so they could get up and walk away or put words to the silent conversation the five now shared in this cold silence. Each looked so real, so unreal, and so dead.

John examined the bodies. Four men and one woman matched the five victims found on the ice. He found nothing else on the bodies. No wallets. No forms of identification. However, none was needed. There was little doubt these were the victims of the brutal and senseless murders that had shocked the area around Lake George.

The only item he found was a gold chain entangled in the fingers of the female body. It had a cross attached to it. He hoped that the woman found a final moment of comfort by holding on to her beliefs before being so brutally murdered. The five black-clad men in the dining hall were guilty of murder, and John intended to do everything he could to see them punished.

He calmed himself as best he could. He knew if he operated from a position of anger, he would make foolish mistakes. There were two things he now needed to do. First, he wanted to sneak up to the dining hall and peek inside to see what he might learn from observing the men. Second, he had to return to Lake George to contact Superintendent Drake and tell him what he had found.

He had found the proof. He had the confirmation Drake insisted upon. It was now up to the state's top cop to launch an all-out assault on the dude ranch to bring these bastards to justice.

But, first things first!

Chapter 26

John stepped out of the shed carefully closing the door. He didn't want the wind to take it and noisily slam it back into place. He then crouched down to hide himself behind the wood pile until he could clearly see the dining hall building again. He took off his backpack and rested it against the stack of cut logs where he could retrieve it later. No sense lugging a heavy pack while trying to sneak up and peek in the windows.

Like any trained agent, before entering the danger zone, he searched for an exit route. He wanted to be sure that should he be seen and needed to escape, he had a way out. The road was not an option. He could never outrun the vehicles these guys had at their disposal. They would run him down in seconds.

That left only a cross-country exit, just like the one he took to get here. Bushwhacking through the dense underbrush and deep snow would be to his advantage. He felt certain that he was better equipped and more experienced to do this than the five men who might be pursuing him. Men of the desert and treeless mountains of sand didn't usually fare well in deep snow and forested hills. Mother Nature would help even up the current five-to-one odds against him.

However, he would be leaving a clear trail in the snow for them to follow. With or without snowshoes, he would leave a trail wide and deep enough for a total novice to follow with a blindfold on. He would have to use speed and his outdoor skills to avoid capture or death. The 9mm handgun he was carrying wasn't enough for him to defend himself or to hold them off. And it didn't have the range to deal with them across any distance that would be safe. He knew the limitations of what he could do… but they didn't.

Keeping within the tree line, he snuck up to the target building and flattened himself against the outside wall. He slowly worked his way to the nearest window, slowly rising until his eyes cleared the sill and he could see into the building. The first room he observed was a bedroom. It held two twin-size beds and two matching dressers. But no men in black.

He continued working his way around the building. There were three more bedrooms, two of which were dark and unused. The third was a duplicate of the first. The next room he reached was totally different. It was a combination of a den and a dining room. It was a large room. On one end, there were four large round tables with chairs tucked under them. The designated dining area.

At the other end of the room, he could see the pewter glow of a big flat-screen television surrounded by three couches and a half dozen overstuffed lounge chairs. In the far corner of the room, there was a fireplace currently not in use. The last major feature in the room was five men dressed in black slouching down on the overstuffed furniture, watching television. Very relaxed.

No one was on guard…no one was on watch… no apparent concern for their discovery. Very stupid. These men were clearly killers, as evidenced by five bodies frozen stiff in the shed only yards away. But, it was equally clear to John that they were amateurs.

All the men in the room were watching the television with their eyes directed away from his position. Therefore, he could observe them without fear of being seen. He watched them for about fifteen minutes until one of them stood and walked toward a doorway leading to another room. He was gone for only a couple of minutes before returning and resuming his seat. John guessed he had made a visit to the bathroom.

He continued to watch the men. Finally, he checked his wristwatch to see what time it was. Much to his surprise, it was nearly ten o'clock. It was time for him to decide his next move. Suddenly, two of the men stood and said something to those remaining seated.

John could neither hear them nor understand what was being said. The two men who stood began walking toward the bedrooms John had first peeked into from the other side of the building. Must be bedtime.

To avoid the risk of being seen, John ducked down below the window sill and made his way back around the building and returned to where he had left his backpack. He had to decide what to do next. He leaned up against the outside wall of the shed containing the five dead bodies and slid down into a sitting position. He thought about the hike in from the interstate. It had taken him a little over seven hours to traverse the distance from the interstate highway to the dude ranch.

Seven hours! It had taken him seven hours to reach the ranch while it was daylight. Deep snow, bushwhacking cross country in the dark, even with his experience in land navigation, it would be a difficult hike out under those conditions.

Even though he had left a clear trail in the snow on the way in, it would be difficult to follow it on the way out. And, it would slow him down trying to stay on his old track in the dark. And, he felt certain that the light snow that fell during the day, along with the light wind, had, at the very least, filled in his tracks partway. That would make it even more difficult to follow his incoming trail.

To top that off, he also knew that there was a cranky black bear in the neighborhood. Something he did not want to mess with during the day, much less in the dark. And lastly, it was forecasted to snow again starting during the overnight hours. New snow would cover his tracks completely and quickly making it even harder and slower to retrace his steps.

Everything pointed toward his hunkering down somewhere to spend the night or at least a few hours. He knew he had to find someplace to get out of the cold. He knew he could easily slip into the shed housing the murder victims, but that didn't intrigue him much. Secondly, one of the killers might just decide to check on the bodies and find a live one with its head still attached. That could very well result in a shootout... Not a good idea going to a gunfight with five-to-one odds against you.

So, he decided to check out the other buildings surrounding the frozen lake. It didn't take him long to find one that was unlocked. He slipped inside. As he did, he looked back to see if everything was quiet.

"Damn it!" He realized his search had left a track in the snow leading right to where he now stood. When the men in the dining hall came out in the morning, they would plainly see his footprints through in the snow and be able to follow them right to him.

Not good! He would have to wake himself early enough to leave the cabin and retrace his steps back to the clearing. Once there, his footprints would blend in with all the other tire and foot traffic. However, there would be no hiding the fact from the men in black that he was there and they had an unknown... and unwelcome visitor.

Hopefully, by the time his presence was known, he would be well on his way back through the woods to meet up with Bob. In the meantime, he needed to get warm and get some rest. The cabin he had gotten into had two small bedrooms and a den-kitchen combo great room. Each of the bedrooms held two twin beds, and each bed was covered with a medium-weight quilt.

There was also a small wood-burning stove in the center of the living area. However, John knew he could not start a fire to warm himself. Doing so would immediately alert the people he most wanted to avoid.

He took two of the quilts and returned to the den. He then took off his backpack and wedged it against the front door. If anyone tried to enter while he was asleep, at the very least, he would have a short warning before being killed. He didn't want to die without knowing it.

Before settling himself, he pulled out his cell phone to see if there was any signal service. He could barely see one bar, indicating a very weak signal. He decided to give it a try anyway. He searched his contacts and pressed Bob's number when it appeared. Finally hearing what he knew to be Bob's voicemail, he attempted to leave his old friend a message. He had no clue if the signal was strong enough to make a clear connection.

He then sat in a comfortable armchair, wrapping himself in the two quilts. The day of pushing through the snow and watching and waiting in the cold had sucked more of his energy than he realized. It took a while until he felt the warmth returning to his body. It didn't take long after that for him to fall asleep.

The distant slam of a door shocked him awake! It was still pitch-black outside, but someone was moving around within the dude ranch grounds. There it was again! Not loud! Just loud enough to trigger his raw senses. He sprang up from the chair, throwing off the quilts. He rushed to a window facing where he thought the sound came from. Lights were on inside the dining hall.

He glanced at his wristwatch. It was five-thirty in the morning. He was surprised that he had slept for so long and so hard. He should have been on his way by this time. He needed to leave. He returned to the den to retrieve his backpack. Before exiting the cabin, he once again glanced out of the window. Just then, the door leading into the kitchen opened. One of the men in black stepped outside carrying a large black plastic bag. He walked to the dumpster and tossed it in.

Routine activity. 'These guys are early risers,' John thought to himself. He should have been, too. Now, he found himself in a position where he had to cross a portion of the clearing to get to his escape route with a highly increased chance of being seen. He knew he couldn't stay in the cabin. Soon, it would be daylight, and his foot trail through the snow from the shed to the cabin would stick out like a bleached blonde at an Italian funeral.

He would have to position himself to make a dash to the woods in hope of not being seen. Even if he made it, he knew that it wouldn't take long for his trail to the cabin to be seen. When it was discovered by his four new friends, and they realized that someone had been at the ranch, they would begin a search that would soon lead to the trail he left through the woods to get here as well as to escape. And he knew that he had at least one snowmobile to run him down with.

Should he run and leave yet another trail, or should he stand and fight, he tossed in his mind. Stand and fight with what? He had only a handgun, no heavy weapon to protect himself with, much less to launch any kind of an attack on five murderers. He knew they had at least one weapon, the one used to shoot at his cabin and wound Kristin and Bob.

Five! Five to one. Only one handgun. It left him with only one other option: hand-to-hand combat, or he had to find a 2x4 somewhere to use as a war club. He knew he was good … but not good enough to risk five-to-one odds… and he didn't have a 2x4. If he only knew if his voice message had reached Bob, the cavalry would be on its way.

He couldn't wait to find out. He would have to make a dash for it and hope that he could get far enough out in front of these guys that they couldn't catch him. He was confident that once in the forest, the odds shifted in his favor. He strapped his pack on his back, cinched it tight and looked out of the window one last time.

To his surprise, there were now two men standing outside of the dining hall door. Both were looking in the direction of the cabin he was in. One was pointing toward the ground. Even in the low light from the security flood lamps scattered around the area, they had seen his footprints in the snow. Time to go!

Luckily, the front door on the cabin faced away from the dining hall. John slipped out through the door as quietly as he could. He snuck up to the corner of the cabin, knowing the building would conceal him from the view of the two men. He peeked around the corner. As he did, one of the men nearly jumped out of his boots. He spotted John. With arms flailing in excitement, he turned and ran back into the dining hall. The second man stood outside of the door continuing to look in John's direction.

To reach the trail he came in on, John would have to run toward the dining hall and across a large portion of the clearing in plain view of the man standing outside. He would be slowed by the heavy pack on his back.

Another option was for him to run toward the north end of the complex. Instead of being fifty yards from the dining hall, he would be more like two hundred yards away giving him a couple of additional precious minute's head start. Not much, but like someone once said, 'Every little bit helps'".

With his backpack strapped down tight, he started off toward the tree line at the north end of the complex, trying to keep one of the buildings between him and the man standing outside of the dining hall. He almost made it. Just a few yards before reaching the trees, he heard loud shouting behind him. He could only conclude that he had been seen running toward the trees.

More voices joined the commotion. John was sure that by now all five of the men in black had been alerted and were outside the dining hall watching him disappear into the woods. He felt certain there was an artillery cannon pointed at the center of his backside, ready to launch a rocket right up his butt.

The ground took a sharp upward slant fifty yards after he entered the tree line. The shouting behind him continued, but it wasn't getting any closer. There was a rock out-cropping in front of him. He decided to risk a few seconds by stopping to look back. He wanted to see what the men were doing.

He could clearly see all five of them outside of the building. All five were talking at once with arms flailing wildly in the air. They were surprised and confused by his presence. Finally, one man, the tallest one, gained control and began barking orders. He pointed to one of the other four men before he turned toward where John had left the clearing. He gestured to the remaining three men, and the four began running toward John.

They were leaving one man behind just as they had when they were in town. Four of them were now in pursuit of John, and a rear guard would stay behind. John made a mental note of this for the future. Something else he took note of. The four men coming after him and the way they were dressed. They were wearing only their black coveralls... and lightweight jackets. They had not returned to the dining area to retrieve their heavy cold weather jackets. A new plan immediately formed in John's mind.

He left the rocky area and began moving toward the north once again. The snow was deep, and his backpack weighed him down, but he couldn't leave it behind. He would need everything he had packed in it now more than ever. But, what he needed to do first was to gain enough time to stop and get his snowshoes lashed to his feet.

He scrambled up the slope, fighting the thigh-deep snow. When he reached the top, he looked back to see what progress the four men in pursuit were making. He could not see them, but he could hear them babbling loudly. It sounded as if all four of them were nervously barking orders all at the same time. He could not make out what they were saying for two reasons. First, they were too far away, and secondly... for the first time, he could confirm that they were not speaking English.

He quickly un-lashed his snow shoes from the outside of his pack and secured them to his feet. Under normal conditions, one man could move faster than four people bunched together, the same as one horseman could outrun a posse. With snowshoes, John could now easily out-pace the men after him, even while carrying a backpack. He didn't want to leave them too far behind. The plan taking shape in his mind only required that he stay far enough out in front of them that they could not actually catch him or shoot at him should they be carrying any handguns. He could see that they were not carrying any rifles.

He wanted to stay close enough for them to see him. Not just be able to follow his trail in the snow. He wanted them to see him moving through the trees ahead of them. He wanted to tease them. To entice them and too lure them into chasing after him. To stay too close for them to abandon the chase. The further he drew them away from the dude ranch, the further into the wilderness they followed, the better he liked it.

Finally, the four men reappeared below him. They were struggling up the slope, their legs pushing snow with every step. John waited until one of them finally lifted his head and caught sight of him further up the hill. When the man pointed at John and shouted to his companions, John stood and set off again. The tease was on! With his snowshoes now assisting him, he was able to move far more easily than he did earlier. And, he could now easily out-pace the men in pursuit. He was setting the pace, he was choosing the path and he wasn't stumbling or avoiding others in his efforts.

When the four had caught sight of John, it reinvigorated them to push harder. Exactly what he was hoping for. Their shouting got louder each time they spotted him, and their arms flailed even more than before. But, the snow, the grade of the hill and the footwear they wore all hindered their progress. They were having a difficult time.

The further they got away from the dude ranch, the more difficult the terrain became. The hills got higher, and the angle of the incline got steeper. Plus, as the old saying goes, 'What goes up must come down.' Going downhill in deep snow didn't require as much energy, but the hazards increased.

Every rock and every tree limb lying on the ground buried beneath the snow became a potential ankle breaker. Step on an ice-covered rock or limb, and feet would go flying in unintended directions. Slipping and falling often sucked energy. Hot bodies working hard caused the snow to melt, wetting their clothing from the outside, while the physical exertion caused their sweat to wet them from the inside.

Wet clothes, poor footwear, deep snow, physical exertion, inexperienced men… and sub-freezing temperatures! These all added up to a deadly combination. Mother Nature was assisting John in fulfilling his new plan. The odds had turned in his favor. It was only a matter of time.

"Come on, boys!" he muttered under his breath as he once again looked back at his pursuers. "Come to Daddy."

They did! The four men dressed in lightweight black pants and shirts, each topped only with what appeared to be, at best, a light to medium-weight jacket, continued to huff and puff their way through the woods chasing after John. Each glimpse of him reinvigorated their effort.

He led them up and over the second hill north of the ranch. When he reached the beginning of the third, John made a right turn heading east. He changed direction in hopes of confusing his pursuers. He frequently looked back over his shoulder to be sure the men were still in sight. He knew if he could see them, they could see him.

Another hour passed. John felt himself beginning to tire. He realized that if his energy was running low while wearing snowshoes, the four men behind him had to be in far worst condition, sinking at least knee-deep with every step.

Yet another hour slipped. This time, John turned left, resuming a northerly path. He stopped again to look back. Seeing that he could stop for a moment, he reached into his backpack and, retrieved a couple of the protein bars and rapidly ate one while pocketing the second. Once he saw the men again, and they started pointing at him, he resumed his trek.

John glanced at his wristwatch. Time was in his favor. He had been leading the chase for hours, and things were going his way. He continued north for another hour and then turned to his left again, heading west. He paused… they saw him… he continued… and they followed. He paused… they saw him… he continued… and they followed. But they were slowing. They were tiring. The effort was taking its toll.

A childhood memory flashed in his mind. He remembered when he was a young boy of about seven or eight. Shortly before his dad died, he had bought John a rabbit. A big fat white rabbit. John was thrilled. He loved that damn rabbit. He named it Blackie just to be cute.

But it was as dumb as a stump. It didn't respond to its name. He tried to train it to follow him. No dice. Finally, John came up with the idea of baiting the rabbit. He called out, "Here Blackie" and either the rabbit was stupid or deaf because it still didn't follow. So, John took food pellets and laid them out in a straight line. He spaced them so there were a couple of inches between each pellet. Then he stood on one end of the line with Blackie on the other and tried again. "Here Blackie", and this time the rabbit came to him following the line of pellets. It worked. With a little bait, the rabbit got a whole lot smarter and learned its name. He had a silent laugh remembering this old story.

Here he was again. Laughing inside of his own mind while laying the bait. Except this time, it wasn't rabbit pellets; it was him. He was the bait. He chuckled aloud when he suddenly realized the irony, Blackie had been replaced by four men dressed in black. *History does have a way of repeating itself,* he thought.

Chapter 27

Back on Interstate 87, early morning found Bob pulling off the highway at the same spot he had dropped John the previous day. It was approaching ten o'clock. John had told Bob that he would call him on his cell phone when he got back to this spot. Bob was to stand by and wait for the call before driving here to pick him up. John was now overdue… way overdue.

When he awoke early this morning, Bob checked his voicemail to find a very garbled message that he could not understand. He was able to catch a word then there was a gap of static followed by another word, more static until the message ended after less than a minute. He knew it was from John because of the originating telephone number listed. However, he could not tell what the message said or what John was requesting. That's why he was now sitting alongside the highway, hoping his friend would either appear or contact him.

John told him what he had expected as the time frame for his hike into the dude ranch and then back out to be picked up. He estimated that the earliest he would return would be between midnight and two o'clock in the morning. At the latest, he would expect to be back here no later than six o'clock. Either way, he was hours overdue.

Bob had sat up most of the night waiting for his phone to ring. He had waited in vain for John to call again after the garbled message. It didn't happen. Finally, he couldn't wait any longer. Either there was no telephone signal to support John's call, or his friend was in trouble. He had to find out.

He pulled onto the shoulder of the highway to wait exactly where John had jumped the railing. He hadn't called Kristin to tell her what he was doing. He didn't want to worry her. He was sure she was nervously pacing the floor of their cabin, waiting for her phone to ring or for John to come marching through their front door. Until John was safely back in his truck, Bob felt that calling her would only make matters worse.

He sat in his pickup truck and waited. Every semi-truck that sped by rocked him with a blast of air pushed by the big rigs. After a while, he got out of his vehicle. He was too anxious and nervous to sit still. He paced up and down the length of the guard rail, looking off into the woods to see if anything was moving. Looking for any sign of John returning.

Noon came and went! He decided to call Kristin to see if she might have heard from her husband. He hit speed dial for her number and put the phone to his ear. Hearing nothing, he looked at the screen and saw the 'No service' indicator flashing. Just as he had feared, service in these mountains was very spotty, and right where it was needed, there was none.

He started his truck and drove to the next exit to make a U-turn and return home. He knew he would be facing an extremely upset woman when he got there. When he got close to Lake George village and saw that phone service was now available, instead of calling Kristin, he called his wife.

Bob could feel the temperature beginning to fall. He no sooner began the return trip to the lakeside compound when it began to snow. Off toward the southwest, the skies were a pewter gray. Not a good sign. At this time of the year, the heaviest snowfall of the winter came from the southwest. He feared this one could be trouble.

"Hello," Sally answered.

"Sally, it's me. I need you to do something. Please walk over to Kristin's cabin and wait there for me."

"What's wrong, Bob?" she asked tentatively.

"Something's wrong. John didn't show. I'm worried, and I know Kristin must be frantic. I'm on my way back. She's going to be even more so when she finds out I didn't find John where he was supposed to meet me. She's going to be very upset when I tell her, and I think you being there when I tell her will help."

"I'll walk over right now. How long before you get here?"

"About half an hour."

"Okay. Be safe. It looks like it's going to start snowing here any minute."

He disconnected the call, knowing that Sally would be with Kristin in just a couple of minutes. He felt a minor degree of relief, knowing that he wouldn't have to deal with this alone.

By the time he reached to compound, it was after one o'clock. He very tentatively climbed the steps of John's front porch. He knew that by now, Kristin had figured out what was going on and would be waiting to jump all over the story she was about to hear.

Just as he arrived at the compound, it began to snow. He felt certain that this was the beginning of the forecasted storm coming in from the southwest. Bob entered the cabin to find both Kristin and his wife, Sally sitting on the couch sipping a cup of hot chocolate. To his utter amazement, Kristin was calm and collected.

"Hi, Bob. We've been waiting for you. You've got to be cold from sitting in your truck all this time. Would you like a cup of hot chocolate?" she asked him as if he had just returned from picking flowers in his garden.

"Yes, please," he replied.

As Kristin stood to walk to the kitchen, Bob glanced at his wife. He was confused by Kristin's totally calm demeanor. Sally looked back at him and raised her index finger to her lips signaling him to remain quiet. When Kristin returned with his mug, she sat down on the couch once again.

"Okay," she said, looking at Bob. "Tell me what you know."

Bob went over every minute from the time he and John left the compound the day before, much of which she already knew. He covered the details of what he did this morning and what he observed while waiting at the side of the highway. He finished by filling in everything right up to the time he walked in the front door only minutes ago.

"Okay," she said. "So, at this point, he's somewhere between twelve to fifteen hours overdue, am I correct?"

"Yes," Bob replied.

Her tone was completely business-like, and both Bob and Sally were about to see why.

"Okay, I've sat and waited for John to check in after dozens of assignments over the years I was his control agent. It is not totally unusual for this to happen. Very often, the after-strike timetable doesn't go according to his initial plan. He is extremely precise in planning the exact moment he hits his target.

"However, once that takes place, it alerts everyone around the site and things unfold that he could not anticipate and can not control. When that happens, his entire course of action is to survive, and he will take whatever steps are necessary. And, in this case, he didn't have a precise target or time. Therefore, he would have to see how things unfolded.

In cases like this, he becomes reactive and, as such, isn't always in control of the events or the timing. It can take him a lot longer to end the assignment than originally planned or hoped for. I can remember once it was more than a week before he was able to check in."

"A week!" Sally exclaimed.

"Yes," Kristin answered.

Bob sat listening to her in amazement. She was a total professional. She was dealing with this as if she were back in her office in Washington, D.C., waiting for *agent* Anderson instead of her *husband* John to report in. She personified the terms cool, calm and collected.

"What do we do now?" Sally asked.

"We wait," she answered.

"But…!"

"No buts, Sally. We wait. We give him time. You don't know how good John is at what he does or what he used to do. Under these circumstances, I won't let myself worry quite yet. Let's give it until six this evening."

"Okay," Bob said. "I'll go back up there and park alongside of the road and wait until then."

"I'll come with you," Kristin replied.

"I'll go too," Sally added.

The three stood and put on their warm winter jackets, piled into Bob's truck and drove back to the appointed spot along I-87. They sat silently for the next couple of hours, waiting. John did not show. Six o'clock slipped by. Bob looked at his wristwatch and then at his wife. Sally looked at him, signaling with her glance that he should remain quiet and say nothing.

Finally, at six-thirty, Kristin spoke up.

"Let's go home. We have some work to do."

Bob drove them back home. Along the way, Kristin made one telephone call.

"This is Kristin Anderson," she said to whoever answered her call. "I need to speak to Superintendent Drake. This is an emergency."

There was a slight pause.

"I said this is an emergency. You give him my name, and I can assure you he will take the call."

Another pause.

"Charles, this is Kristin. John is missing. I think he needs our help."

Bob drove back into the lakeside compound shortly after seven thirty that evening. Just as the three of them were getting out of his truck, they heard the thump-thump-thump of helicopter rotor blades slapping the air out over Lake George. They turned toward the lake to see the aircraft with New York State Police markings settle down near the edge of the frozen lake.

When the side door sprang open, two people climbed out. First was a female officer dressed in her uniform. She was immediately followed by Charles Drake dressed in casual clothes. He was obviously not at work when he took Kristin's call.

The state's top cop and his aide came up the slope from the lake and walked directly to John and Kristin's cabin. Following a compulsory greeting, they went inside.

"Okay, tell me what's going on," Drake requested.

Kristin and Bob filled him in completely. They told him everything that John had discussed with them and the plan he had put together. Bob told him about dropping John off by the highway and about waiting for his telephone call to come pick him up. He also filled Drake in on the garbled voicemail message. He then told him about returning to the spot by the road earlier today with Kristin and Sally and finished by filling in all the details right up to the time Kristin called him.

Drake absorbed everything he heard without any comments or questions. When Bob was done talking, Drake lowered his head, contemplating what would come next.

"Bob, how well do you know the area up there by the dude ranch?"

"Fairly well," Bob replied. "Sally and I have driven in there a few times. We were invited to their season-ending cookout a couple of times. That's about it."

"Can you make me a sketch of the grounds?" Drake asked.

"I can do better than that," Sally injected. "I have one of their brochures that has a layout of the grounds, and I have some photos from the cook-outs."

"Great! Can you get them for me, please, Sally?" Drake asked.

Sally left the cabin to return home to retrieve the items she indicated.

Drake then turned to the uniformed female officer who came with him and barked orders at her. She nodded and took out her cell phone to fulfill his directions.

"It's too late for us to do anything tonight. We can't risk barging into a non-surveilled area in the dark. It would be too dangerous for everyone. We'll have to wait for daylight."

"He might be dead by then," Bob injected. "This will be his second night out in the cold. That could kill anyone."

"Do you really think that he is?"

"No!" Kristin injected. "I would know if John was dead. I've been through this too many times with him. I can sense what he is doing. I can feel him. He may be in trouble, but he's alive."

Drake stood and paced around the cabin. He was deep in thought as Kristin spoke again.

"Superintendent Drake, I'll make this easy for you," Kristin spoke up again. "If you don't go in there tonight in force, I'll go in alone."

"I somehow knew you would say that."

Drake turned back to his uniformed aide and barked a series of new orders at her. She immediately began relaying his instructions to whoever was on the other end of her telephone call.

Chapter 28

John continued to monitor the progress of the men chasing him. They were slowing, making his efforts to stay out in front of them much easier. He could feel the temperatures beginning to fall, and it had begun to snow. The air got dense and all the sounds surrounding him seemed muffled and traveled further as it bounced from snowflake to snowflake.

The quiet that came with a snowfall in the forest was magic. The flakes filled the vacuum between the trees. All sound was magnified and intensified, as was the silence. There was no quiet like the forest during a snowfall. It reminded John of when he was a skydiver.

When jumping from an aircraft, once the engine noise was out of range of the jumpers and their parachutes opened, the silence was deafening. He remembered being able to talk to his fellow jumpers thousands of feet away and converse in a normal conversational voice. The quiet was so intense. So peaceful. So totally encompassing he could hear his heart beating.

He could clearly hear the men behind him arguing among themselves. He changed his direction once again. This time, he took a meandering route along the base of a rock-face cliff that was about fifteen feet high. He could tell that the men were tiring. He estimated that the merry chase he had led his pursuers on brought them about six or seven miles away from the dude ranch.

The zig-zag route he has taken made their distance traveled even longer. He guessed that the actual distance they had trudged through the snow was exceeded ten miles. The distance, the cold and, the deep snow and the disorientating zig-zag path he led them on were all adding up and taking their toll on the ill-prepared men giving him chase.

John was sure of a couple of things. First, there was no way these guys could make it back to the dude ranch before dark. If they were from the part of the world that he now suspected, it was clear that they were not experienced cold-weather woodsmen.

Secondly, he knew they were poorly… very poorly equipped. Their clothing and footwear were totally inadequate for this territory and could prove to be fatal.

These two facts, along with the falling snow and dropping temperatures, worked to his advantage. He would continue to bait them and lead them further into the forest in hopes they would soon surrender to the elements and attempt a return to the ranch, breaking off their pursuit. But the new snowfall was rapidly covering all the tracks they left behind, increasing the difficulty and danger of trying to retrace their steps.

Up ahead, he saw an opening in the rocky cliff he was following. He decided to climb to the top of the fifteen-foot high cliff to more clearly see what was going on below and behind him and to make their effort a bit more difficult. It took him only a few minutes to climb to a new vantage point.

From there, off in the distance below him, he could see the men struggling along. The distance between he and them had increased to about three hundred yards. It was difficult to keep them in sight. The combination of the trees and the increasingly heavy snowfall began to limit his visibility, and he was certain theirs as well.

John wanted to be sure that they saw him. He wanted to be sure they continued to be suckered into the chase by thinking he was close enough for them to overtake him. He sat on the rock ledge and waited until he saw one of the men look up and point toward him shouting to the others what he had seen.

John stood and walked away this time, staying on the rocky surface, not leaving any footprints in the surrounding snow. He moved toward the men so that they would pass right below him. Hopefully, this move would confuse them even more by making it difficult to find his trail.

Plus, the light was fading. It was getting late, and the cloud cover from the snowstorm hastened the coming of darkness and excellorated the concealing of his tracks. He hoped that the results would be the men walking in circles looking for him while expending even more time and energy.

It worked! The men in black finally reached the top of the rocky cliff and stopped. They looked around in total confusion, trying to determine which way John had gone. John watched them from atop yet another rocky outcrop a hundred yards away. It was easy for him to see that the men were arguing, confused, disoriented and totally worn out.

Suddenly, an argument broke out among the four men. The tall one, the one John thought to be the leader, stood cowering over one of the others, attempting to dominate. The two men were shouting at each other. John didn't understand the language they spoke but presumed they were arguing about what to do next. The smaller of the two men took a threatening step toward the taller man. When he did, the taller man shoved him, putting his hands on the smaller man's chest and pushing. The smaller man stumbled backward. The taller man took a step forward and pushed the smaller man a second time.

This time, the smaller man stumbled back, slipping on the icy rocks atop the cliff. He attempted to stop himself from losing his balance in the effort. The taller man tried to reach out to grab him to keep him from falling, but it was too late. The smaller man fell backwards, falling head first down over the rocky cliff.

John could plainly see the entire event. The man landed at the bottom of the cliff, smashing his head into the rocks near the base.

John could see his neck twist at an awkward angle when he impacted the ground. He didn't move. He lay there completely still and limp. John knew immediately that neck was broken and that he was dead.

The three remaining men in black looked over the edge of the cliff to see their comrade lying amid the snow and rocks. Two of them scrambled back down the cliff face, leaving the taller leader where he stood. When they reached their companion, they shouted and angrily gestured toward their apparent leader standing on the ledge above them. The man at their feet was clearly dead.

The shouting continued for some time. John continued to watch from his vantage point. He was curious to see what the three remaining men would do next. Clearly, the accident diverted their attention away from him and their pursuit.

It didn't take long to find out what their next move would be. The two men near the corpse sat down on rocks near the body and didn't move. It appeared as if they were praying over their comrade.

Finally, the third man, the taller apparent leader of the group, climbed down to join the other two and their dead comrade. Darkness was rapidly approaching, and it seemed to John as if this was as far as they intended to go today.

John continued to watch the three men. Shortly after sitting down, he saw them wrapping their arms around themselves in an attempt to stay warm. They made no attempt to start a fire. All John could conclude was that they had no way of starting one or they were trying to decide what they would do next. Wait where they were, chase after John or attempt to return to the dude ranch? Their loud arguing continued for a brief period.

John waited. He lost sight of them when darkness finally engulfed the forest. The men were dressed in black blending them into the night, their black clothing blending in with the rocks surrounding them. They became invisible. However, John was sure they would not be going anywhere tonight. He didn't fear them sneaking up on him in the dark. He decided to find a place to huddle up and get some rest.

A few yards from where he sat watching, he found an overhanging rock that offered him a place to get out of the falling snow as well as the wind. He took off his backpack and worked his way into the space. He rummaged through his pack, extracting a couple more protein bars, which he ate quickly, followed by half a bottle of water. He found that his water bottle was partly frozen, but by shaking it hard, he could liquify it enough to satisfy his thirst and his need for fluids.

When he finished his delicious meal, he removed a foil emergency survival bag and a military surplus quilted poncho liner from his pack. He wrapped himself in the liner and pulled the bag up and over his body. The combination of the liner and bag, along with his heavy clothing, was enough to keep himself reasonably comfortable in these conditions.

It wasn't long before the day-long excitement and exertion pulled his eyes down, and the quiet coaxed him to sleep. The snow continued to fall as did the temperature. He wasn't exactly snug as a bug in a rug, but at least he was somewhat protected. The gear he carried with him offered enough comfort and protection to allow him to get some much-needed rest. For John, the day was done.

His thoughts wandered to Kristin. Where was she? What was she thinking? What was she doing? Was she okay? He knew she would be worried, but he also knew that her professional experience would surface, and she would once again become his control agent. He was confident that her professional experience and instincts would kick in.

She had been through this with him before. She had lived through his delayed return from missions in remote areas of the world. He had faith in her and knew she had faith in him. Most of all, he knew they would be together again in a very short time.

He fell asleep warmed by her presence.

Chapter 29

The gravel parking lot near the Warrensburg exit off I-87 became the staging area. By eight o'clock that evening, a dozen highway patrol cars plus two ambulances, a couple of Warren County Sheriff vehicles, and four hunter-green Forest Ranger pickup trucks were all assembled with red, white and blue lights flashing. Anyone driving by on the interstate and seeing the concentration of official vehicles and flashing lights would imagine a major event had just taken place.

Kristin, Bob and Sally were parked among the gaggle of official vehicles, sitting warmly inside Bob's truck. Superintendent Drake was due at any moment. He had clearly organized a task force large enough to handle anything that might come their way from the unknown suspects and the unknown conditions within the dude ranch. What the three of them were witnessing was a typical government overkill response to anything.

Drake finally arrived in his unmarked black sedan. Only moments behind him was another official-looking sedan with two men inside. Kristin immediately recognized the occupant to be Don Costa from the Department of Homeland Security.

All the law enforcement personnel quickly gathered around the superintendent to get their final orders. However, it wasn't Drake who issued the marching orders. As any good commander should, Drake directed his senior officers to take control of the operation as he stood aside to add his authority to their orders for carrying out the plan that had been developed within the past couple of hours.

After a few minutes, Drake walked to Bob's truck. Bob rolled down the two windows on the driver's side so Drake could speak to both he and Kristin.

"Okay, here's what we're going to do. We can't put our helicopter in the air because of the heavy snow. So, we're going to go in hard and fast on the ground. We'll drive in two abreast with no sirens and no lights until we get within a quarter of a mile. One of the Rangers from the local barracks knows the area well and will lead the way. Once we reach a point close to the main camp, all vehicles will turn on their lights and sirens. The display will overwhelm anyone in the camp.

"You guys are to come in last. One of our patrol cars will stop about a half mile from the ranch. You are to stop there with him. I don't what you anywhere near the front should there be any shooting. We don't know what to expect. We must be prepared for the worst, and putting something like this together this fast makes a lot of people with guns very nervous, and we have to assume they are armed.

"Once we're in there and get things secured, we'll radio the patrol car that is with you, and he will escort you to the main camp. Then, we'll deal with whatever we find. Got it?"

Kristin and Bob both nodded in understanding. They remained in the truck awaiting further instructions. In less than five minutes, the State Police vehicles began moving down the ramp onto the highway. Bob followed the last official vehicle. The entire caravan drove north on Interstate 87 to the next exit, where all vehicles took the off-ramp. One of the state patrol cars pulled into and blocked all traffic on the road leading to the iron bridge, allowing the remaining official cars and pick-up trucks to proceed in an uninterrupted line.

When they reached the snow-covered dirt road leading to the dude ranch, the patrol cars realigned themselves two abreast. Once the entire task force was properly in place, the vehicles began moving along the dirt road, two abreast at a slow, even pace. No cars approached from either direction anywhere along the route to the dude ranch.

The line-up of law enforcement vehicles slowly closed the gap toward the dude ranch. Then, suddenly, as if done with a single switch, all the rooftop-mounted light bars lit up, and sirens of all the vehicles came screeching to life at the same instant.

Following at the rear of the pact, Bob was damn near blinded by the bright lights destroying the total darkness of the surrounding forest. The blaring of the sirens bouncing off the trees bordering the road was deafening. The falling snow made matters worse. Red, blue and white lights reflecting off the snowflakes were both beautifully and blinding, creating a holiday atmosphere.

The vehicles scattered as they entered the clearing surrounding the ranch buildings. Their movement seemed to be choreographed and rehearsed for days instead of minutes. The maneuver looked like a well-planned military attack. From their distant observation point, Bob, Kristin and Sally were totally impressed by the way the multi-jurisdictional units carried out the maneuver as if they had practiced together for years.

All the vehicles came to a sliding stop with the two front doors of each flying open, an armed officer jumping out of each. A loud bullhorn blasted the area with new commands. Any human inside any of the buildings who had half a brain and any sense of self-preservation would be scared shitless by this display of force.

"Inside the building. Come out with your hands over your head. Do it now!" the command came blasting from a bullhorn.

Most of the officers held hand guns pointed toward the dining hall. A few held rifles, and a few others, shotguns. In all, there were nearly three dozen weapons pointed at the door they awaited to open.

"Inside the dining hall. Come out with your hands above your head. Do not have anything in your hands, or you will be shot. Do it now!"

Nothing moved! The tension stiffened. Once more…

"Anybody inside the dining hall, come out now. Put your hands above your head and come outside. Do it now, or we will we release our dogs. Do it now!"

Two officers flanked the building armed with tear gas guns. They would await the signal from the officer in command before firing the canisters into the building. Once they did, other officers would storm the doorways.

It would not be necessary. The front door slowly swung open. One lone man dressed in black slowly stepped out into the night. He had one arm raised over his head and the other across his forehead, shielding his eyes from all of the flashing lights.

"Move forward. Walk to the vehicle right in front of you," he was commanded.

When he reached the nearest patrol car, he was tackled to the ground by two officers and placed in handcuffs. The same two officers got him up on his feet. Another placed his face less than two inches from his nose and began shouting questions at him.

"How many more people are inside? Where are the other men? Where is the man who came here alone?"

The man in black was clearly shaken. He was very young and very frightened. He began to tremble, followed by tears rolling down his face. He was shaking his head.

"No one is inside. I am alone."

"Where is the man who came here yesterday?" the questioning officer barked.

"They… they went after him. He was hiding over there. He ran into the forest. All the other went after him."

"How many? How many men went after him?"

"Four!"

A hand signal was given, and half a dozen state police with guns drawn rushed toward the doorway leading into the dining hall. Their tactical approach looked like a prime-time television show.

Kristin, Bob and Sally had driven to the edge of the clearing and continued to wait in Bob's truck. They had rolled down the windows to hear what was going on. They could hear all the orders and questions being shouted around the clearing. They could also hear the officers who rushed the building shouting the 'clear' signal as they went from room to room searching for additional people.

"Search all the other buildings in the compound," the officer in charge instructed his men. "Consider anyone you see to be armed and dangerous. No one goes into a building alone. Report anything unusual immediately."

His men scattered running in pairs toward the other buildings encircling the clearing as well as the lake. It took less than five minutes before one of the searching men yelled out to his boss.

"Sir, I think you'd better take a look at this," he yelled, standing next to a small shed near a wood pile.

The officer in charge of the operation, as well as his boss, Superintendent Drake, walked toward the small shed next to a wood pile. Bob and Kristin exchanged a glance, both thinking the same thing. There must be something in that shed, but what? Was it John? Was he dead? Did they find his body? Bob decided to find out.

He jumped out of this truck and started to walk across the clearing toward the shed. Before he got there, Superintendent Drake emerged from the shed and walked toward Bob.

"What's in there?" Bob asked him.

"Bodies!"

"Bodies!? Is John…?"

"No, John is not in there."

"Who… how many…?" Bob stumbled to get the question out.

"There are five bodies in there. All have been beheaded. Looks like we found our clergymen."

"Damn!"

"Yeah," Drake responded. "This seals the deal on these guys being our killers. John was right. He found them. Now we have to find him."

"Superintendent!" came another call. This time, it was one of the state policemen inside the dining hall. "You need to see this."

Drake and his incident commander walked toward the dining hall. Bob returned to his truck to calm Kristin and to tell her what had been found. Most of all, he needed to tell her what was not found. That John was not among the dead. That he was still missing.

Ten minutes later, Superintendent Drake came back out into the clearing and walked to Bob's truck. Bob lowered his window to hear what Drake reported.

"We found two more bodies in a food locker behind the kitchen. A man and a woman. One of my local guys knows them. It's the owners of the dude ranch. Husband and wife. They've been shot in the back of the head. Bodies are frozen solid. Looks like they've been dead for quite some time. I'm guessing they were the first victims and were killed when these guys first got here and took over the ranch."

"What now?" Kristin asked.

Just then, yet another call came. This time on the radio. Drake listened and then responded. The call came from officers searching one of the buildings at the far end of the compound. Drake turned and started walking toward the call. This time, he was followed by three anxious people wanting to know where their friend and husband were.

When they reached the officer making the call, he reported that they had found what looked like where someone had been sleeping. He then pointed down at the snow and aimed his flashlight toward the woods. There was a clear trail of footprints leading away from the clearing and up the hill away from the dude ranch. It was clear that the trail was made by more than one person.

"Get the Forest Rangers up here," Drake commanded.

It took only a minute or two before four uniformed New York State Forest Rangers arrived where there was now a group gathering.

"What do you think?" Drake asked the senior Ranger.

"Looks to me like at least three or four people have plowed their way up the hill. Hard to tell for sure, the fresh snowfall has partially obscured the tracks."

"Can you follow the trail?" Drake asked.

"Sure, we can, but not tonight. At least not until we can get some equipment up here. It would be much easier and much faster if we had our snow machines here. Following on foot in this snow will be very difficult and very slow going."

"How long will it take to get your equipment here?"

"Let me check. I believe we have equipment in the Warrensburg garage. I'll be back with you in a few minutes," the Ranger lieutenant said.

Drake turned back to address Kristin, Bob and Sally.

"Look, you guys, this is going to take a while for us to get things sorted and figure out what's going on and how we are going to proceed. I can't let you into any of these buildings to warm up. Right now, they're all part of the crime scene. Why don't you go back home, warm up and get some rest? I'll call you as soon as we know anything."

"Are you out of your friggin' mind?" Kristin blurred out. "That's my husband you're trying to find. I'm not going anywhere."

"Neither are we," Sally added vehemently without even looking at her husband. "We stay right here until we know John is okay."

Bob looked at Drake and shrugged his shoulders in submissive agreement.

"Looks like we're here no matter how long things might take," he told Superintendent Drake.

"Okay, go back to your truck and try to stay warm. I'm afraid we're going to be here all night. Try to rest. I'm going to order my field support unit to get some hot food and drinks up here ASAP. When they get here, I'll let you know."

The roar of a revved-up angry truck engine roaring toward the dude ranch clearing, being chased by a police car with lights flashing, caught everyone's attention. Everyone was aware of the action tensed in anticipation of an attack of some sort. Maybe the four missing men had returned. Maybe they were on a suicide charge against the authorities on the scene.

"That's Gretchen's truck," Bob blurted out.

His recognition and declaration immediately eased the situation. Drake and his commander yelled out commands for his men not to fire upon the approaching vehicle. Gretchen slid to a stop only yards away from where Kristin and the others were standing. The driver's side door flew open, and a very angry-looking woman stepped out of the truck and stomped toward the group, watching her approach.

"Why didn't you call me?" she demanded.

"Gretchen, I…" Kristin stammered.

"Gretchen, my ass! Why didn't you call me?"

Drake stepped between the two women. "Calm down! Who are you, and how did you get in here?" he demanded.

Gretchen totally ignored the state's top cop and continued to address Kristin and Bob over Drake's shoulder.

"That's my boy out there; why didn't you let me know what was going on?"

Bob took over. "Gretchen, everything happened so fast. We didn't have time."

"The hell you didn't! It would have taken only a few seconds to make a telephone call."

Kristin stepped up to the distraught woman she had grown to love and laced her arms around her neck.

"I'm sorry, Gretchen," she said in a soft, loving voice. "Everything happened so fast. We were so absorbed with helping John."

Gretchen softened immediately. "Where is he? Is he okay?"

"Let's sit in the truck to keep warm, and I'll fill you in on everything," Kristin said. "How did you find out what's going on and where to find us?"

"Kristin, this is Lake George, not Washington, D.C. You can't have this many vehicles charging up the road with their lights flashing, looking like Christmas trees on steroids in this area without everyone knowing something's going on. Besides, I work part-time for the police department, remember?"

The four retreated to Bob's truck to get out of the cold as best they could. The commotion around the dude ranch and Gretchen's splashy arrival increased as the night progressed. Police units came and went. The medical examiner arrived to inspect the bodies.

Around two o'clock in the morning, two plain black sedans pulled into the clearing. Four people emerged from each car. They were dressed in business attire, including low-cut street shoes.

"F.B.I.," Kristin said to no one in particular. "They stick out like a sore thumb. I've worked with them for years. They're here for a reason. See that guy standing over there next to Drake's car? That's Don Costa. He's with DHS. He's the top dog on the scene. The F.B.I. will run everything through him."

The federal agents found Superintendent Drake and had an impromptu meeting standing in the snow. Drake summoned the task force, and together, they provided the feds with an update on the situation. When they were done, all the federal agents moved into the center of action. Six walked into the dining hall, while two went to the shed where the five bodies were found.

The wind died down, and the snow finally came to an end. The entire dude ranch became engulfed in the exhaust fumes being emitted from the nearly two dozen federal, state, county and local police vehicles and ambulances gathered around the compound clearing. The hot fumes pumped into the cold still air creating a heavy cloud trying to suffocate all life forms within the area. It was almost impossible to see from one side of the clearing to the other.

"I wonder why these guys never turn off their engines," Bob asked. "Seems like a lot of gas is being wasted."

"They don't care," Sally added. "It's government gas. They're not paying for it. We are."

The clock continued to drag by. Sally finally gave in and dozed off in the back seat of Bob's truck. Bob rested his head on the steering wheel and managed to squeeze in a few minutes of sleep as well. Kristin and Gretchen remained totally focused on the activities taking place around them.

At six-thirty in the morning, the EMT people from the ambulances began carrying out the five headless bodies as well as the owners of the ranch. First came the two from the freezer locker near the rear of the kitchen. Shortly after them, the five from the shed were loaded into the rear of the waiting white and red vehicles and driven away. After a brief discussion with the scene commander, one of the federal agents, along with the medical examiner, left the area for parts unknown.

At first light, five well-armed Forest Rangers mounted high-powered snowmobiles that had finally arrived from Warrensburg aboard two trailers hauled in by Ranger trucks. They took off with engines roaring as the sky began turning from black to grey. The machines quickly penetrated the surrounding forest and disappeared. It promised to be a cold, dull day with ground-hugging fog shrouding the activities that continued all around the dude ranch.

Eight o'clock came and went. Then nine! By ten o'clock, most of the medically related vehicles had departed from the compound. Their work was completed with the removal of the seven bodies found on the premises. For each of the medical personnel who left, it seemed as if they were replaced by two new faces. Kristin knew these new people on the scene were the crime scene investigators. They would comb through every nook and cranny of every building as well as every square inch of the property, looking for clues.

Who were these strangers? Where did they come from? Why did they kill seven people? Why all clergy except for the owners? Why were they dressed in black? Where and how did they kill and decapitate the victims? The "who, what, when and where" wouldn't end until they extracted every possible bit of information they could find. Individual hairs, dust particles, fingerprints, toothbrushes and dirty socks. Anything and everything connected to or associated with the five culprits found to be living there and… killing people.

Kristin watched. Riveted to the activity unfolding all around her. And she waited! As she had so many times in their previous professional life, she waited. Waited for her husband to magically appear before her.

Chapter 30

And he did!

Finally, he did!

It was nearly two o'clock in the afternoon. A loud commotion coming from the north end of the compound drew everyone's attention. A noisy snowmobile, driven by one of the Forest Rangers, emerged from the tree line. It carried two people. The man in front driving wore a white uniform, clearly showing his official insignia. The man seated behind the driver with his arms wrapped around the Ranger, holding on tight, was wearing clothes she recognized.

She knew immediately. She didn't need to see his face. She knew. The doors to Bob's truck flew open, and Kristin, Gretchen, Bob and Sally dashed toward the oncoming snow machine. Superintendent Drake, as well as the senior officer on the scene, came rushing out of the dining hall. The Ranger driving the machine brought it to a stop next to the lone remaining ambulance on the scene.

Kristin was in a full run when she reached the two men. She ran past a dozen police officers and knocked another half dozen out of her way as she ran toward the snowmobile. She looked like an NFL fullback plowing through a Pop Warner team of fifth graders. She launched herself into John's arms, knocking both to the ground. She lay on top of him, sobbing uncontrollably.

They lay there for what seemed like forever. Sally stepped up to Kristin and whispered in her ear.

"Kristin, honey. You need to let him up. I think these people want to speak to him."

Kristin lifted her head. She peeked from beneath her hat that had slid down over her forehead. She saw that she and John were surrounded by a large group of broadly smiling, gun-toting police officers, including Superintendent Drake. She uncurled herself from around John's body, permitting him to get to his feet, and was helped by two state patrolmen to do the same.

Drake stepped in, taking John by the hand. He tried to lead John to a quiet area. Kristin would not let go of her husband. She clung to him like ivy to a brick wall. Drake led them into a large command post tent that had been set up to house the investigative process underway. Gretchen, Bob and Sally followed close behind when they entered the tent; all four embraced, sharing their joy at John's return.

"Clear the area," Drake commanded. "I need some quiet privacy with Mr. Anderson." Within seconds, the five were alone inside the tent.

"Got any hot coffee in this joint?', John asked while holding Kristen tightly and closely with his arm wrapped around her shoulders.

"I'll take care of it," Drake said as the four close friends continued to absorb John's safe return. "Please bring a pot of hot coffee and some food," Drake ordered one of his officers standing near the entrance to the tent. He let the celebration continue until the coffee and food arrived.

John took a cup and held it with both hands wrapped around the hot ceramic. He then took a sandwich of unknown content and gobbled it down.

"We need to talk," Drake said after a few minutes had elapsed.

"Yeah, I know," John answered.

"Where are the four guys who came after you?" Drake asked.

"The other Rangers are bringing them in. They were having a hard time loading them onto their sleds."

"How were they handcuffing two prisoners per sled?"

"They weren't cuffing them. They were loading them on."

"Loading them?! What do you mean loading?"

"They're dead."

"Dead!?" Drake shouted. "What do you mean… Damn it, John. I warned you. I made it clear that you didn't have the authority to do anything with these people. I told you that you couldn't apprehend them or arrest them, and I damn sure made it clear that you couldn't walk up and kill them like you did in your old life."

"Calm down, Charles."

"Calm down my ass. I told you that if you did anything, I'd run your ass in. What the hell were you thinking going after these guys?"

"I didn't go after them; they came after me," John said with a smirk painted across his face.

"You think this is funny? You think you can laugh your way through this?"

"Nope!" John responded, still displaying a big grin, now enjoying the annoyance he was causing the superintendent.

"So, what are you going to do, claim self-defense? That won't cut it. Not with me, John. Damn it, this pisses me off to no end. This really pisses me off. I gave you very clear and direct orders!"

Drake was shouting at this point. He stood and paced back and forth in front of John and Kristin. Gretchen, Bob and Sally sat as silent onlookers, not knowing what to do or expect. Just as Drake was about to start lashing into John once again, a head poked into the tent. John stood by, allowing Drake to shout and vent.

"Superintendent," the man poking his head in the tent shouted.

"WHAT?" Drake shouted in response.

"They're coming in."

"Who's coming in? What are you talking about?"

"The other Rangers. They just got back. They have the four bodies with them."

Drake turned back to John. "Don't move. This isn't over. Not by a long shot. I'll be right back, and you can plan on me cuffing you and dragging your ass off to jail."

"I'll be right here," John replied with a smirk still on his face.

"You think this is funny? You won't think this is funny when I get back, John. Don't move from this tent." Drake left the tent in a huff. Kristin took her husband by the arm.

"John, what did you do? What's going to happen?"

"What's my middle name, baby girl?" he asked her, smiling.

"Nothi…"

"Exactly!"

The four of them sat in the tent, hearing the Ranger-driven snowmobiles pulling up to the waiting crowd of officers. There was suddenly a great deal of commotion outside of the tent, with so many people talking and shouting orders that nothing could be understood.

The few minutes Drake expected to be delayed from hauling John off to jail stretched to almost half an hour. When he returned, he was subdued to the point of having his tail between his legs.

"Why didn't you tell me?" he asked John.

"Well, Charles. You didn't exactly give me a chance to say much. You sort of got your ass on your shoulders and stormed off with your mind made up that I killed them and you were going to slap cuffs on me. Remember?" John said sarcastically.

"Okay, you're right," Drake said as he took a chair and sat down. "Please start at the beginning and tell me everything. I want all the details from the time Bob dropped you off by the interstate."

John relayed the entire story to the Superintendent as well as to Kristin and the others. He provided all the detail he could, including the crossing of the river at the very beginning of his hike making a mental note to himself that he needed to return there to retrieve his waders.

Then he told them about encountering the bear and how close a call he had with the wild critter. Next, he told them about how he first came upon the dude ranch and, observed the men in black and learned that there was a fifth individual.

Next, he told them how he had discovered the bodies in the shed and how he had sat in the snow between the shed and the wood pile. He told them about breaking into the cabin to find a place to get out of the weather and spend the night and instead found the bodies.

He filled them in about finding another building open and finding a place to get some sleep. Then, the next morning and how, he was first seen trying to dash across the clearing to get back on his own trail to the interstate. He gave Drake a blow-by-blow account of the day-long chase through the woods to the north of the dude ranch and how poorly dressed and ill-equipped his pursuers were.

He told them how he zigged and zagged, stretching out the effort in hopes of leading them further and further away from the ranch. How they tired and slowed as the day progressed while he continued to lead them on a wild goose chase. Then he told them about the man taking a header off the cliff after being pushed twice by the tallest of the men, the apparent leader of the group.

Next, he told them how the remaining three circled the corpse and argued amongst themselves and how he didn't understand a word of what they were saying or what language they were saying it in.

Then he told them how he sat and watched the three remaining men sit near the body as darkness approached and how he found a nook in the cliff face to wrap himself up and spend the night.

"I knew that by the time the sun came up, I would be alone out there. All three of them were shaking before dark, and it was getting colder every minute. When I woke up this morning, I walked to the edge of the cliff and looked over. Three of them were sitting up like cement statues. The fourth guy, the one who fell, was covered in snow. The other three were frozen stiff, deader than a doornail.

"I started hiking back here right away. There was no way I could do anything with the bodies, and I knew they would be retrieved by you guys either now or in the spring. Either way, they were just as dead.

"After I hiked for a couple of hours, I heard the snow machines. Figured it was you guys finally coming out looking for me? It was one of the Rangers tracking me. When they found the four dead guys and then found my separate fresh tracks leaving the area, one came after me. When he finally caught up to me, he told me the others that were with him stayed with the bodies to load them up somehow and get them back here to the ranch.

"So, you see, Charles. I didn't touch them which I'm sure you found out from the Rangers. Once the M.E. examines the bodies, you'll see that I never got close to them until they were already dead. I didn't have to. My dear old pal, Mother Nature took care of the problem for me as well as for you and the State of New York. Those guys got exactly what they deserved."

They all sat quietly, letting John's story sink in. Kristin held onto her husband as if he might lift off and float away. Drake let out a deep sigh before speaking again.

"Okay, John. What you're telling me matches up with what the Rangers told me outside."

"Hold it a second, Charles," John butted in. "What happened to the fifth guy, the one that stayed behind?"

"We have him in custody. He came out of the dining hall whimpering like a little girl when we came at him with our little army of officers. We scared the crap out of him. I got a radio call about an hour ago. Turns out he's only fourteen years old.

"Oh, in addition to the five bodies in the shed, we also found the ranch owner and his wife out back in a food locker. They've been dead for a while. M.E. has them back in Albany for examination. He'll come up with a time and cause of death, but I don't expect he'll come up with any surprises."

"Damn," John said. "These bastards needed dying!"

"Yeah, now go home and get some rest. I'll bet a hot shower would feel fantastic right about now."

"What about you?" John asked.

"Looks like we'll be here at least for the rest of today. There's a lot to clean up before we leave and then we need to secure this place since the owners are now dead. I'm sure there are going to be a lot of nosey folks poking around with their little cameras, trying to add to their scrapbooks. We are trying to contact their next of kin and get someone in here to care for the place.

"You guys go home," Drake continued. "Get some rest and that hot shower. I'll call you when we wrap things up here. Might not be today or even tomorrow. There are a lot of loose ends we need to grab ahold of with this case. I think our lab techs will stir up even more stuff we're going to have to examine once they finish processing the main building.

'Right now, I will bring the feds up-to-date. Your buddy Costa and his minions from the F.B.I. have been hanging around all night waiting to see if you came out of this in one piece."

"Okay," John answered. "We'll just kick back and wait for your call."

Chapter 31

It didn't take a day or even two days. It took nearly a week before Superintendent Drake called John. The media coverage of the story was running wild. Speculation about the men in black, their motive, how they were found, the owners of the dude ranch.

Who was the mysterious civilian said to have solved the case. Rumors ran wild. But fortunately, John and his tight knit little group living in a secluded compound on the shores of Lake George remained anonymous. Nothing in the news led the press to their doorstep. John's phone finally rang.

"Hello!"

"John, it's Charles Drake."

"Hey, how are you?"

"Fine, thanks. Things have been rather hectic, as you can imagine."

"I'm sure they have been. How are things coming along?"

"Well, that's why I'm calling. I'd like to meet with you to discuss a few things. And I'd like to have Bob and Kristin there as well."

"What about Sally?"

"She's welcome to attend if she would like."

"When and where?"

"How about here in my office the day after tomorrow? Say ten o'clock? I think I can get the State to spring for lunch."

"Okay, we'll be there."

"Good! See you then," Drake added as he ended the call.

John talked with Bob and Kristin to coordinate the trip to Albany. Sally decided to sit at home and not attend. She announced that she would rather stay at home and prepare a nice hot dinner for them to return to. Bob directed a question to John and Kristin.

"What should we expect from this meeting?"

"This is standard," Kristin answered. "After every mission, or in this instance, a criminal case, there is debrief. I went through dozens and dozens of them. They will tell us as much as they think we need to know. Do not expect to get all the details. And, they will ask us some questions to fill in a few blanks they may still have. And then, if we're lucky, we get a free lunch.

"But," she continued. "Take your time answering any questions they might throw at us. You'll never know what they know and what they don't know. And you'll never know if they are probing and trying to catch you in a lie. So, say what's necessary and only what's necessary."

"Kristin knows far more about this part of the activity than I do," John added. "She had to attend all these meetings when we worked together. I was somewhere else in the world, and coming in for meetings wasn't a smart thing for me to be doing. So, I think we'll have to let her take the lead when we meet with Drake."

"Sounds good to me," Bob replied.

They arrived at Superintendent Drake's office shortly before ten in the morning on the appointed day. They were greeted warmly with nods, smiles and lots of hand-shakes. Drake's secretary met them at the elevator and led them to the sprawling conference room next to his office.

They were greeted by Drake and a dozen other of his top assistant superintendents and aides. They all stood and applauded as John entered the room. Sitting quietly at the far end of the table was DHS agent Don Costa. When the room finally quieted, Drake took the lead.

"John, we obviously want to thank you for your efforts in solving these murders and for putting your life at risk to bring these guys to justice. We would like to wrap things up by filling in any blanks, answering any questions you might have and presenting a few questions of our own."

"Fine by me. However, if you don't mind, I'm going to defer to Kristin as our lead. She's a lot better and far more experienced with these kinds of meetings than either Bob or me."

"Fair enough," Drake added. "I'm going to do something similar and let each of my department heads provide you with the information they have."

He gestured to his left toward the first of his assistant Superintendents. One department head after the other presented the portion of the case within their area of responsibility. Much of the information was already known to the three civilian guests. They already knew all the information leading up to the final couple of days prior to John hiking into the dude ranch. In fact, they knew the information long before these men ever got involved.

But, the game required a full review so as not to make anyone feel left out of the process and have their efforts overlooked. This was one of those mission recap meetings where all egos needed a bit of stroking.

The finding of the heads on the ice, the determination of who each head belonged to, the name of each, where they came from, etc, etc, etc. Finally, the presentation reached the information John had hoped to hear.

First, the fifth man. He was alive and healthy, currently being held in the basement of the very building the meeting was being held in. From the questioning of this individual, a lot has been learned. He was the youngest of the group of five. That's why he was left behind each time a head was being placed on the ice and when the others went after John. He was some sort of a trainee.

The kid was scared to death, being alone and surrounded by the police. When questioned, it was reported that he was talking faster than the interrogators and translators could ask questions. Information was pouring out of him.

All five were originally from the same Middle Eastern country and came separately to the United States via Belgium. They all entered by walking across the U.S./Canadian border at various tourist attractions where security was soft, including Niagara Falls.

Each was met by a different contact person and brought to a farm somewhere in central Ohio. They all arrived at different times. He told them that there were others there when they arrived and that the others were assigned to other teams. Once all five were there, they spent the next three months planning and practicing their assignment.

"Assignment!?" John interrupted.

"Yes, assignment," the officer making the presentation continued. "That's the way he described it. They were matched up and assigned as teams and each team was designated an assignment. Sounded more like a mission to me."

The captive claimed that all five had been trained and selected for this specific assignment. The killing of only clergy representing different Christian religions was designed to send a message to the "Christian devils" and strike fear in all other clergy members.

Lake George had been selected because of its remote location particularly at this time of year. Plus, winter offered additional advantages, further isolating the area while having an interstate highway close by should a dash and escape to Canada be necessary. They believed that being in a rural area, it was less likely they would be caught. They were trained to believe that all local law enforcement in the United States was conducted by the F.B.I. and only in Washington, D.C. and New York City.

He also provided the identity of the other four members of the team. John had been correct; the tallest man was the team leader. One sobering bit of information was that the men were not finished. Their assignment called for the killing of a total of ten clergy in this area, five more than they managed thus far.

They were supposed to stay at the dude ranch until their assignment was complete, and then they were to move on to another location. He didn't know where that was to be. They were to be told that when their time and killing here was complete.

When the last officer completed his report, the room quieted. John spoke first.

"Is this a state or federal case," he directed at Superintendent Drake.

"Federal," Drake answered. "The F.B.I. and Homeland Security took once it was confirmed that the five team members came from another country. The whole issue is now classified and being treated as a terrorist attack. We are cooperation with the feds and providing them with access to our facilities."

"Makes sense," John added.

"Yeah, and it gets it off our plate. I don't think this will be the end of the story. I think our friend down in the basement is going to lead the D.C. guys to bigger and better things. And I'm sure Agent Costa would agree," Drake added, glancing toward the man seated at the far end of the table.

"John," Drake continued. "We have an issue of major concern… at least potentially of major concern."

The two men looked at one another, knowing that what was about to be said wasn't good news. Drake continued.

"The guy in the basement also told us that there is a second team currently operating or in the process of setting up for their mission somewhere else in the U.S."

"Doesn't surprise me," John said.

"No, it doesn't. However, he also told us that each team was told that if one team was captured or killed, the second was to take revenge. They were to infiltrate the area where the first team failed and take out those responsible for their failure. I'm afraid that puts the three of you, as well as Sally and potentially even Gretchen, in danger."

Once again, the room went completely silent. It was Kristin who spoke first this time. She also very deliberately made eye contact with Agent Costa.

"Superintendent Drake," she addressed the man in charge formally for effect. "You and I and my husband have talked about his former life. And mine, as well. From all you have said, I believe you... and others in this room think that you know who he is and what he has done in the past.

"Let me assure you. You don't! If you have a dossier on John that's an inch thick, it's lacking another foot. If you think you know all there is to know about him, I can assure you that you're not even close.

"The only person alive who knows him besides himself is me. I was his control officer for years. I ran his missions and monitored every day of his life. I know what he did, where he did it and how his assignments were completed. Every detail.

What I'm getting at is this. Should you find out who the second team is, please send them our way if you need assistance. Call us. If you need training on how to deal with them, call us. And if you need them dead… call us.

"What I can also tell you is that should anyone decide to come after us, to do us harm or try to kill us, they will be met with… shall we say, stiff and swift reaction. Reaction they will not survive."

She made eye contact with only two of the many people in the room. She looked only at Drake and at Costa.

Agent Costa spoke for the first time since the meeting began.

"Superintendent Drake, may I please ask you to clear the room of all but yourself?"

All the other senior people in the room looked at their boss. Drake gave them a dismissal nod, and two minutes later, the room was cleared with the exception of the three civilians, Superintendent Drake and Department of Homeland Security Special Agent in Charge Don Costa.

The room quieted with four sets of eyes focused on Costa waiting for him to explain why he wanted the room cleared.

"First, Kristin, even though we worked together for only a very brief time, it's good seeing you again, and I'm very glad to see you happy, doing well and recovering from your wounds."

"Thank you," she replied very stiffly.

"John… or do you prefer Lucas now?"

"John will do just fine."

"Very well. And Bob, I know your background and connection to John, and I applaud you for your loyalty, and I'm sure John does as well. And I'd like to thank you for your service to our country in uniform and out."

"Thank you, but why am I here? I was never employed by the agency. I never got through the training program."

"Yes, I know. However, your continued support and relationship with John connects you to him and to the things that might affect him. And you were certainly a vital part of the recent operations. So, I thought you would like to hear what I've got to say."

"Okay, got it!" Bob acknowledged.

"Good. Okay, so let me begin. John, I know my presence and my revealing that I know who you are… or at least who you were, and your past history might be somewhat upsetting to you and your wife. And I know that Superintendent Drake has some knowledge as well. So, I wanted to put your concerns to rest.

"I know of your history only because of the time I spent in the same office as Kristin. I want to assure you that your file has indeed been removed from the federal records. Totally removed and, so far as I know, destroyed. You technically never existed.

"However, like Superintendent Drake, I recognize a potentially valuable resource when I see one. After all, that's why he approached you and got you involved in this very complex case at the very beginning. The proof of his foresight has been proven by what you did to that led us to this very moment.

"What I wanted to let you know… to ask you… is what the future might hold for you in other difficult cases. You see, you bring a totally different perspective to the table, one that we don't have and, quite frankly, don't necessarily understand. In addition, you have, shall I call it, a certain skill set that the superintendent's people don't have and aren't permitted to obtain nor use even if they did.

"I know I have a certain reputation, but exposing private citizens is not part of my resume' no matter what Mr. LaBue might want you to believe. So, I'm asking you, would you and your wife consider lending your assistance in future cases? If you agree to do so, I will assure you that your identity, along with those of everyone close to you, will be protected and that you will be provided with an extremely high level of security."

John was about to respond when Kristin grabbed his hand, sensing the emotion that began to stiffen her husband's body. He paused at the touch of her hand composing himself.

"Agent Costa," he began. "I heard that exact speech not so very long ago. It didn't hold up. In addition, as my beautiful wife said earlier, if you think you know me, you don't. If you think you know what I have done, you don't. If you think you know what I'm capable of, once again, you don't.

"Kristin and I, along with Bob and his wife Sally, currently live a fairly simple life. We feel safe and secure and appreciate knowing that our past is history."

"I know the roll you played in the death of the president," Costa interrupted.

"No, you don't. You only think you do. What you think you know is not fact; it's purely speculation, and I assure you it's wrong," John replied. "And your statement alone makes me believe you would attempt to hold that suspicion over my head… to blackmail me. Let me assure you, that would be a mistake… a very big mistake.

"I intend to return to our home and renew our life. What I will do as any husband should do… I will protect and provide for my family, and I will love those close to me and do whatever I can for them. And should anything threaten us, should anyone threaten us… . any of us, in any way, I will react. Those things I will promise you.

"What I will not do is willingly and knowingly expose those that I love to any threats to their safety and security. And, should anyone… anyone… in any way come into our lives in any unwelcome manner, then and only then will you truly come to know and understand what I am capable of."

The two men stared into each other's eyes, communicating in ways words could not. The tension in the room was stifling. Agent Costa finally broke the silence.

"Understood, John. I would expect nothing less. Before I end this meeting, I once again want to assure you that whatever secrets you may have are safe with me. I wish to leave here, hoping we can be friends, not enemies. That is my sincerest wish."

John studied the man for a moment. "I accept that Agent Costa, and I hope that if we ever meet or talk again, it will be with that understanding. Superintendent Drake and his wife have offered us the same, and we have begun to develop just such a much-welcomed relationship with them. Kristin and I leave that door open to you as well."

"Good," Costa replied. "Now, let me fill you in on a couple of other pieces of information resulting from your breaking this case.

The young man we have in custody has been providing us with a lot of information. As a result, we have strong leads to similar groups in at least four other states. We have also found that the incidents in Michigan were not conducted by this group but by another who we now believe has left the United States. However, from the information we were able to get from our young friend in the basement, we were able to provide the Michigan authorities with enough information to lead them to finding the missing bodies, providing some peace to the families.

"So, you see, your actions have had some far-reaching positive effects. I hope these results help you understand why I had to ask you if you would work with us in the future. You have proven to be a very valuable team member. I would be remiss if I didn't attempt to recruit you once again."

"Fair enough," John replied.

Chapter 32

They skipped lunch. Neither John, Kristin, nor Bob were in the mood for what would surely have been a stiffly forced time together. This was not a social gathering of drinking buddies and their wives.

Instead, Bob called ahead to Sally and had her meet them at their favorite pizza joint in the middle of Lake George village. The four friends sat in the nearly empty restaurant and talked quietly among themselves. The village had finally returned to its normal, sleepy wintertime existence.

Bob took the lead in bringing his wife up to date on all the information presented at the meeting. When she heard what Kristin contributed to the meeting, Sally burst out laughing and high-fived Kristin in a girl-on-girl celebration.

After Bob completed his report updating Sally, the four friends kicked back to enjoy their own company. John decided to order a bottle of wine. By the time it was half gone, the tense edge of the day had disappeared into the bottom of their empty glasses. By the time the wine totally disappeared and a second bottle was ordered, hardy laughs were being shared and enjoyed.

Following their lunch together, they all returned to their home. As they approached the cement-filled six-inch diameter steel pipe barrier guarding the entrance to the lakefront compound, they saw an unmarked black sedan waiting for them. Superintendent Drake followed them to John and Kristin's cabin. Bob and Sally joined them.

The four friends greeted their unexpected visitors warmly. The effects of the bottle of wine, along with their pizza, elevated their expression of welcome. Once inside John's cabin, they all sat down, circling the fireplace.

"Do I need to arrest you for DWI? Drake jabbed.

"To what do we owe this unexpected pleasure," John replied, taking Drake's extended hand.

"Well," Drake began. "Kristin's speech at the end of our meeting was very impressive. Got the attention of my guys and, quite frankly, scared the crap out of a few of them.

"But it doesn't change the fact that you guys might get some unwelcome visitors in the future. I don't want to see anything happen to any of you."

"Look, Charles," John began. "My wife sometimes scares the crap out of me, too, so you guys should seriously consider what she had to say. But, here's the skinny of this whole thing.

"We are not going to live our lives looking over our shoulders. Bob and I will re-examine our security setup for the entire compound as well as our individual homes. Should anyone approach the compound, we'll know about it. Should anyone manage to enter the compound … well, we'll deal with it as necessary.

"Besides, nobody knows who we are or what we did. The media have never included our names or where we live or anything about us. The only people who have seen my face are dead. So, unless your people leak information, we're good! And, as far as the media goes, this story is over. They've already moved on. In a day or two, we'll be old news."

"You may be right," the Superintendent replied. "But, forgive me if I worry. That's part of my job. You have proven to be a valuable guy to have around, and my wife and I have enjoyed getting to know the two of you on a social level. I just want to be sure that you'll be around to expand our relationship."

"Fear not, Charles," Kristin added. "I intend to keep him alive and well for a very long, long time."

"That goes for us as well," Sally added.

"Okay," Charles said. "One last thing. I heard everything you said to Agent Costa, but I'd like to be able to call on you to assist in other cases. The experience the four of you have could be of great value to me and to my officers."

"Hold on," Kristin blurted out. "Are you offering him a job?"

"No, not a full-time job. Sort of continuing in a consultant position. You know, sort of on call when something pops up."

"Charles," Kristin spoke up again. "This is a big state. There are lots of people in this state. Lots of people can create lots of 'pop up' situations."

"Yeah, I know! That's why I'm asking."

"Don't forget, Charles, we are a team. We come as a package deal. If you take me, you also take Kristin," John added.

"Understood."

A short time later, Sally and Bob excused themselves and returned to their house. Kristin left her husband and the Superintendent alone to further discuss the future while she went inside to get some rest.

She relinquished her concerns, leaving the limits of future involvement up to John. It was approaching five o'clock by the time the two men completed their discussions concerning the potential parameters for John and Kristin's participation in future cases.

Darkness had blanketed their world, and the temperatures were once more dropping toward zero. John accompanied his new friend out to his car. The two were huddled against the cold, finding themselves staring out across the lake with nothing more to say until Superintendent Drake broke the silence.

"I don't trust Costa."

"Glad to hear you say that, Charles. Neither do I. I think he's dirty."

"I agree. I'll stay alert to anything he might stick his nose into anywhere near you."

"Thank you," John said.

The two men stood quietly in the dark, absorbed by the frozen surface of Lake George and the surrounding snow-covered mountains.

"Night skies are beautiful up here in the North Country," Charles said quietly.

"They sure are," John added.

"More stars than I've ever seen anywhere else I've traveled. We're lucky. All we have to do is look up, and there they are. Sparkling and bright."

"Yeah," John answered. "And I'm the luckiest of all. I go to bed every night with the brightest of all in my arms."

Chapter 33

Kristin found her husband the following morning exactly where he should be, sitting out on their deck wrapped in a down-filled quilt, looking out over Lake George with a mug of coffee in his hand.

She snuggled up with him, taking his mug and sipping his coffee.

"I have an idea," she said.

"I suppose you're going to share it with me."

"Yes!"

"Okay, I'm all ears."

"Okay! I think we should pack up the motorhome and head south for a while."

"Really? And how long a trip do you see us taking?"

"At least a couple of months."

"Done!"

She was elated. A long trip with her husband all to herself after the tension-packed events that had engulfed them in recent months would be a very welcomed change. Only, she seemed to be alone in her excitement. John sat staring out across the lake.

"What is it, John?

"What?"

"Come back to our world," she said to him. "What is it? There's something troubling you."

"It's not over, baby. This isn't over."

"What do you mean?"

"We haven't seen the end of this yet."

"Why do you say that?"

"This group of yoyos didn't act along. Somebody is pulling their strings. There's someone behind all of this."

"Who?"

"I don't know… at least not yet."

"You really think there's someone else?"

"I'd stake my life on it. These guys aren't smart enough to put all of this together. Someone has been financing them, and I'd bet there are other groups just like this one and the one at Lake George floating around the country."

"You really believe that, John?"

"My gut tells me we haven't seen the end of this. There are too many dangling ends that need to fit somewhere."

"What will you do?"

He stood up and reached down to pull his wife into his arms.

"First thing is that I'm taking my beautiful wife on a long road trip. We are getting away from all of this crap for a while."

"Then what?"

"I don't know. We'll have to wait and see what develops. Just remember what I just told you: this isn't over. Whoever is behind all of this is watching. They have been watching everything that has happened up here. They've been watching everything and everybody… including us. There's more to come, Kristin. I'd bet on it."

About the Author

Richard Totino was raised on an apple farm in the town of Marlboro in the mid-Hudson Valley of New York. His small-town roots and values have guided him throughout his entire life. Although he has traveled extensively, he still considers himself a small-town boy with small-town values. After he enlisted in the U.S. Army, he returned to college to complete his graduate degrees at the ripe old age of 34. His work in international sales and marketing provided him with an insight into many cultures and customs beyond our borders, and his extensive travel in the U.S. taught him that people everywhere are as open and friendly as you give them the opportunity to be. He likes to tell people, "I have slept in 49 states," which leads his wife to describe him as George Washington, who seems to have slept everywhere.

Together with his wife Sharon, Dick now resides in North Carolina, where they soak up the sunshine and sea breezes. Their combined family includes eight children and five grandchildren, providing them with plenty to do and all the related challenges that go with keeping up with a large family. An avid hunter and outdoorsman, his personal experiences enhance his writing. He refers to fall as "scrapbooking season," that is when he leaves Sharon at home to occupy herself with her crafts while he escapes to the wilderness of North Carolina and the Adirondack Mountains of New York. He has been active in the Knights of Columbus, the Elks, Disabled American Veterans, and the American Legion and as a crew boss with Lower Adirondack Search and Rescue (LASAR), participating in numerous search and rescue efforts throughout the region.